WOMAN WITH A GUN

ALSO BY PHILLIP MARGOLIN

Lost Lake
Sleeping Beauty
The Associate
The Undertaker's Widow
The Burning Man
After Dark
Gone, but Not Forgotten
The Last Innocent Man
Heartstone
Worthy Brown's Daughter

DANA CUTLER NOVELS
Washington Trilogy

Executive Privilege
Supreme Justice
Capitol Murder

Sleight of Hand

AMANDA JAFFE NOVELS
Wild Justice
Ties That Bind
Proof Positive
Fugitive
Vanishing Acts (with Ami Margolin Rome)

WOMAN WITH A GUN

A Novel

PHILLIP MARGOLIN

HARPER
An Imprint of HarperCollins*Publishers*

This book is a work of fiction. The characters, incidents, and dialogue are drawn from the author's imagination and are not to be construed as real. Any resemblance to actual events or persons, living or dead, is entirely coincidental.

HarperCollins books may be purchased for educational, business, or sales promotional use. For information, please e-mail the Special Markets Department at SPsales@harpercollins.com.

FIRST EDITION

Designed by Joy O'Meara

Library of Congress Cataloging-in-Publication Data

Margolin, Phillip.
Woman with a gun : a novel / Phillip Margolin—First edition.
pages cm
ISBN: 978-0-06-226652-1
1. Photographs—fiction. 2. Murder—investigation—fiction. I. Title.
PS3563.A649 W66 2014
813'.54 2014023462

14 15 16 17 18 OV/RRD 10 9 8 7 6 5 4 3 2 1

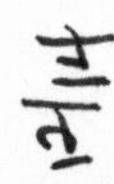

This book is dedicated to Robin Haggard, my longtime,
super-extraordinary legal secretary and assistant,
without whom my life would spiral downward into total chaos;
and to Leslie Jeter, whose amazing photograph was the inspiration for
Woman with a Gun.

Part One

WOMAN WITH A GUN

2015

CHAPTER ONE

"Wilde, Levine and Barstow, how may I direct your call?" Stacey Kim said, trying to sound perky and barely succeeding.

"Perky" was getting harder and harder each mind-numbing day she worked as the law firm's receptionist. The pep talks she gave herself on the subway didn't work. Neither did the triple-shot espressos they made in the coffee bar in the midtown Manhattan office building where she toiled.

From nine in the morning until five in the afternoon, with an hour off for lunch, Stacey manned the firm's reception desk and stared at the glass doors that opened into the hall near the elevators. Wilde, Levine and Barstow had a lot of clients, so she was always asking callers to whom they wished to speak or serious-looking people whom they wanted to see. That's all she did, over and over. There were times when Stacey wondered if she was trapped in a hideous nightmare where every boring day was like every other boring day for all eternity.

Everything had been so different eight months ago when Stacey had moved from the Midwest to Manhattan.

"I'm a struggling artist in New York City! It doesn't get much better than this!" Stacey told herself during those early days. Her enthusiasm had been fueled by the comments of Morris DeFord, winner of the PEN/Faulkner Award for Fiction and a finalist for the National Book Award. Professor DeFord had told Stacey that her short story "A Fragment of the Day" was one of the finest pieces of fiction he had read during his tenure in the MFA program at State. The vibrant characters, the complexity of the plot, and the quality of her prose were unique, he proclaimed. Then he urged her to let those characters run free and transform her miniature gem into a magnificent novel.

As soon as she received her MFA, Stacey headed to New York City, convinced that simply living in the Big Apple would ignite a fire that would turn the tiny flame generated by "A Fragment of the Day" into a towering literary inferno. She had sought out a low-paying job that was not mentally taxing so she would be free to think about her novel. Working as a receptionist at a law firm had sounded perfect, and she was thrilled when she was hired. Stacey had watched a lot of law-related shows on television. She fantasized about the sexy young associates who would make all sorts of witty comments she could use in her book and she looked forward to encountering a wonderful mix of quirky characters she could use to populate her novel. Reality had intruded very quickly.

First, Stacey was so busy answering the phone and greeting clients that she had no time to think about her book. Second, the partners at Wilde, Levine and Barstow practiced bankruptcy, probate, and tax law, and the partners and their clients were as dull as the firm's specialties. Finally, there were several associates but they were as boring as the partners. None of them made witty comments.

Another thing Stacey fantasized about on the way to New

York was the men she might meet. Stacey had wide, brown eyes, silky black hair, an engaging smile, and an attractive figure. At twenty-eight, she was still a romantic who wanted to fall in love with that special someone who would return her love and share her life, just like the character of Bill did with Angela in "A Fragment of the Day." In Manhattan, Stacey believed she would hobnob with the literati, lunch with actors and artists, and date dynamic young men who shared her love of literature and art. The secretaries at the firm invited Stacey to the bars near her office building and to parties, but none of the men she met were budding Hemingways or Picassos. She had gone out with a few of them, but her dates just wanted to sleep with her, which she would have done if they had even hinted at being interested in a relationship.

Stacey's nonexistent social life and mind-numbing job would not have mattered if she were making progress on her novel, but she wasn't. The idea for her short story had struck her like lightning one sunny afternoon, and she had torn through her first draft like an Olympic sprinter. Moving on from those initial twenty-seven pages was proving hopeless. Stacey had scribbled some ideas in a notebook, but none of the ideas excited her. Each time Stacey stared at the blank page on her laptop, she tried to rekindle the hope and excitement she had felt during her first days in New York, but all she felt was despair.

That was about to change.

"Hey," said Miranda Perez as she walked up to the reception desk to take Stacey's place during the lunch hour. Stacey breathed a sigh of relief. It was noon, that wonderful time of day when she was paroled from her prison.

"Can you cover for me if I'm a little late?" Stacey asked.

"Sure, what's up? Got a hot date?"

"No such luck. There's a Salvador Dalí exhibit at the Museum of Modern Art that sounded interesting. What with the crowds and all, I might not make it back on time."

"No prob. Have fun."

It was hot and muggy outside her air-conditioned building, and Stacey began to perspire as she fought her way through the shoulder-to-shoulder crowds on Fifth Avenue, a daunting task for someone who was five foot two. Stacey had been dying to see the Dalí exhibit ever since she'd read about it in the Sunday *Times*. She loved surrealism. In fact, it had been the surrealistic aspects of her short story that had enchanted Professor DeFord.

To her surprise, there wasn't much of a line at the ticket counter inside the museum. Stacey paid and found the exhibit. It was small, and it was only 12:35 when she finished viewing all of Salvador Dalí's paintings.

The photography of Kathy Moran was on display next to the Dalí exhibit. Stacey had never heard of Kathy Moran, but her eye was drawn immediately to a series of photographs on the wall in front of her. Moran had taken one of her shots through the window of a diner in the dead of night, and the streetlights and neon signs in the stores across the way were reflected in the panes of glass. Seated at the counter was a girl with multiple piercings and bare arms covered with tattoos. She was engrossed in a book and sipping from a coffee cup. A few stools down, two weary men, who looked like they'd just gotten off the night shift at a factory, worked on a midnight breakfast while a harried waitress took an order from two cops seated in a booth.

The next photograph was of a bearded man sitting on a barstool, staring morosely into a half-filled shot glass. Moran had set up behind the man, and her subject's careworn face could be seen in a gap in the liquor bottles arrayed in front of the mirror behind the bar. The man's despair was so evident that Stacey wanted to comfort him.

Stacey was about to move to the next picture when she caught sight of a photograph that was hanging on the wall to her left. Unlike the other works, it was displayed alone and a group of people wearing the earphones supplied for self-guided tours was gathered in front of it. Stacey walked over to see what was attracting the crowd. A young couple moved on and Stacey leaned forward.

The title of the black-and-white photograph was *Woman with a Gun*. A placard affixed to the wall next to the photograph informed Stacey that the photograph had been awarded a Pulitzer Prize ten years earlier. In the photograph, a woman was standing on a beach, staring out to sea. It was night and she was bathed in moonlight. A line of foam left by a retreating wave stretched down the beach inches from her bare feet. The shot had been taken from behind and slightly to the right of the subject. Stacey could not see the woman's face, but the white strapless wedding gown she wore showed off deeply tanned shoulders partially covered by long black hair. The woman's left fist was pressed against her hip and her right arm was angled behind her, as if gripped loosely in a hammerlock. What made the photo unique was the long-barreled six-shooter she held behind her back in her right hand, barrel down.

Stacey walked closer. What was going on here? Had the woman killed her husband on her wedding night? Was she waiting for someone in a boat who was coming in to shore? Was she going to murder that person? Was she contemplating suicide? Stacey's mind raced through one possibility after another and each one suggested others.

And what was the woman doing with an ancient six-shooter? The photo would have been interesting if the woman were holding a modern gun, but a revolver from the Old West added a mysterious element that made the photograph fascinating.

Stacey glanced at her watch. Her lunch break would be over in a few minutes. She didn't want to get in trouble so she tore herself away. Stacey made a brief stop in the gift shop to buy a catalog of the photographs in the Moran exhibition. As she walked back to her office, she felt the same electric feeling she had experienced when the idea for "A Fragment of the Day" had come to her. There was a story behind *Woman with a Gun* and she vowed to discover it. And when she did, maybe—just maybe—she would have the plot for the novel she had come to New York to write.

Part Two

THE *CAHILL* CASE

2005

CHAPTER TWO

Jack Booth was pouring himself a cup of coffee when Elaine Rostow, the Oregon attorney general, called. Jack knew Rostow, but he didn't know her well, and she had never phoned him at home.

"I didn't wake you, did I?" Rostow asked.

"No. I'm just finishing breakfast."

"Good. Do you know Teddy Winston?"

"He's a DA, right?"

"In Siletz County."

"I know who he is. I've met him at some legal conferences. But I can't say I *know* him. Why?"

"There was a murder this morning in Palisades Heights and he wants me to send someone to help him with the case."

"This is pretty early in the game, isn't it?"

"Yes, but Teddy is one of my strongest supporters on the coast and I owe him. When he called, he sounded very concerned, so I said we'd help."

"What do you want me to do?" Jack asked. He wondered why

Rostow couldn't wait until he was in the office to talk about the case.

"Teddy wants you to see the crime scene while it's fresh."

"He wants me to drive to Palisades Heights now?"

"Exactly. Can you do it?"

"Yeah. I was set to go to trial in a murder case in Union County but the defendant pled two days ago, so I'm free."

"Good. Keep me posted."

Rostow hung up and Jack frowned. The assistant attorney general was a shade over six feet tall with a wiry build. He had dark green eyes, a Roman nose, and curly black hair. Jack had been a Multnomah County district attorney in Portland for many years. Then, a year and a half ago, he had heard there was an opening in the Oregon Department of Justice District Attorney Assistance Program. The program sent experienced prosecutors to small towns to assist local DAs who weren't experienced enough to handle complex cases. It usually took a while for these small-town DAs to admit to themselves that they were in over their heads. He wondered what it was about this case that made his immediate involvement necessary.

It took Jack two and a half hours to drive to Palisades Heights, the county seat for Siletz County. The trip west started in farmland and continued through forests and a low mountain range. Then Jack hit the coast highway, a narrow, twisting road on the edge of the ocean. When Jack risked a westward glance, he saw jagged rock formations that rose like giants from the Pacific and waves crashing on beaches that ended below high, weatherworn cliffs.

Jack took the Dune Road exit and stopped at the bottom of the ramp. He'd been to Palisades Heights before, and he knew that a right turn would send him toward the Pacific on a two-lane street that curved past bed-and-breakfasts and a scattering of Cape Cod–style homes until it arrived at Ocean Avenue. A left on Ocean would bring him to bars, restaurants, art galleries, clothing boutiques, an amateur theater, and other attractions of the popular resort town. If he turned right on Ocean he would find seaside motels, restaurants with ocean views, the country club, and, eventually, a residential area with million-dollar beachfront properties.

Jack took a left on Dune Road and drove away from the sea. As soon as he passed under the highway he found himself in the business district with its less expensive motels, two- and three-story office buildings, discount stores, and his destination, the Siletz County Courthouse, a dull, gray, functional concrete building that had replaced the original courthouse in the mid-eighties.

Jack climbed the stairs to the second floor and found the district attorney's office. The door opened into a waiting area guarded by a receptionist who was ensconced at a wooden counter. Behind the receptionist stood a row of gunmetal filing cabinets that turned a corner and continued down a hall. A low gate at the end of the counter could be opened to permit entry to that hall and whatever lay beyond.

Booth identified himself to the receptionist. Two minutes later a harried-looking man dressed in tan slacks and a mismatched gray-blue, checked sports jacket appeared. Teddy Winston was short, thin, and in his late thirties. He was balding but had compensated by growing a bushy mustache that did not look good on him.

"Thanks for getting here so quickly, Mr. Booth . . ."

"Jack, please."

"Jack it is. And you should call me Teddy. I appreciate the speed," the DA said as he walked through the gate into the reception area. "If you don't mind, I'd like to take you straight to the crime scene. The state police forensic unit is already there. We can talk on the way. I want you to see it while it's relatively untouched."

"Fill me in," Jack said as soon as they were on the road. "Elaine didn't tell me much."

"Do you know who Raymond Cahill is?" Winston asked.

"No."

"He's a California businessman; a multimillionaire. He lives in Los Angeles most of the year. When he was a kid, he spent his summers in Palisades Heights at a relative's beach house, and he's always had a soft spot for this town. After he made his money, he built a house that overlooks the ocean and he spent a few weeks here every year.

"Yesterday evening, Ray married Megan Cahill at the country club. There was a reception at the club after the ceremony. The Cahills drove home from the reception a little after midnight. The police were called to the house around three in the morning. The first officers on the scene found Cahill in his den. He'd been shot to death.

"Cahill was a collector. There's a vault in his home where he kept some of his collection: valuable coins, stamps, and antique guns. The guns may be important. Anyway, the vault door was open. There's evidence that Cahill was beaten before he was shot, so he may have been forced to open the vault. It looks like there are items missing."

"Any idea who robbed him?"

"No."

"So you don't have any suspects?"

"We may. A witness was walking on the beach and found

Megan Cahill standing at the waterline, holding an antique revolver. We think it's from his collection but we won't know if it's the murder weapon until they run ballistics tests."

"What does Mrs. Cahill say?"

"That's the problem. She's in shock and she hasn't said a word. Not to anyone. She's in the hospital but the doctors won't let us see her."

"Did she say anything to the witness who found her?"

"No."

"If you don't mind my asking, why do you feel that it's so important to have me involved at such an early stage in the investigation?"

"Most of the crime in Siletz County involves drunks and domestic violence. I've handled four murders, but two of the killers confessed and the two who went to trial had public defenders and were obviously guilty. Raymond Cahill's personal fortune is larger than the county budget. If I indict Megan Cahill, she can dip into it for her defense. I'm okay going up against public defenders in murder cases involving bar brawls and domestic abuse, but Megan will be able to hire a dream team. If she does, I'll need all the help I can get."

It didn't take long to drive to the crime scene. A mile and a half after turning right on Ocean Avenue, a driveway appeared on the sea side of the road. Above him and in the near distance, Jack saw the flat roof of a house that stretched along the top of a cliff. The side facing away from the Pacific was painted a subdued gray that weathered well and blended into the colors of the surrounding dunes and sky.

An officer posted at the entrance to the driveway recognized the DA and waved him in. Police vehicles were parked in a turnaround and Winston pulled in behind one of them. The Cahills' front door was open and Booth could see police officers and forensic experts moving around inside.

Jack followed the DA into a polished stone entry hall. On his left was an unobstructed view of the ocean through massive floor-to-ceiling windows. Jack leaned on a low wood banister for a moment and looked down into a spacious living room. A door in the living room opened onto a large deck outfitted with lounge chairs and glass tables shaded by wide umbrellas. Jack could see a hot tub off to one side.

A slender African-American man dressed in a tan suit and open-necked blue shirt was talking to a state trooper near the top of the stairs that led down to the living room. His hair was salt-and-pepper. He turned when he heard the two men enter the house and lasered his sharp blue eyes at them. Then he smiled.

"Archie," Booth said.

"You know Detective Denning?" Winston asked.

"We worked a case in eastern Oregon right after I joined the Justice Department."

"Hey, Jack," Denning said.

"Are your forensic guys through with the den?" Winston asked. "I want Jack to see the scene."

"Come on back," the detective said.

Jack followed Winston and Denning down a hall decorated with oils and photographs of seascapes. They stopped in front of an open door.

"The body was found in here," Winston said, pointing into a large den.

There were no windows in the room and it was illuminated by bright, recessed lighting. The odors left behind by violent death had dissipated to some extent but there were still enough left to wrinkle Jack's nose.

A huge television hung on one wall over a cabinet. The cabinet was open and Jack could see electronic equipment and stacks of DVDs. Trophies decorated the top of the cabinet. Some looked like golf trophies and others looked like they were for shooting. On another wall, pennants celebrating UCLA, the Los Angeles Lakers, and the Oakland Raiders were mixed with photos of Raymond Cahill standing with well-known sports and entertainment figures.

Jack took in the decorations quickly because his eye was drawn to a chair that had tipped over in the center of the room. The body had been removed but the gore remained. There was dried blood on the floor behind the chair and something else that looked like brain. There was more blood spatter on either side of the chair and in front of it. Jack wasn't surprised. Winston had said that the victim had been beaten.

Denning saw where Jack was looking. "Mr. Cahill was tied to the chair. It must have gone over when he was shot in the head. The criminalists took the rope to the lab. The body is at the hospital where they do the autopsies out here."

"Do we know how the killer got in?" Jack asked.

"No," Winston said. "If he was waiting when the Cahills got back from the wedding he may have forced them to let him in. There's the front door and a door that opens onto the deck. You can get to the deck from the beach. The door to the deck was open because that's how the witness got into the house, and we're pretty sure that's how Megan Cahill left when she walked down to the beach. But we don't know if it was open or locked when Megan left the house, only that she didn't lock it when she walked down to the beach. None of the doors were forced."

"Okay. Is there anything else I need to see here?"

"Definitely," Winston said. He pointed to the left side of the cabinet that held the television. A section of the wall was in shadow. Jack squinted at the spot. Then he walked to it and discovered that what he had taken for a wall was actually the door to a vault. The door was barely open, but Jack could see that it was thick steel covered by wood that blended into the wood used for the rest of the room.

"That's where Cahill kept his collection," Winston said.

When Jack drew closer, he spotted a keypad on the wall next to the door to the vault. He pulled back the door and stepped into a large, temperature-controlled room. A gun collection hung on one wall. When Jack was a deputy district attorney, a disgruntled defendant had threatened him and he had been given a gun for protection, but he knew nothing about antique guns. He recognized a blunderbuss and another rifle that looked like something from the American Revolution. There was a derringer he had once seen in a TV show. But what drew his eye were several blank spaces.

Winston saw where Jack was staring. "We're pretty sure that the revolver Megan Cahill was holding is from the collection but we won't know for sure until we talk to Frank Janowitz, the curator who looked after Mr. Cahill's collection. He's flying up from L.A. and should be here tomorrow."

There were several glass cases arranged in an orderly manner in the center of the vault. Some were intact and Jack saw coins in them. The glass in several had been smashed and shards littered the floor. Winston pointed to a small gold coin that was partially hidden behind the leg that supported one of the cases.

"Some of these cases contained Cahill's coin collection. The thief took some and left others, but we won't know why until we get an expert opinion from Janowitz."

Winston pointed toward rows of wide metal drawers. Some were in the wall but others had been pulled out.

"Cahill's stamp collection," he explained. "It's been looted, too."

Jack looked around and asked a few questions, which Winston said he wouldn't be able to answer until Janowitz assessed the damage.

"None of the other rooms in the house appear to have been disturbed. We think the killer tortured Cahill to get the combination to the vault, then took what he wanted, killed Cahill, and left."

"So Megan Cahill might have been a victim, too?" Jack said.

"Or an accomplice," Denning said.

Jack took a look around the rest of the house. When he was done he agreed that whatever had happened had been confined to the den. Jack followed Winston and Denning to the stairs that led down to the living room.

"There are tracks leading up from the beach and into the house that were left by the witness and Mrs. Cahill when the witness brought Mrs. Cahill back to the house after she found her on the beach," Winston said. "The witness said that the door to the deck was wide open."

Winston led Jack down the stairs to the living room and onto the deck. Denning followed them. The view was spectacular. Some waves rushed into shore while others crashed against the shining black hides of massive rock formations, sending spray flashing through the clear summer sky. And while the shore was wracked by turbulence, a little way out, the sea was flat blue calm. Jack decided that money might not buy happiness but there was a lot it could buy.

"Show me where the witness found Mrs. Cahill," Jack said. Winston led him down a set of weathered wooden steps to the beach and across the sand in the direction of the main part of town. They didn't go far before the DA stopped to point out the spot. Jack walked to the water's edge and stared. A seagull swooped down to the beach and two more glided on the updrafts, making lazy circles over the open water. The ebb and flow of the waves and the light sea breeze hypnotized him.

With an effort, Jack turned his back on the Pacific and broke the spell. Above him loomed the beach house, all glass. In winter you could take in the storms through the picture windows. In the summer, you could sit on the wide decks and watch the sunsets.

"Where's the witness now?" he asked Winston.

"She's at the courthouse, giving a statement."

"Let's go back so I can talk to her."

CHAPTER THREE

Archie Denning stayed at the house to supervise the investigation and Teddy Winston phoned ahead to make sure that the detective who was taking the witness's statement kept her at the courthouse. When Jack and Winston arrived, the DA led Jack to an interrogation room in the rear of the police bureau. Winston opened the door and stood aside to let Jack enter. Jack took one step into the room and froze.

"Jack Booth, this is Kathy Moran," Winston said. "She found Megan Cahill on the beach behind the Cahills' house."

Kathy and Jack stared at each other. Kathy recovered first.

"It's been a while, Jack."

Winston looked back and forth between the prosecutor and the witness.

"You know each other?"

"From Portland," Jack answered. "Kathy practiced law there when I was with the Multnomah County DA."

"You're a lawyer?" Winston asked. Kathy smiled.

Jack turned to Winston. "Ted, would you mind not sitting in while I debrief Kathy?"

Winston's brow furrowed and it appeared for a moment that he might protest. Then he gave in.

"Sure, Jack, if that works better for you."

"Thanks for being so understanding. I'll give you a full report when we're through, and I assume that Miss Moran won't object to talking to you at a later date if you have something else you need to discuss."

"That would be fine," Kathy said, and the DA left the room.

Kathy was sitting in a straight-back chair on one side of a small table. A black windbreaker was draped over the back of the chair. She was wearing jeans and a green-blue cable-knit sweater. It was summer, but the coast was always several degrees cooler than the valley. And, Jack remembered, she had been walking the beach in the early-morning hours when the wind coming off the water would have chilled the air.

"You look good," Jack said, and he wasn't lying. The last time Jack had seen Kathy, she had looked unnaturally thin and strung out. In the five intervening years, Kathy had gained back any weight she'd lost and she was sporting a healthy tan.

"Thanks," Kathy answered with a smile. "Six months in rehab and four and a half years in the ocean air work wonders. Why are you here, Jack?"

"I'm with the District Attorney Assistance Program at the Department of Justice. The DA asked for help on the case."

"So Teddy Winston thinks Megan killed her husband?"

"Why do you say that?"

"Everyone in Palisades Heights knows everyone else. Teddy's scared of his shadow. If Megan Cahill is charged she'll be represented by some heavy hitters. Teddy doesn't have the self-confidence to go up against that level of legal firepower."

"Winston told me you found Megan Cahill on the beach around two in the morning and called the police. Have you gotten any sleep?"

Kathy shook her head.

"You must be exhausted. Have you had anything to eat? Do you want a sandwich or coffee?"

"Seeing Cahill's body killed my appetite, but I could use some coffee."

Jack went to the door and asked the policeman outside for two cups.

"I'll try to make this quick so you can get out of here."

"Thanks."

"Why don't you tell me why you were walking on the beach at two in the morning?"

The door opened and a policeman entered with two cups of coffee. Kathy took one healthy sip, then another. Then she put the cup down and answered Jack's question.

"After I resigned from the bar I had to find a job. I'd represented Grady Cox in a divorce case in my first year in practice. After his divorce I did odds and ends for him: contracts, a real estate deal. Grady owns the Seafarer. It's a bar on Ocean Avenue. I earned money in college bartending. Moving to a small town and away from temptation after I finished rehab sounded like a good idea. I called Grady and explained my situation. He gave me a job.

"This morning, my shift ended at one thirty. It was a beautiful night, full moon, no clouds, lots of stars. A friend, Ellen Devereaux, has a gallery in Palisades Heights. She shows my photographs. We'd talked about a one-woman show. I wanted to feature beach scenes. I always have my camera with me and I decided to walk along the beach."

"Do you live near the Cahills?"

"Lord, no." Kathy laughed. "I couldn't afford their garage. I have a bungalow I rent from Grady. It's a few blocks from the Seafarer. But I wasn't tired, and the night was so perfect. There was a full moon, and I thought I might get a few shots I could use for the show. The rock formations near the Cahills are spectacular."

"I've seen them. So you walked down the beach?"

"And I'd taken a few shots when I saw Megan Cahill standing on the shoreline."

Kathy paused. She'd looked exhausted when Jack entered the interrogation room but her eyes suddenly regained the sparkle he'd noticed the first time they'd met and her features came alive.

"That scene," she said. Her voice filled with wonder. "It was something I would never have imagined seeing in my lifetime. This woman, bathed in moonlight, her tanned shoulders in sharp contrast to the pure white of her strapless wedding gown, barefoot, staring out to sea, the foam from the last, retreating wave inches in front of her. And that gun . . . It was so out of place. It was the gun that made the scene unique, bizarre. So I took the shot."

"Weren't you worried that she would shoot you?"

"Honestly, I didn't think about that right then because everything was so surreal. I just took the shot. Then I draped the camera's carrying strap over my shoulder so my hands would be free and I walked toward her.

"I moved slowly, carefully, because I had no idea what state Megan was in or what she planned to do with that gun. You know, would she try to shoot me? Was she moments away from suicide?"

"Had you met her before?"

"No, but I'd met Raymond Cahill."

"Oh?"

"Not socially. A reporter who was writing an article in the *Palisades Heights Gazette* about the Cahills' wedding had seen some of my work at Ellen's gallery. He came to the Seafarer and asked me if I wanted to photograph the house for the article."

Kathy shrugged. "I needed the money and I'd always wondered what the inside of the house looked like, so I said I'd do it. That's when I met Raymond. But Megan wasn't at the house then. Of course, I knew what she looked like. I'd seen her picture in the society section of the *Gazette.* And, of course, the gossip columns covered her divorce."

"Her divorce?"

"She was married to Parnell Crouse. He played for the Oakland Raiders. The divorce was very messy. Raymond had an interest in the team. I think Megan and Raymond met at a team party."

Jack wasn't interested in society gossip so he pressed on.

"What happened when you got close to Mrs. Cahill?"

"She turned. Her eyes were unfocused. She looked dazed, disoriented, and I could see blood in her hair. I asked if she was all right."

"Did she answer you?"

"No, she just stared. That's when I started thinking about the gun. It was dangling at her side, just hanging there. I wasn't even sure Megan knew she was holding it and I didn't know what would happen if she realized that she was in possession of a deadly weapon. So I approached cautiously, the way you would approach a wild animal. I held up my hands, palms toward her, to show that I meant her no harm. I asked again if she was okay but I didn't get an answer, just a vacant stare.

"A gust of wind reminded me that we were out in the open.

My windbreaker offered some protection but Megan was wearing a strapless wedding gown. I knew she had to be cold and that I had to get her to a warm place. Then I was going to call for an ambulance and the police.

"When I got close enough to take the gun, I reached out slowly and covered the hand that held the weapon. Megan stared down at the gun. She looked surprised to see that she was holding it.

"I said, 'Let me take this so no one gets hurt.' Megan didn't resist. I took the gun. Then I wrapped my windbreaker around Megan's shoulders, took her by the hand, and brought her across the sand to the wooden steps that led up from the beach."

"Did she resist when you led her back to the crime scene?"

Kathy shook her head. "She was docile, unresisting like a sleepy child. So I kept talking to her as I led her up the steps; talking about the weather, how nice the house looked, anything to keep her calm, because I was certain that whatever had broken her was in the house. And I was right."

She shuddered. "When we got to the den . . . Cahill was sprawled on the floor. I could see the blood. His face . . . I pulled my eyes away pretty quickly but . . ."

"That's okay. You don't have to describe the crime scene. I'll see the photos. Did Mrs. Cahill say anything about the circumstances of her husband's death?"

"She didn't utter a word about anything. When I saw the body, I pulled her away from the den and got her settled in the living room. Then I called the police."

"Did you see anyone at the crime scene?"

Kathy shook her head. "I'm sorry but I can't help you."

"Okay. I think that's enough for now. Go home and try to get some rest. We'll get in touch if we need anything else and you should call if you remember something that might help."

"Okay," Kathy said. She stood up and started to put on her jacket. Then she paused.

"Are you staying in town, Jack?"

"Winston got me a room at the Surfside Motel."

"So you'll be here for a few days?"

"Yes."

"I'm working tonight but tomorrow is my day off. Do you want to have dinner? They serve a mean chowder at the Seafarer."

Jack hesitated. Kathy Moran was a key witness in the Cahill murder case. But he was curious and he was still attracted to her.

Kathy knew why he hesitated. "We won't talk about the case. I'd rather not think about it anyway. We'll just catch up on the last five years."

"Dinner sounds good."

"Is seven okay?"

"I'll be there."

CHAPTER FOUR

Glen Kraft was employed as Henry Baker's associate because it was the only job he could get after he graduated from law school. It wasn't that Glen was a poor student. He was in the top quarter of his class at Lewis & Clark, a fine law school in Portland. The problem was the market, which was tight. No one was leaving the public defender's or district attorney's offices because of the economy. The big Portland firms only wanted you if you were at the very top of your class in an Oregon law school or had graduated from some place like Harvard, Stanford, or NYU. Most midsize firms weren't hiring at all, and the ones that had an opening had their pick of the litter. Glen's father had told Henry Baker about Glen's depressing job search during a round of golf at the Palisades Heights Country Club, and Henry had told him to have Glen give him a call because his associate had just quit.

Coming back to his hometown was depressing. Glen had such big dreams when he graduated first in his high school class and was accepted at Amherst. But the competition at Amherst had been a lot stiffer than the competition at Palisades Heights High. A middle B average and so-so LSATs hadn't gotten Glen into a top-ten law school. Instead of going to Boston or New York, Glen found himself returning to Oregon. And now he was back where he'd started, in Palisades Heights. In his darker moments, Glen realized that he wasn't just going nowhere, he was going backward.

Henry Baker was a nice guy to work for and a competent lawyer, but he had a small-town practice, which meant he survived by handling whatever came in the door. Most of the work was dull as dust: real estate closings, simple wills and contracts. Every once in a while Henry would go to court on a criminal case, but they were never the kind of cases that Perry Mason handled, because Perry didn't take DUIIs or shoplifts. Glen kept his spirits up by convincing himself that he was getting experience that he could parlay into something better somewhere down the line, although he had no idea what that might be.

When his intercom buzzed, Glen was working on an appeal for a local CPA who had been caught sharing a joint with an underage girl. Henry Baker's secretary sounded excited.

"There's a call for Mr. Baker. I told her that he wasn't in. She wants to talk to you."

"Who does?" Glen asked.

"Megan Cahill!"

Glen couldn't have sat up faster if he'd been jabbed by a cattle prod. Raymond Cahill's murder was front-page news in Palisades Heights. More important, Perry Mason did take cases where the victim was a multimillionaire and the defendant was his beautiful wife.

"Did she say why she was calling?" Glen asked.

"No. So, do you want to talk to her?"

Glen's mouth was dry but he managed to tell the secretary to put the call through. He knew that Megan Cahill lived in L.A. most of the year and he found it hard to believe that she would want a Palisades Heights lawyer to represent her in a murder case but what if . . . ?

Glen drove four miles south to the small hospital that served Palisades Heights and the coastal towns near the county seat. After going to the nurses' station, he was directed to a private room. Glen had gone to high school with the Palisades Heights police officer who was stationed outside the room, and they talked about the prospects for the football team for a few minutes before Glen explained why he was at the hospital. The officer went into Megan Cahill's room to find out if she was expecting Glen. Glen had checked himself in the mirror in the restroom before going to the nurses' station but he smoothed down his hair and adjusted his clothes again while he waited in the hallway.

"Good afternoon, Mrs. Cahill," Glen said when the policeman stepped aside so he could go in. "I'm Glen Kraft, the lawyer. We spoke on the phone."

"Thank you for coming so quickly," Megan said. Her voice was so low that Glen had to strain to hear her. He closed the door and pulled a straight-back, gray metal chair next to the bed. Megan was wearing a hospital gown, her hair was unwashed and her face was bruised, but Glen knew that she was a beautiful woman because he had a vivid memory of the first time they had met. It had been a sultry summer night and Glen was dining with his parents and Henry and Alma Baker on the flagstone patio of the Palisades Heights Country Club. A light breeze gently ruffled the leaves of the trees that lined the fairway and a luminous moon bathed the verdant green of the eighteenth hole in silver light. Into this magical setting walked one of the most beautiful women Glen Kraft had ever seen. Henry Baker had done some simple real estate work for Raymond Cahill and they'd played golf a few times, so Ray, fresh from divorcing wife number two, led Megan to a table next to Henry's and introduced his new friend to everyone.

Alma Baker walked out on Henry two weeks later, and Glen guessed that Henry had probably been working hard at keeping up appearances that evening. His boss probably thought that he had kept his composure during the introduction and small talk that followed, but something about the way Henry acted made Glen think that his boss had been as affected by Megan's beauty as he had been.

"How are you feeling?" Glen asked.

"I'm shaky. I was hit on the head really hard."

"Do the doctors think there's anything seriously wrong?"

"They say I have a concussion. My biggest problem is that I can't remember what happened to me and . . ."

Megan took a deep breath. Her eyes teared. Glen scrambled to her bedside and poured her a glass of water.

"Thank you," Megan said after she'd calmed down enough to continue. "I've been doing a lot of that lately, crying. I just can't remember anything that happened after we left the wedding reception . . . Have you ever lost your memory?"

Glen shook his head.

"I'm frightened. What if I never remember and Ray's killer is never caught?"

Megan lost focus and Glen fidgeted for a few seconds. Then he remembered why he was there.

"Mrs. Cahill, can you tell me why you called Mr. Baker, so I can tell him what you need."

Megan looked at Glen. He was worried that she might start crying again.

"Do you know that I was holding a gun when she found me on the beach?" she asked.

"I don't know anything about what happened except what I read in the *Gazette*."

"The police wanted to know why I had a gun and I can't remember."

She broke down again. "What if they think I killed Ray?"

"I'm sure you didn't," Glen said. "I can't imagine you wouldn't remember something like that. And how could you hit yourself hard enough to get a concussion and amnesia?"

Megan flashed Glen a weak smile. "Thank you. It's so nice to know that someone believes me. That's very important to me, because I'm afraid they think I killed Ray. That's why I called Henry. I need someone to protect me."

Megan sounded so sad and so lost that Glen's heart went out to her.

"Don't worry, Mrs. Cahill. Mr. Baker is a very good attorney. I'll call him as soon as I get back to the office. When he hears that you're in trouble, I'm sure he'll be here right away."

During the drive to his office, Glen could barely contain his excitement. A murder case! This murder case! It would be huge. There would be national coverage—television, the press—he might even be interviewed, although Henry would probably do all the talking because he would be lead counsel.

Glen mulled over his first impressions of Megan Cahill. There had been no mention of a gun in the report in the *Palisades Heights Gazette*, but she'd told him she was holding one when she was found on the beach behind her house. She seemed genuine when she said she had no memory of why she was holding a gun or how she got to the beach. Did he believe her? He wanted to. She seemed so helpless. Did he want to believe her because she was a beautiful damsel in distress? By the time Glen parked, he decided that it was too early to draw any conclusions because he didn't have all the facts. Still, he thought, it would be nice to represent an innocent person.

Glen raced to the phone as soon as he was in his office. Henry Baker was in court in Portland and it took forever to get through to him.

"Mr. Baker, this is Glen."

"Yes, Glen. I know your voice. You sound out of breath."

"You have to come back to Palisades Heights right away. We just got a big case and she wants you to be her lawyer."

"Calm down. Who wants me to be her lawyer?"

"Megan Cahill."

"Why does Megan need a lawyer?"

"Don't you know about the murder?"

"I've been in court. What murder are you talking about?"

"Raymond Cahill was murdered late Sunday night or early this morning."

"You're kidding? I was at the wedding."

"That must be why Mrs. Cahill called you. She was found on the beach holding a gun. She's a suspect."

Megan Cahill and Glen Kraft were killing time by talking about a movie they'd both seen when Henry Baker walked into Megan's hospital room. She stopped in midsentence.

"Henry! Thank you so much for coming. Glen told me you were in Portland and drove all the way back."

Henry stood by the side of Megan's bed. "This is unbelievable. I just saw you and Ray at the wedding. How could something like this happen? I am so sorry."

Megan's eyes teared. "I can't process it, Henry. It's like some bad dream."

Henry pulled a chair next to the bed and took Megan's hand in his.

"You're going to be okay. I'll talk to Teddy Winston, the DA. I'm sure they don't think you had anything to do with Ray's death."

"Don't be too sure. I was holding a gun when Kathy Moran found me on the beach."

"Was it the murder weapon?" Henry asked.

"I don't know," Megan answered. "I can't remember anything from the time we left the country club until Kathy found me."

Glen could hear the desperation in her voice and tried to imagine how he would feel if he were in her situation.

Henry turned to his associate. "Do you know whether Megan was holding the murder weapon?"

"No. I called Teddy Winston. The police don't know, either. They're waiting on the results of the ballistics tests."

"Okay," Henry said. "But even if it is the murder weapon no one can think you'd shoot Ray on your wedding night. Everyone at the wedding could see how much in love you two were."

Megan squeezed Henry's hand. "Thank you for that, and thank you for coming to see me. Will you be my lawyer? Will you protect me?"

Henry hesitated. "I'd like to say yes, but there are a few things you have to think about before you hire me to represent you."

"What things?"

"I can foresee several ways this could go, and I might not be the best person to represent you in some of the scenarios. Best case, Teddy Winston doesn't think you're involved or they find the person who did this. In that situation, you won't need a lawyer. But sometimes the police don't get it right and they go after the wrong person.

"Now, I believe you didn't kill Ray but innocent people are sometimes accused of crimes they didn't commit. If you're charged with aggravated murder you'll be facing the death penalty. I'll be honest with you, Megan, handling a death penalty murder case requires special expertise. I've never handled a capital case. I've never even represented anyone charged with murder. If Teddy indicts you for aggravated murder I shouldn't be the attorney who represents you. You'll need an expert, and they're expensive, very expensive."

"Ray was rich. I'm his wife. Can't I use Ray's money if that happens?"

"I'm not sure. I'll have to talk to Ray's attorney and find out the terms of his will. But all this may not be necessary. Glen told me that the person who killed Ray stole valuable items from his collection. I'm certain that the police are concentrating on finding the person who robbed you. He's the obvious suspect. I think the odds are good that you will never be accused of a crime. In the meantime, I'll be here for you."

"Thank you, Henry. I knew I could count on you."

Peter Fleischer, a reporter from the *Palisades Heights Gazette*, and an *Oregonian* reporter were waiting for Glen and Henry when they left Megan's room.

"Are you representing Mrs. Cahill?" Fleischer asked.

"For now, Pete."

"Did she kill her husband?" the *Oregonian* reporter asked.

Henry laughed. "Of course not. They were just married. Now I have nothing more to say."

The reporters pestered them with more questions until it was obvious that they weren't going to get any more answers. When they were in the hospital's parking lot and away from the reporters Henry turned to his associate.

"What do you think?"

"Mrs. Cahill seems genuinely confused. It doesn't look like she's faking amnesia. But I don't have the training to spot someone who's pretending to have lost their memory."

"Well, I believe Megan," Henry said firmly. "And I'm going to make sure that there's no rush to judgment. The first thing we have to do is convince Teddy to give us the police reports so we can see what the investigation has turned up. Then we have to contact the executor of Ray's estate to see if she'll have access to funds for her defense if the worst happens."

"And if she doesn't."

"I said I'd protect her, and I'm not going to let her down."

Glen walked to his car with a smile on his face. He was happy his boss was so enthusiastic about this case because Henry had been severely depressed since Alma Baker had filed for divorce. After Alma walked out, Henry had put on a brave front in public, but Glen had caught him crying in his office and he was certain that Henry was drinking.

There had been a serious physical toll, too. Henry Baker was a big man but he'd kept his weight in check by jogging, tennis, golf, and the occasional gym workout. After Alma left, he'd lost the will to exercise so the pounds had rolled on, his cheeks had puffed up, his jowls had sagged, and his once tight gut had begun to inch over his belt line. Since the divorce, Henry had just been going through the motions, working just hard enough to keep his practice afloat. Glen hoped that the Cahill case would bring Henry back to the living.

CHAPTER FIVE

Frank Janowitz had been hired by Raymond Cahill to be the curator of his collection and he had flown up from L.A. as soon as Teddy Winston called. Janowitz and the DA were talking in the living room of the Cahills' house when a policeman opened the front door for Jack Booth. Jack took in the view as he walked down the staircase. The bright sunshine and frolicking waves were in sharp contrast to the tragedy that had occurred in the house.

Winston made the introductions, and Jack and the curator shook hands. Janowitz surprised Jack, who had expected a curator to be an absentminded, wizened old man with a pince-nez and mismatched socks. Janowitz had blond hair, blue eyes, and a square jaw, and he was wearing pressed jeans and a black T-shirt that molded to a wide chest and showed off boulder-size biceps. His only concession to Jack's stereotype was a pair of gold, wire-rimmed glasses.

"Frank's had a chance to look at the collection and examine the gun. I asked him to wait to tell me his conclusions until you got here," Winston said.

"The robber definitely knew what he was looking for," Janowitz said. "The items that were stolen are the cream of the collection."

"Frank is going to prepare a detailed list of the stolen items with photographs, which I'll circulate to local and national law enforcement agencies," Winston said.

"I wouldn't hold my breath about making an arrest," Janowitz told them. "It would be impossible to sell the stolen stamps, coins, and firearms on the open market. Any legitimate buyer would know that Ray owned them. But there are unscrupulous collectors who will buy stolen items for their private collections at high prices. I'm betting that our thief not only knew what to look for but who would pay top dollar for the items and ask no questions about how they were acquired."

"Do we know if the gun Megan Cahill was holding is the murder weapon?" Jack asked Winston.

Winston nodded. "The ballistics tests say it is."

"What an odd choice for a murder," Jack mused.

"My thought exactly," Winston said. "You'd think the robber would have brought a gun with him if he wanted to shoot Cahill. How would he know that an antique gun would work?"

Winston turned to the curator. "What can you tell us about the murder weapon?"

"You've heard of the Gunfight at the OK Corral?" Janowitz asked.

Jack and the DA nodded.

"On October twenty-sixth, 1881, Wyatt, Morgan, and Virgil Earp and John Henry 'Doc' Holliday faced off against Frank and Tom McLaury, Ike and Billy Clanton, and Billy Claiborne. The fight only took thirty seconds and it didn't really take place at the OK Corral. The confrontation actually took place in a vacant lot several blocks east near C. S. Fly's photo studio.

"When the smoke cleared, Billy Clanton and the McLaurys were dead. Holliday had a few bullet holes in his coat, Virgil Earp was shot in the calf, and Morgan Earp had been shot in the shoulder. Wyatt Earp was uninjured, and Ike Clanton and Claiborne fled when the shooting started.

"No one knows for certain what gun Wyatt Earp used during the gunfight. The best guess is that his six-shooter was either a Colt Single-Action Army or a Schofield .44 Smith and Wesson revolver. The gun Mrs. Cahill was holding is a Schofield .44 Smith and Wesson revolver that Ray believed was Wyatt Earp's gun."

"Was it?" Jack asked.

"Ray never showed me conclusive evidence to substantiate his belief."

"Are you surprised that the gun worked?"

"No. Ray kept it in pristine condition in one of the glass cases that was broken into. He liked to display the type of bullets that would have been used in the gun in the case with the Schofield. The killer only had to load it."

"Have you been able to get anything out of Mrs. Cahill?" Jack asked Winston.

"No. I talked to her doctors. She's awake but she says she can't remember what happened. She suffered a vicious blow to the head and that could account for her amnesia."

"Did you find any gunshot residue on Mrs. Cahill's hands?" Jack asked.

"No. She was rushed to the hospital and no one thought to test her. And the fact that there's no gunshot residue is not conclusive anyway," Winston answered. "You don't always find GSR on the hands of someone, even when you know for a fact that they fired a weapon."

Jack was quiet for a moment. Then he turned to the curator.

"Can you tell us a little about the relationship between Mr. and Mrs. Cahill?"

"Not really. They didn't start dating until I'd known Ray for quite a while. I knew him because of my work with his collection. I've only met Mrs. Cahill a few times, and that was just to say hello when I was at his place in California. But I never saw anything that made me think they weren't getting along."

"How did they meet?"

"Parnell Crouse was a running back who played for the Oakland Raiders. Then he had a serious knee injury and several concussions. The injuries ended his career. As I understand it, Mrs. Cahill filed for divorce soon after Crouse was cut from the team. She had Crouse arrested for domestic abuse; there was a restraining order, allegations of 'roid rage. Ray was a minority owner of the Oakland Raiders. From what I heard, Ray and Mrs. Cahill met at a team party. He was also recently divorced."

Janowitz smiled. He looked embarrassed. "I should make it clear that almost none of what I told you is firsthand knowledge. The divorce was very public, and I got most of what I told you from the gossip columns or stuff I heard at parties."

"Do you know if Cahill had enemies? Maybe a rival collector or someone from his business dealings?" Jack asked.

"I really don't know much about his business or private life. I deal in antiques, rare coins, stamps. We met when I sold him some stamps from a lot I'd picked up at an estate sale. The work I did on his collection was a side job. We didn't socialize."

"Okay," Jack said. "Teddy, do you have anything else for Mr. Janowitz?"

"No," Winston said.

"I appreciate your flying up on such short notice, Frank," the DA told the curator. "What should we do about the rest of the collection?"

"That's really Mrs. Cahill's call," Janowitz said. "It should be safe in the vault. I'm working on an inventory so you'll know what was stolen. I'll talk with Mrs. Cahill when she's better."

Janowitz went back to the den.

"What are you thinking?" Jack asked when they were alone.

"The way I see it, we have two possibilities. Raymond Cahill was the victim of a burglar or his wife killed him. I'd go with the burglar."

"What if she and the burglar were working together?" Jack said. "She was holding the murder weapon."

Winston thought about that for a moment. Then he shook his head.

"If she killed him, why would she be on the beach?"

"Working up a story about being attacked."

"She wouldn't have known that Kathy Moran would come by on a photo shoot," Winston argued.

"What if she went down to the beach to get rid of the gun but Moran came by before she could ditch it?"

"What about the blow to her head?" Winston asked. "It sounds like she was hit really hard."

"Her accomplice could have done that to make her look like a victim."

Winston thought some more. Then he shook his head. "We're just guessing. Hopefully Mrs. Cahill will clear up our confusion when she remembers what happened."

"When am I going to be able to speak to her?" Jack asked.

"She's going to be released today."

Jack looked alarmed. "Will she be staying in Palisades Heights? I don't want her skipping to California."

"The doctors don't want her to travel and we're done with the crime scene, so she'll be staying here. By the way, she's hired Henry Baker to represent her. We had a short talk earlier today."

"So, Mrs. Cahill thinks she needs a lawyer."

"Megan is no dummy. We questioned her about the gun she was holding, she saw that her husband was shot, and she says she can't remember what happened. You'd probably lawyer up under those circumstances, wouldn't you?"

Jack frowned. "Is Baker local?"

"His office is on Ocean Avenue."

"Has he done a lot of criminal defense?"

"Henry has a general practice. You have to if you want to earn a living out here. His criminal defense experience is limited to DUIIs and minor stuff, but he's smart."

"Has he ever defended a murder case?"

"I know he won a vehicular homicide in Lincoln County but I don't think he's ever been involved in something like this."

"I wonder why she hasn't contacted one of the heavy hitters you were so worried about."

"She knows Henry from the country club. I'm guessing that he's the first name that popped into her head. And she's been in the hospital since the murder. She wouldn't have had an opportunity to do any research."

Jack nodded. "Okay, that makes sense. When are we talking to her?"

"We're going to meet here this afternoon around five."

CHAPTER SIX

Megan Cahill was seated at a round glass table under the shade of an umbrella on the deck behind her house, staring at the sea. The cool breeze drifting in from the ocean made the edges of the umbrella sway. Megan didn't turn when the door to the deck opened, so all Jack could see was the hood of the sweatshirt she was wearing to combat the chill in the air.

The two men seated at the table with Megan stood when Jack, Winston, and Archie Denning walked onto the deck. Henry Baker, a large man with thinning, sandy blond hair and pale blue eyes, was dressed in a sky blue shirt, yellow tie, and tan suit. The lawyer wasn't obese but he was sloppy fat with a small gut that lapped over his belt and the beginning of a double chin. When Henry saw the prosecutors and the detective he walked over to them. The young man who was sitting with him followed.

"Hey, Henry," Winston said.

"Pleased to meet you, Mr. Baker. I'm Jack Booth and this is Archie Denning. He's a detective with the state police and I'm with the Oregon Department of Justice."

"The hired gun from the capital," Henry said with a smile as they shook.

Jack shrugged. "I've been called that before but I'm really here as an adviser."

Henry turned to the young man who stood beside him.

"This is Glen Kraft, my associate. He's going to be assisting me."

Glen was five foot ten with an athletic build. Jack took him for a recent law school graduate because of his full head of wavy brown hair and smooth skin. The young lawyer was wearing a cheap gray suit, a white shirt, and a blue tie with narrow white stripes. He looked very serious. Jack remembered his first murder case and he bet defending a homicide had gotten the young man's blood racing.

"Pleased to meet you, Glen," Jack said.

"Can we step inside for a moment before you talk to Mrs. Cahill?" Henry asked.

"Sure," Winston said.

"What's your position on Mrs. Cahill?" Henry asked when they were in the living room.

"What do you mean?" Winston asked.

"Is she a suspect? Are you going to Mirandize her?"

"Right now I consider Mrs. Cahill to be a victim and a witness," Winston said hastily.

"That's not exactly accurate, Teddy," Jack interjected. "I consider her to be a person of interest. She was holding the murder weapon when Kathy Moran found her and she's probably in line to inherit Raymond Cahill's fortune. So she had the motive, the means, and the opportunity to commit the crime."

"She was hit on the head hard enough to give her a concussion, for Christ's sake," Henry said.

Jack shrugged. "If she had an accomplice he could have hit her to take suspicion off of her."

"Do you really believe that?"

"Look, Mr. Baker, this is early days in the investigation. I'm just throwing out possibilities. I haven't talked to Mrs. Cahill yet so I have no opinion. If she's innocent then what happened here is truly horrible. I can't imagine what it must be like to lose a spouse right after you're married."

"It's been awful for her. So be very gentle when you talk to her."

"You have my word," Jack said.

They walked back outside and Jack turned his attention to Megan Cahill, who continued to stare out to sea. Jack walked past Henry and stopped in front of her, blocking her view. She looked up at Jack. Megan had an olive complexion, full lips, high cheekbones, and liquid brown eyes. Strands of black hair strayed from the confines of her hood.

"How are you feeling?" Jack asked.

Megan didn't answer right away. Jack had the impression that she had to work to process what he'd just said. Then again, she could be faking.

Henry hurried over and stood at Megan's shoulder. "Mrs. Cahill is still feeling the effects of the blow to her head and she tires quickly, so we need to keep this meeting short."

There were four chairs set around the table where Megan Cahill was sitting. Jack gestured toward one of them.

"May I?" he asked the injured woman. Megan stared for a moment before dipping her chin. Jack took the chair next to her. Henry took a chair next to his client and pulled it close to her. Winston took the last chair and Glen stood behind his boss while Denning stood off to the side where he could see Megan's face.

"First, let me say how sorry I am," Jack said. "I can't imagine how you must feel, but I want you to know that we are going to try our hardest to find the person who hurt you and your husband."

Jack waited for a reaction and he got one when Megan teared up.

"What do you remember about that evening?" Jack asked.

Megan shook her head slowly. "I . . . I've tried but . . ."

"My client and I have talked about this, Jack," Henry said. "Mrs. Cahill remembers the wedding but her last clear memory is getting in their car outside the country club. Megan's doctor says that this type of short-term memory loss is normal after a serious blow to the head."

Jack kept his eyes on Megan's face. "So you have no memory of what happened after you came home?" He asked.

"No," she answered, her voice barely above a whisper.

"The doctors say that her memory should return, but they can't say how soon," Henry said.

"Can you think of anything that might help us catch your husband's killer?" Jack persisted.

Megan responded with a brief shake of her head.

"What about enemies. Mr. Cahill was a successful businessman. Was there anyone whom he may have bested in a business deal who was upset with him?"

"I was divorced a little over a year ago. I knew Ray from team parties. We didn't start dating until I filed for divorce so we haven't . . . hadn't known each other that long." Megan's voice caught and her eyes watered again. "Ray didn't talk about his business." She paused. "There was someone at the wedding reception—a man. He and Ray were arguing but I was too far away to hear what they were saying. You should talk to Kevin Mercer, his partner in the investment firm. He would be able to tell you about business problems."

"Thank you. Can you think of anything else that can help us catch your husband's killer?" Jack asked.

"I . . . No. I just remember standing on the beach and Miss Moran helping me back to the house and seeing . . ."

Megan started to sob.

"I can see how painful this must be for you, Mrs. Cahill, so I'll cut this short. If you remember anything about that night or anything else you think might help us catch your husband's killer, call Mr. Winston. Will you do that?"

Megan nodded. Jack stood up. "I hope you feel better soon. And, again, my condolences."

Henry followed Jack, Winston, and Denning to the door.

"Mrs. Cahill jogged my memory about the scene at the wedding reception. A man did crash the party. I don't remember his name, but Kevin Mercer, Ray's business partner, might. The man was very angry and he had to be escorted out by security."

"Where does Mercer live?" Jack asked.

"In L.A."

"Okay. Does he know about Mr. Cahill?"

Henry nodded. "He was at the wedding but he flew back to L.A. on a private jet right after the reception started. He's staying in California to deal with the business problems caused by Ray's death."

The prosecutors left and Henry sat down next to Megan Cahill.

"Are you okay?" he asked.

Megan nodded.

"Look, I hate to bring up business but I have to. When I saw you at the hospital I told you that I probably shouldn't represent you in a murder case where the state is seeking the death penalty. We agreed that I would represent you until you decided who you would hire as lead counsel—someone from

Portland or L.A., whoever you felt would best represent your interests."

"Those men don't think I killed Ray, do they? They didn't seem to suspect me."

"Remember we went into the house before they talked to you?"

"Yes."

"Jack Booth was very clear that you're a suspect."

"But he was so nice to me."

"He puts on that act to fool people. I called around. Jack Booth is not a nice person where his cases are concerned. He is single-minded and driven and he will do anything to win."

"Why would he think I killed Ray? Someone hit me, Henry. Someone stole Ray's stamps, his coins."

"Booth suggested that you may have had an accomplice who hit you to make it look like you weren't in on the murder and the robbery."

Megan's eyes grew wide. She looked terrified. "That's insane. We just got married. Why would I kill my husband on our wedding night? That makes no sense. You told me that's what you thought at the hospital."

"And I still do, but Booth pointed out that Ray's money could have been your motive. You are Ray's heir."

"That's good news, isn't it? That means I can afford to hire a top criminal defense lawyer if I'm indicted."

"There may be a problem. Denice Bailey, the executor of Ray's will, told me that she's not freeing up any money until it's clear that you weren't involved in Ray's death."

"Can she do that?" Megan asked. She sounded panicky.

"I'm afraid so. But you have money of your own, don't you, from the divorce?"

"Not enough for the fees you thought a top lawyer would

charge. My parents were dirt-poor, so I never had a dime of my own. If it wasn't for scholarships and part-time jobs there's no way I would have gotten through school.

"By the time we split, Parnell had gone through most of his money. That's why I started putting money into an account he couldn't tap. We were almost bankrupt, even after we sold the house."

Baker looked troubled. Megan suddenly perked up.

"Ms. Bailey will free up the money if I'm not indicted or if they arrest the murderer, won't she?"

"Well, yes. Then she would have no basis for keeping it from you."

"Do you think you can find me a lawyer who will wait for his fee until after he wins or they arrest the real killer?"

"That won't work. It's unethical for a criminal lawyer to take a case on a contingent fee. The bar is worried that a lawyer in that position might do something unethical to win so he could get his money."

"This is so unfair," Megan said. She began to sob again. Her shoulders shook and she beat her fists against her pant legs.

Henry wrapped an arm around her shoulders. "Don't lose hope, Megan. I'll keep representing you until we think of a way out of this mess."

Megan looked up into Henry's eyes. "Would you? I'd be so grateful."

Jack, Denning, and the DA had taken separate cars. After a few more minutes of conversation, they split up and Jack drove to his motel. On the way, he remembered something Frank Janowitz had said. The curator had told them how hard it would be to sell Cahill's rare items because reputable dealers and collectors wouldn't touch them. He'd also told them about disreputable collectors who would stash stolen items in private collections. To sell the items, you'd have to know who those disreputable collectors were. Jack bet Janowitz would know. And Janowitz was one hell of a good-looking guy. Were he and Megan Cahill lovers? Jack decided to find out.

The balcony outside his room was the only place Jack could smoke, so he went there and lit up. It was sunny and warm. A young woman was running on the beach with a Labrador retriever, and a father was helping his daughter build a sand castle. A couple was walking slowly, hand in hand, deep in conversation.

Jack checked his watch. He was meeting Kathy at seven. It had been quite a shock seeing her again, and being with her had unearthed memories and emotions best left buried. But the mere sight of her had also awakened feelings he thought he'd shaken. The first time they'd met, everything had gone horribly wrong for both of them. Now Jack wondered if fate had given them a second chance.

Part Three

THE *KILBRIDE* DISASTER

2000

CHAPTER SEVEN

The phone call jarred Jack Booth out of a deep, alcohol-induced sleep. He jerked up, eyes wide, heart beating rapidly. Where was he? The phone rang again and the nerve-jangling ring sounded strange. The room didn't look right, either. Jack groped for the receiver and couldn't find it. Then he remembered why everything seemed so odd. The phone wasn't where it should be because he wasn't where he should be. He was in a cheap apartment in a strange bed.

Jack turned on the light, located the phone, and grabbed the receiver. "What?" was all he could manage. His mouth felt like it was filled with packing material and the words coming out of the receiver took ages to penetrate his brain.

"Wait," he said. He swung his legs over the side of the bed and sat up. He felt light-headed and he paused a second before turning on the lamp on the nightstand. The light stabbed into his eyes. He closed them and groped for the pen and pad he kept next to the phone. He opened his eyes slowly and took a deep breath. The air irritated his throat and he coughed.

"Okay," he croaked. Oscar Llewellyn was on the other end of the line. He made a hangover joke. Jack didn't laugh. Llewellyn read off an address and gave him directions. Jack repeated the address to make sure he had it right. Then he said, "I'm on my way."

Jack hung up and buried his head in his hands. After a moment, he leaned over and pulled a cigarette out of the open pack on his end table. Jack lit up, inhaled, and coughed. He took another drag, stabbed out the cigarette, and stared at the floor.

After a moment, Jack stood up. It took an extraordinary effort to get to his feet. He felt light-headed again. While he waited to regain his equilibrium, Jack looked at the bed. It was a single. Adrianna would be curled up on her side of the king in their bedroom, which would become her bedroom as soon as the divorce became final.

Jack felt bad. He'd fucked up big-time. Adrianna was a good person and he'd taken her for granted, burying himself in his job and in strange beds with any woman to whom he took a temporary fancy. He was seized by regret, but only for a few seconds. Jack was an expert at anesthetizing his feelings and he'd shaken off this one by the time he staggered into the bathroom.

The bigger they are, the harder they fall was the first thought that popped into Jack's head when he saw Joey Kneeland sprawled on his back on the floor of room 107 of the Weary Traveler Motel. Joey was huge. Jack eyeballed him as at least six foot seven, and he didn't have to wait for the autopsy report to put his weight around three hundred and fifty pounds.

Jack knew all about Joey Kneeland. He'd played a year of college ball at Portland State but was too dumb to keep himself academically eligible, so he'd engaged in the only profession for which he was suited, muscle for the drug dealers in his neighborhood. From what Jack had heard, Joey wasn't that great at roughing up people. He was too slow, both mentally and physically, and Jack knew of at least two times Joey had been put in the hospital.

"What a mess, huh?" said Oscar Llewellyn. Detective Llewellyn was a twenty-year veteran who'd been investigating homicides for eleven years. He was five foot ten, wore his hair in a Marine cut, and dressed like a blind man had chosen his outfit. Jack had worked with him before and he was very good.

Jack walked around the body. If it weren't for Joey's unique physique, he wouldn't have been able to ID the victim. Joey had been shot in the face, probably with a shotgun. Jack studied Joey's massive, pear-shaped torso, which was also riddled with entry wounds and bathed in blood.

"How many times do you think he was shot?" the deputy district attorney asked.

Llewellyn shrugged. "With all that blood, who can tell? Talk about overkill."

Jack cocked his head and looked at the detective. "You think one shot would have brought Joey down? If it was me, I'd have used every bullet I had."

"Point taken," Llewellyn said.

"Where are the witnesses?" Jack asked.

"The guests who saw something are in their rooms. The two from this room are in separate squad cars."

"They stuck around?"

"The manager called 911 as soon as he heard the shots, so there was a car here in no time. First responders found the two of them cowering behind the bed. There are more bullet holes in the walls behind them. The guys who shot Joey told them to stay put for ten minutes. I guess they were too scared to run."

Jack took another look at Joey. "Can't say as I blame them."

"Room one eleven is vacant. You can use it if you want to talk to the witnesses here."

"Sounds good. Bring in Joey's roommates, one at a time."

On the way to the motel, Jack had stopped to get a large black coffee. He took a sip as he walked down to room 111. The caffeine helped a little but he was still groggy.

Room 111 was as seedy as the crime scene and only a few steps down from his apartment. The bed was covered by a cheap quilt, and the mattress sagged in the middle. The motel advertised HBO and adult movies. The TV was a flat-screen, but it was the only thing in the room that looked like it didn't predate World War II.

Jack looked for someplace to sit. There was an armchair next to a lamp and a wooden straight-back chair at the desk. He chose the armchair and was about to sit down when Llewellyn escorted a woman into the room.

"Mr. Booth, this is Sally Russo," Detective Llewellyn said. "Sally, Mr. Booth is the prosecutor in charge of this case."

Jack put Russo at five seven and two fifty and she looked like she had a lot of miles on her. She appeared to be exhausted and shaky. Her eyes were bloodshot and her stringy hair looked like it hadn't been washed in a few days. Russo was wearing an extra large sweatshirt and pants with a stretch waist. There were blood spots on both garments.

Jack held out his hand. "I'm pleased to meet you, although I regret that it has to be under these circumstances."

Russo seemed surprised by the way the DA had greeted her. He guessed that she'd had run-ins with the authorities before and had not been treated courteously.

"Take a seat," Jack said. "Can I get you some water, coffee?"

"I could use some coffee," Russo said. Jack nodded at

Llewellyn, who stepped outside for a minute to give one of the uniforms the order.

"Please sit down." Jack pointed at the straight-back chair. Russo lowered herself onto the chair slowly. It wobbled a little as she settled.

"Are you doing okay?"

"Not really," Russo said. She sounded subdued and she was staring at the floor.

"Detective Llewellyn told me a little about what happened. I can tell you, I'd be messed up if I'd been here."

"They just shot him," Russo said. Her voice quivered. Then she started to cry. "Joey never hurt nobody. He looked scary but he wasn't mean."

Jack nodded. "I never met Mr. Kneeland, but that's what I heard, too. So why was he murdered, Sally? Did he do something to scare the guys who did this?'

Russo wiped her nose with the back of her sleeve and rubbed the tears away.

"They didn't give him a chance. As soon as he opened the door, they started shooting."

"Did you recognize the shooters?"

"They were wearing masks, and even if they weren't . . . Man, I was on the floor behind the bed as soon as the shotgun went off."

"Okay. Can you tell me anything about them?"

"Not really. It happened so fast. I didn't even see the other men. Just the guy who shot Joey with the sawed-off. He had jeans." She shook her head.

"Were they white, black, Asian?"

"They sounded white and the guy who pointed the shotgun at me, he was wearing gloves but his wrists were white."

"Did you see any tattoos or scars?"

"No. I was so scared I just looked at the ground. I didn't want to see anything. I didn't want them thinking I could be a witness against them. Then they might have killed me."

"Did anyone say anything?"

"Yeah. The one with the shotgun. He told me and Carl to stay on the floor for ten minutes. He said they had a guy outside who would shoot us if we stuck our heads out the door."

"Would you recognize the voice if you heard it again?"

"I doubt it."

"Okay, Sally. You've been great so far. Now, I'm going to ask you a question that you're probably not going to want to answer. But I promise you won't get in trouble if you answer honestly. I'm not going to give you your *Miranda* warnings, so a judge wouldn't let me use what you say against you. Understand?"

Russo nodded.

"I prosecute murder cases. I'm not interested in what you were doing in this room if it doesn't involve you, Carl, or Joey killing someone."

"We never did anything like that," Sally assured him.

Jack nodded. "Why did these guys bust in here? What did they take?"

On his way to view the crime scene, one of the forensic experts had told Jack that he'd found cocaine residue on the desk in room 107. He watched Sally debate how much she should say.

"Tell me the truth and I'll treat you right."

Jack didn't add a threat. Sally knew she was in trouble and Jack was the only one who could help her.

"What if we were doing something we shouldn't be?"

"I can give you immunity if it didn't involve violence. Look, I know you're scared. I can't even imagine how I would feel if I saw a good friend gunned down and I thought I was next. That's why I want to help you. Let me do that."

Sally looked Jack in the eye. She was scared, but Jack could see that she was clinging to hope.

"We had some coke. Not a lot. We were down on our luck and thought we could score."

"You were dealing out of the room?"

Sally nodded.

"How many people knew?"

"A few. We got friends who know people who use. We weren't gonna get rich," she said quickly.

"What did the killers take?"

"Our coke and all the money."

"Do you have any idea who did this?"

"No." Sally's jaw clenched. She wasn't sad anymore. She was angry. "But the guy with the sawed-off said we'd end up like Joey if he ever caught us selling again."

"You think he's a dealer and you were in his territory?"

"That's what I thought, but I don't know any more than what he said. Believe me, if I could help you get the bastards who killed Joey, I would."

Jack was about to answer when Llewellyn walked in with the coffee. He handed it to Russo. Then he bent down and whispered in Jack's ear.

"We may have caught a break. One of the guests heard the shots and peeked through the blinds on his window. He saw one of the shooters run by his room. The guy braced himself on the guy's car. He wasn't wearing gloves."

"Did you . . . ?" Jack started to ask.

Llewellyn nodded. "Dave lifted a beautiful set of prints."

CHAPTER EIGHT

Bernie Chartres's foot had been tapping like a telegraph key since Jack walked into the interrogation room in Oklahoma City, where Bernie had been arrested. Jack had flown to Oklahoma as soon as he got the news. The prisoner was a sloppy-looking man with a pockmarked face, who was not much brighter than Joey Kneeland. Bernie's straight black hair was tied back in a greasy ponytail and he had trouble making eye contact. This wasn't Chartres's first brush with the law, but he'd never been in trouble like this before.

Bernie's court-appointed attorney was driving Jack crazy. Every few seconds she'd either brush her frizzy black hair off her face or adjust her glasses. Jack thought she might have obsessive-compulsive disorder.

"You know you're fucked, right?" Jack asked Bernie Chartres.

"Don't answer that," the lawyer said.

"She's right," Jack said. "Anything you say can and will be used against you. Unfortunately for you, we don't need a confession. An eyewitness saw you tear out of the room where Joey

Kneeland was shot. Your mistake was pushing off his car. He'd just had it cleaned and your prints look really great. So don't talk. I've sent three guys to death row and I can use another notch in my gun."

"I didn't shoot him!"

Chartres looked panicky. His attorney told him to shut up.

"Look, Bernie, I'm gonna be honest. You've got a pretty clean record. A couple of minor assaults but nothing that would indicate you'd blow the shit out of someone. But you're also the only suspect I've got. So, unless you help me—and, by helping me, help yourself—I'm going to be forced to bring the full weight of the law down on you. You know that old saying about a bird in the hand being worth two in the bush?"

Bernie didn't look like he had any idea why Jack was talking about birds.

"Well, you're the bird I have in my hand, and I don't have any other birds or any idea who the other little birds at the motel were." Jack squeezed his open hand into a tight fist. "So you're the only bird I can crush at this time.

"Now I'm going to step outside. You talk with your lawyer. Give me the names of the shooters and I'll treat you right. Exercise your right to remain silent and I promise to bring popcorn to your execution."

Twenty minutes later, Chartres's attorney beckoned Jack into the room to talk about the deal. A few minutes after they had agreed on a disposition, Bernie was talking like his life depended on it—which it did.

"Gary Kilbride shot Joey. I didn't know he was going to shoot him, honest."

Jack was a trial lawyer and any good trial lawyer can keep from reacting to a surprise, no matter how devastating. In this case, the surprise was really great. Gary Kilbride wasn't the biggest drug dealer in Portland but he was big enough, and he was a very bad person who liked to hurt people. Jack was a very ambitious prosecutor. Putting a scumbag like Gary Kilbride on death row would definitely give his career a boost.

"Why would Gary waste time with a penny ante operation like the one at the motel?"

"They were selling in his territory. He wanted to make an example out of them. The plan was we beat them up, take their drugs and money, and tell them we'd do worse if we caught them selling again. But we didn't know Joey would be there."

Bernie shook his head.

"Joey looks like King Kong. When he opened the door, Gary freaked and started shooting."

"What did you do?" Jack asked.

"I got out of there. I didn't want anything to do with that shit."

"Okay. Now who was shooter number two?"

"Nick French. He's how we learned about everything. I think he got spooked and opened fire because Gary opened fire."

"How did you learn they were selling out of the motel?"

"Angie Reed is Nick's girlfriend. Nick was over at her house with a bunch of other people and one of them knew. He said he was going to score some coke the next day at the motel. So Nick told Gary at this bar. And I was there and Gary was pissed because he didn't want anyone selling to his customers. He said Nick and me could have some of the coke and money if we backed him up. He said he wouldn't do anything really bad. All he wanted was to scare them. I thought he'd smack them around a little. I never thought he'd shoot anyone."

"Whose idea was it to bring the guns?"

"Gary. I don't even own a gun. He gave me one. I didn't want it but he said I had to wave it around to look like I meant business."

"Where's the gun now?"

"I tossed it in some bushes. I don't even know if it was loaded."

Jack asked for the location of the bushes. Then he made some notes. When he was finished he looked across the table.

"You done good, Bernie, and I'm going to do right by you. We'll polygraph you. If it turns out that you didn't shoot anyone, you walk after you tell a grand jury what you told me and testify in court. I'll get an immunity agreement to your lawyer. We'll keep you here for your safety. Then we'll fly you to Portland when the time is right."

CHAPTER NINE

It strained the limits of Jack's self-control to keep from staring when Gary Kilbride's attorney walked into his office. She had long ash-blond hair, high cheekbones, and liquid blue eyes. Her white silk blouse was open at the neck, and her severe black business suit came with a skirt that was cut just long enough to be tasteful but short enough to show off her long legs. The legs and face were tanned gold.

When the *Kilbride* case ended and Jack had been thoroughly humiliated, he blamed his disastrous loss on Kathy Moran's amazing looks and killer body. Overactive hormones and the desire to come out on top in every competition had always been the twin drives in Jack's life. During *Kilbride,* however, his hormones redirected the blood that would normally have flowed to his brain, causing Jack to spend time that should have been spent on legal research fantasizing about what might happen between him and Kathy Moran when the case concluded.

But Jack's downfall was several months down the line on the day he met Miss Moran. On that day, he was sitting pretty. True, he had fucked up his marriage, but he was only twenty-seven and already a top prosecutor in the Multnomah County district attorney's office, fast-tracked into Homicide because of his stellar record and gaining a statewide reputation he hoped to parlay into a partnership at a prestigious law firm where he would make the big bucks he believed he deserved.

"We haven't met, Mr. Booth. My name is Kathy Moran and I'm Gary Kilbride's lawyer."

Jack walked around his desk and shook Kathy's hand. It was soft and warm. Jack's palm tingled and his heart and nether regions went haywire. He was certain that something electric had passed between them when they touched and he believed Kathy felt it, too, because her eyes widened briefly.

"Pleased to meet you, Ms. Moran. Take a seat."

"Are you with the public defender?" Jack asked when he was back behind his desk.

Kathy smiled. "No. Mr. Kilbride has retained my firm to represent him."

"Oh? Who are you with?"

"Well, actually, I'm with two friends from law school, Nancy Hong and Ronnie Ireland. Our firm is Hong, Moran and Ireland."

"Haven't heard of it."

"I'm not surprised. We're small and we don't do much criminal law."

Jack frowned. "Have you been practicing for a while?"

"No. We all graduated from Boalt Hall four years ago. Nancy and Ron are from Oregon and they convinced me to move up here."

"Aren't you a little inexperienced to be handling a death penalty case?"

Kathy blushed. "I explained that to Mr. Kilbride, but I

represented a friend of his successfully in a criminal matter and he insisted that I handle his case. I did win a manslaughter trial in Washington County a few months ago."

"There's a big difference between handling a manslaughter case and trying an aggravated murder with a potential death penalty," Jack said, hoping that he sounded wise beyond his years.

"So I'm learning. Anyway, I wanted to introduce myself and get a copy of the indictment and the discovery."

Jack leaned back. "It won't do you much good. I've got Kilbride nailed."

Jack wasn't bragging. He saw the *Kilbride* case as a slam dunk. That opinion was based on an objective evaluation of the facts, as *he* saw them. There were two victim eyewitnesses to the shooting, and Bernie Chartres had been terrific in the grand jury. To say that Jack was overconfident about his chances in *Kilbride* would have been an understatement. His overconfidence explained why he spent so little time thinking about possible problems with his case.

"You have way more experience then I have," Kathy conceded with a shy smile, "so you're probably right. But I won't be able to advise my client until I've read the police reports."

"Fair enough. I'll give you everything we've got. When you've gone through the discovery, let's talk."

"So you might entertain a plea?"

"Right now, Kilbride can plead to aggravated murder and take his chances in the penalty phase."

"You won't consider life without parole?"

Jack shrugged. "Make the offer and I'll take it to my boss. He has the final say in capital cases, but I'll probably oppose leniency. Your client gunned down a human being in cold blood because he didn't like some low-level dealers selling minute amounts of coke in his bailiwick. Kilbride is a vicious thug and the world will be better off without him."

Kathy didn't defend her client and Jack thought she looked scared like any lawyer would be who was handling a death case for the first time and was starting to realize that she was out of her depth.

"Thank you for your time. I'll get back to you when I finish going through the discovery," Kathy said.

Jack flashed what he hoped was a winning smile. "I'll look forward to it. It's been nice meeting you."

Kathy stood and turned, presenting Jack with a wonderful view as she walked out of his office.

CHAPTER TEN

On the day set for the trial in *State v. Kilbride,* Jack showered, shaved, and donned his best suit. He wanted to make a good impression on the judge and jury, but impressing Kathy Moran was his first priority. He considered a guilty verdict and, most probably, a sentence of death to be a done deal. Getting Kilbride's lawyer in the sack was an ongoing project that had become a bit more challenging because of the lack of contact he'd had with Kathy after their first meeting. She had filed the motions all defense lawyers filed in death cases—constitutional challenges to the statute, motions to suppress, and the like—so Jack had seen her in court. But he hadn't had a real chance to talk to her because she'd left court with her client and gone directly to the jail after each hearing. Jack assumed he'd have a good chance to turn on the charm during plea negotiations, but, strangely, Kathy had not followed up on the possibility of a plea. Jack might have spent time wondering why she had not pursued a plea if he weren't so preoccupied with wondering how Kathy's breasts would feel when he cupped them or how smooth her thighs would feel when he stroked them.

The Honorable Albert Haber had been assigned the *Kilbride* case. The judge was tall and thin with steel gray hair and an iron temperament. He had been a prosecutor before going on the bench and he was definitely a law and order jurist. On the other hand, he was a stickler for the law and followed it regardless of where it led him. Haber demanded that attorneys come to court prepared and on time, and he would take them to task in front of the jury for the slightest deviation from proper decorum.

"Are the parties ready to proceed?" Haber asked as soon as he took the bench.

"Jack Booth for the State, Your Honor. We're ready."

"Kathy Moran for Mr. Kilbride."

Jack looked across the room at the defense table. Kathy was wearing the same suit she'd worn to his office and she looked just as stunning. Gary Kilbride was also wearing a suit. It was charcoal gray. The fabric at the shoulders and sleeves strained against his bulging muscles. Kilbride had a large head and black hair he wore short and tight to his skull. His eyes were an unsettling gray color and his nose was crooked, like that of a boxer with poor defensive skills. Kilbride caught Jack's eye and grinned. He looked way too cocky, which was fine with Jack. He'd enjoy wiping the smirk off the killer's face.

"Okay," Judge Haber said. "Let's call in the jury."

It was not unusual for jury selection in a death penalty case to go on for days with both sides asking potential witnesses question after question in an attempt to determine if they could count on the jurors to deliver a prosecution or defense verdict during the penalty phase. Jack was shocked when Kathy asked few questions and jury selection was over by the end of the day, but he chalked up her ineffective voir dire to inexperience. Handling capital cases was a specialty, and even attorneys with vast experience trying noncapital homicides were not equipped to handle a death case without special training.

Jack realized that he would have an excellent excuse for asking Kathy to dinner when the case was over. He could volunteer to do a postmortem and act as a mentor, thus gaining her trust and making the other steps in his planned seduction much easier.

Court recessed after the alternate jurors were chosen and it reconvened in the morning with both sides giving their opening statements. Jack took an hour during which he outlined his case. Kathy took fifteen minutes and spoke about burdens of proof and the reasonable doubt standard, never mentioning a single piece of evidence or one witness that might clear her client. Jack suspected that she had spoken in generalities because no such witness or evidence existed. He was feeling supremely confident up to the point where his first witness was sworn.

"I have a motion for the court," Kathy said after the first officer on the scene told Judge Haber that he would tell the truth, the whole truth, and nothing but the truth.

Judge Haber peered at Kathy through his wire-frame glasses. He did not look pleased to have the orderly presentation of evidence interrupted.

"Mr. Booth hasn't asked a single question, Miss Moran. What motion could you possibly make?"

"One best heard out of the presence of the jury, Your Honor," she said as she strode over to the dais and handed the judge her motion and the very thick memo in support of it. While Haber was reading the motion, Kathy walked over to Jack. When she handed him his copy of the motion, she looked down as if she were embarrassed.

"Bailiff, please take the jury out," Judge Haber said when he had finished reading the motion and memo.

Jack didn't hear the judge. He felt light-headed. By the time he had finished the memo he thought he might throw up.

"All right, Miss Moran, let's get this on the record."

"Thank you, Your Honor. You heard Mr. Booth outline his case. I have attached to my memo the discovery provided by the State. Almost all of it was covered in Mr. Booth's opening statement. I assume he has no surprise witnesses who would add to what he told the jury because he would not be able to present a surprise witness without violating the discovery rules.

"The basis for my Motion for Judgment of Acquittal is simple. Mr. Kilbride is prepared to stipulate that Mr. Booth's witnesses will say what he told the jury they would say in his opening statement and that his physical evidence will prove everything he said it would. It is our position that all of Mr. Booth's evidence when taken in the light most favorable to the State cannot support a finding of guilt beyond a reasonable doubt.

"Let me sum up the State's evidence in the light most favorable to the State. Mr. Kneeland was definitely murdered in room one oh seven of the Weary Traveler Motel, but none of the eyewitnesses who shared the room with Mr. Kneeland were able to identify any of the people who committed the murder.

"A witness has unequivocally identified Mr. Kilbride as the killer. This witness is his alleged accomplice, Bernard Chartres. Other than Mr. Chartres no witness or piece of evidence is able to connect Mr. Kilbride to the shooting. And that is the problem for the State.

"Oregon Revised Statute 136.440 defines an accomplice as 'a witness in a criminal action who, according to the evidence adduced in the action, is criminally liable for the conduct of the defendant' under certain circumstances defined in ORS 161.155 or ORS 161.165. This would include aiding and abetting. In his opening statement, Mr. Booth contended that Mr. Chartres aided and abetted Mr. Kilbride in the commission of this felony.

"ORS 136.440 goes on to say that 'a conviction cannot be had upon the testimony of an accomplice unless it is corroborated by other evidence that tends to connect the defendant to the commission of the offense.' If the court listened carefully to Mr. Booth's opening statement and read all of the reports provided in discovery, you would be forced to conclude that only the testimony of the alleged accomplice Bernard Chartres connects Mr. Kilbride to the incident at the motel. No other witnesses place him there, nor does any forensic evidence like DNA, fingerprints, hair, or fibers.

"Therefore, taking the evidence the State will produce in its most favorable light, any trier of fact would be forced to conclude that the State had failed to meet its burden."

When Kathy sat down she did not look at Jack. Jack didn't notice. He was stunned.

"What do you have to say, Mr. Booth?" Judge Haber asked.

Jack was speechless. He couldn't think. Finally, desperately, he asked for time to read and research Kathy's motion carefully. Judge Haber granted his request, but everyone in the courtroom knew that Gary Kilbride was going to walk because of Jack Booth's incompetence.

CHAPTER ELEVEN

The debacle in *State v. Kilbride* marked the end of Jack's ascent in the district attorney's office. Gary Kilbride walked because Jack had screwed up, and Jack was so overwhelmed by self-pity that he forgot about his witness. Three months after the end of the trial, Bernard Chartres went missing. Two months after that, his body was found off an old logging road by hikers. He had been tortured before he was killed. Oscar Llewellyn broke the news to Jack, who drank himself unconscious and didn't show up for work for two days.

Then, nine months after Kathy Moran ran him out of court, a phone call from Detective Llewellyn presented Jack with an opportunity for revenge.

"Hey, Jack," Llewellyn said. "I'm glad I caught you."

"What's up, Oscar?"

"Grab a quick bite to eat. Then get back to your office by seven tonight. I have someone who wants to talk to you."

"Why can't they come over now?"

"They don't want to be seen?"

"Why?"

"Don't ask so many questions. Just be in your office at seven. You won't be sorry."

Other than the cleaning crew, there were few people working in the district attorney's office at seven o'clock. At 7:05, Oscar Llewellyn ushered a slender Chinese woman into Jack Booth's office. Jack figured her age at late twenties or early thirties. She was dressed in a gray skirt and wore a matching gray jacket over a rust red blouse. The woman looked upset.

"Nancy Hong, meet Jack Booth."

The name sounded familiar but Jack couldn't remember where he had heard it.

"Miss Hong has something to tell you," Llewellyn said when they were all seated.

Hong sat with her hands clasped in her lap. She looked very uncomfortable.

"I wish I wasn't here," Hong said, "but the situation has become intolerable. Detective Llewellyn was the chief investigator in one of my cases and I came to trust him. That's why I went to him."

"What did you want to tell me?" Jack said.

"It's about my law partner Kathy Moran."

Bingo! Jack thought. Hong, Moran and Ireland was Kathy Moran's law firm. Jack had tried to forget about Kathy. When her name came up in a conversation its very mention elicited feelings of anger, shame, and embarrassment.

Hong looked down at her lap. Her shoulders were hunched. When she looked up, anger had overcome any discomfort she felt.

"Kathy is a criminal, Mr. Booth. She's a drug user and an embezzler. I've tried to reason with her, but she lies. I can't trust her." She paused. "Coming here was a last resort."

"Can you go back a bit?" Jack asked. "Can you start at the beginning?"

Hong nodded. "Kathy, Ron Ireland, and I met at Boalt Hall during our first year in law school. We were in a study group. Ron and I are from Portland. When we graduated we talked Kathy into coming to Oregon and starting a law firm. She's very smart, brilliant. We were very excited."

Hong shook her head. Her distress was obvious.

"It all started with that *Kilbride* case."

Jack's face reddened. Hong noticed and she looked embarrassed.

"Shortly after the case ended, Kathy's behavior changed. She couldn't stop bragging about her coup. She was giddy, revved up. I wrote off her enthusiasm to having won a big case in spectacular fashion. Then she started coming into the office late; she missed court appearances. Ron and I couldn't figure it out. Then Ron began acting oddly."

Hong paused again. She was very upset. "Ron is married. He was married in law school to his college sweetheart. But he always had the hots for Kathy. You can see why. She's gorgeous and she uses sex to get what she wants," Hong said bitterly. "Ron found out what she was up to and she seduced him to shut him up."

"What did Ron find out?" Jack asked.

"Kathy is addicted to cocaine. I think Gary Kilbride hooked her so he wouldn't have to pay for her representation in his murder case. I know he never paid the entire fee. And Kathy's been embezzling. She was our managing partner. She kept the books and paid the bills. We trusted her, so we never checked up on her. But I did after she started acting oddly. I don't know how much she's stolen but our bank accounts are very low."

"You said coming to me was a last resort."

Hong nodded. "I confronted her. She was defiant at first. She said there was nothing wrong with the books. She wouldn't explain why she was missing work and court on a regular basis. So I cornered Ron and he broke down and confessed.

"Ron and Kathy were working late one night and he walked in on her snorting coke in her office. He said that he was going to tell me. Kathy offered to fuck him if he kept quiet. Ron's marriage hasn't been great. He gave in to temptation. She even talked him into trying cocaine. Then she kept him on a string while she looted our accounts to pay for her habit. Ron's wife found out about the affair and wants a divorce. The firm is probably going to break up. And it's all her fault."

"Would you press charges if it meant Miss Moran would go to jail?"

"At this point, yes. She betrayed me and she's ruining Ron's life. I worked hard to build our firm and she's sent it straight down the toilet. I'm just praying she didn't do anything that will lead to a malpractice suit."

"Can you prove Miss Moran is embezzling funds?" Jack asked.

"I had a friend who's a CPA take a look at the books on a weekend when Kathy was out of town. The drugs must have made her overconfident and sloppy because she left a paper trail. I also found a Baggie in her desk and I brought it to Detective Llewellyn."

"The lab confirmed it's cocaine," Llewellyn said.

"Okay, then. Let's have a chat with Miss Moran," Jack said.

Hong and Llewellyn worked out a plan. Then the lawyer and the detective left. Jack had kept his demeanor businesslike until he was alone. Then he leaned back in his chair and smiled.

CHAPTER TWELVE

Detective Llewellyn arrested Kathy Moran at five in the afternoon and placed her in a holding cell in the offices of the police bureau where only police personnel would see her. Kathy demanded a chance to call a lawyer, but Llewellyn stalled so the frightened attorney could give her imagination a workout.

Shortly before eight o'clock, the cell door opened and Jack walked in. He had looked forward to his confrontation with Kathy, but any sense of satisfaction melted away when he saw her. He remembered how vibrant Kathy had looked on the day they met. Now she looked skeletal and there were dark circles under her eyes. The lustrous blond hair Jack remembered looked lifeless, and Kathy was twitchy, shifting in her seat, tapping her foot.

"I'm sorry we're meeting under these circumstances," Jack said as he sat opposite her.

"I'll bet," Kathy said. She wouldn't look Jack in the eye.

"You probably think I'm still upset about the outcome in *Kilbride*," Jack said, "but I'm not. You taught me a valuable lesson and I'm grateful. I was too cocky and my ego got in the way. If I'd been less self-assured and a little more insecure I might have figured out that my case wasn't anywhere near as good as it seemed."

Now Kathy did look up. Her expression was one of contempt.

"Don't try to play good cop, Jack. You can't pull it off. And don't lie to me. Everyone knows how badly I humiliated you. You were the laughingstock of the defense bar, and I hear your boss wasn't too pleased."

If Kathy didn't look so pathetic, Jack might have reacted differently.

"Do you think it's in your best interest to antagonize me, Kathy?"

Jack could see how much Kathy hated him. "I want a lawyer," she snapped.

"That's your right, but hear me out first. You could be looking at prison. Ron is going to testify that you hooked him on cocaine. That's distribution. If I decide to ship your case across the street to the Feds you could do serious time."

Kathy suddenly looked panicky. She started to say something. Then she paused and smiled coquettishly at Jack.

"I'm sorry if I insulted you. I'm just exhausted and scared."

Kathy looked into Jack's eyes.

"We don't have to be enemies, Jack. Let me out and we can continue this talk later this evening in my apartment."

If she'd come on to him like this when they'd met for the first time, Jack would have been across his desk in a flash. Now he found her attempt at seduction desperate and pathetic.

"Come on, Kathy. This isn't going to get you anywhere."

The anger and hate he'd seen in her eyes moments before were back in a flash.

"I want my phone call. I'm not going to talk anymore without a lawyer present."

"You don't have to talk. Just listen. There's a way out of this mess."

Kathy drew her lips into a defiant line, but Jack could tell that she was paying attention.

"We want Gary Kilbride. If you help us get him we'll help you stay out of jail."

Kathy's features shifted from intense interest to real fear. "Are you crazy? You've seen Kilbride's file. He's not just a killer, he's a sadist. Have you forgotten what happened to Bernie Chartres?"

Jack leaned forward and looked Kathy in the eye. "This can go one of two ways. Cooperate and no embezzlement and drug charges will be filed. You'll voluntarily resign from the bar, which will give you a chance to reapply without a criminal record at some point in the future. We'll have to figure out when that will be. But no one will bring your past up if you help us. Your law partners have agreed to keep quiet if you make restitution for the funds you embezzled. You're young, Kathy. You're very bright. Cooperate and you can get out of this in one piece and have a chance at a future.

"If you decide to fight the charges you *will* be reported to the bar and the chances are pretty good that you'll be disbarred permanently. You'll also go to prison. When you get out, there will be nothing waiting for you.

"Right now, only I, Detective Llewellyn, and your partners know you've been arrested. Your reputation is still pristine. You can keep it that way or you can throw your life away. It's your choice."

"What . . . what would I have to do?"

"I talked this over with Detective Llewellyn. This would be a one-time deal. We want you to get Kilbride to sell you a kilo of cocaine. We'll have you wired . . ."

Kathy looked like she might throw up. She shook her head violently back and forth.

"No, no! I can't do that. You don't understand."

Jack leaned forward. "Talk to me, Kathy."

Kathy's eyes lost focus and she stared at the floor. Jack was certain she was seeing something that wasn't there.

"He . . . he debases me. He . . . I'm an animal to him. He . . ."

Kathy paused and gagged.

"Do you want some water? Are you okay?"

Kathy started to cry. Jack wanted to comfort her, but he knew he could never touch her while she was under arrest and they were being taped.

After a minute, Kathy got her emotions in check. When she looked up at Jack he saw the face of a woman who had lost all hope.

"I can't wear a wire."

"We'll fix it so he won't know you're wired."

She looked down again, too embarrassed to look at Jack.

"Whenever I go to his house he . . ." She licked her lips. "He makes me take off all of my clothes, everything. I . . . I have to beg him for my drugs. That's when he . . . He does things to me."

She looked up again, pleading. "Please, Jack. Don't make me do this."

Jack felt sick and he wasn't sure that he could go along with Llewellyn's plan anymore. He stood up.

"I'm going to get you some water and give you a chance to pull yourself together."

Llewellyn was waiting in a small room near the holding cell where he was watching the video feed. Jack walked in and shook his head.

"We can't do it, Oscar. She's terrified."

Llewellyn's stony expression didn't change. "Of course she's scared. She's facing jail time and she's gonna be disbarred. Anyone would be scared."

"I said terrified. There's a difference. And she's right to be terrified. You know what Kilbride is capable of doing."

Llewellyn flashed Jack a paternal smile. "You're young, Jack, and she's hot. She got to you. It's understandable. She's using her pussy to affect your judgment. Get over it. She got into bed with Kilbride. Now she regrets it. I feel for her, but we need her to take him down."

"What if he catches on?"

"He won't, believe me. I talked to the tech guys. He won't make her."

"How is she going to pull it off in this state?"

Llewellyn shrugged. "That's her problem. She knows she'll walk if she helps us set up Kilbride and she knows she'll go to jail and lose her license if she doesn't. That's powerful motivation, Jack. She'll keep her shit together when she has a little time to think."

"I don't know."

Llewellyn put his hand on Jack's shoulder. "This isn't the first time I've done something like this. We're gonna nail Kilbride and Miss Moran will be fine. Trust me."

CHAPTER THIRTEEN

Gary Kilbride's parents were well off and they had tried to give their only child every opportunity for success. His test scores and early grades proved that he was bright and they anticipated a career as a doctor or lawyer or maybe something in finance. They had been shocked when he was arrested for assault in high school, but they accepted his explanation that the brutal beating he had administered to a gay student was a reaction to a sexual advance. An out-of-court settlement crafted by a high-priced attorney had kept Kilbride's record clean.

Kilbride had earned a football scholarship to Oregon State, where he planned to play linebacker. His father died shortly before he dropped out of college and his mother was so consumed by grief that she didn't have the energy to question his decision. Kilbride told his mother that he was going to take a year off to deal with his dad's death, but Kilbride did not have a choice about leaving school. His departure was part of a deal brokered with the administration by his football coach after the coach discovered that Kilbride was supplying steroids to some of the other players. Kilbride—ever resourceful—used his father's death as his ace in the hole during negotiations. No one wanted to cause his mother more grief by saddling her only child with a criminal record.

Kilbride never returned to school. Selling drugs was too profitable and time-consuming. And it provided ample opportunities to satisfy his need to inflict pain and humiliation. It also gave him enough money to purchase a conservative Tudor house in a respectable residential neighborhood near Reed College in southeast Portland. His home, like the others on his block, was well tended. A gardener cut the grass and trimmed the hedges. Beautiful flowers adorned the property. Kilbride didn't have a lot of contact with his neighbors, but those who had spoken to him were under the impression that he was "in sales."

Kilbride laundered his profits through legitimate businesses and he insulated himself from the police by constructing numerous buffers between him and his customers. Some of those customers were students at the college. Others inhabited the shadier segments of society. All of them had a driving need that Kilbride could satisfy for a price. Kilbride's lieutenants ran street dealers who stored his cocaine in houses and apartments in which he had a well-concealed interest. The storehouses changed frequently. The police had raided a few of them but were never able to connect the dealers or the drugs to Kilbride.

Kilbride was watching the Trail Blazers play the Lakers on his sixty-inch plasma TV when Kathy Moran called.

"How's my favorite lawyer?" Kilbride asked as soon as he picked up.

"I need a, uh, a favor, Gary."

"Oh?"

"I wondered if I could stop over. I'm not far."

Kathy provided an excellent outlet for Kilbride's sadistic

tendencies and just hearing her beg for an audience gave him a hard-on.

"I don't know," he teased. "I'm watching a game. We're playing the Lakers and the score is tight."

"I wouldn't be long. I'm just . . . you know."

"How's business?" Kilbride asked. "Lots of new cases with healthy retainers?"

"That's what I wanted to talk about."

"We should do this in person. I don't want to tie up my phone line."

Kilbride suspected his phone might be tapped so he always kept his conversations vague and short.

"Okay, I'll come right over."

Kilbride hadn't thought of Kathy Moran as his lawyer since he'd gotten her hooked. Now he thought of her as his sex slave and he enjoyed humiliating her whenever she came around begging for product. The sexual aspects of their deals had developed slowly as Kathy's need increased and her financial resources began to tank. Usually Kilbride only accepted cash, but he got a kick out of dominating Kathy. He loved to hear her beg and it made his day when he forced her to degrade herself.

Ten minutes after their phone call ended, Kilbride's doorbell rang. He let Kathy wait while Kobe Bryant sank two free throws. Then he opened the door. Kathy flashed an anxious smile. Kilbride studied her. She looked sexy as hell in tight jeans and a T-shirt with no bra. Kilbride could see a hint of nipple where it pressed against the fabric.

Kilbride stood aside and Kathy walked by him. He could tell she was nervous.

"You look good," Kilbride said.

"Thank you."

"You'd look better without those clothes."

Kathy lost some color. "Please, Gary, can't we just . . . ?"

Kilbride held up a hand. "No talking. You know the drill. Obey or leave. If we're going to have the conversation I think we're going to have, I need to be sure that you're not wearing a wire. So what do you want to do? It's your choice."

Kathy looked at the floor. Kilbride enjoyed her discomfort and the view as she stripped off everything but her thong.

"Everything off, Kathy. I'm going to have to do a search. There's no telling where a mike can be hidden nowadays, what with modern technology."

Kathy kept her eyes down as she stripped. She had been through this before, but she still felt sick to her stomach. Kilbride stroked her thighs before inserting a finger. Kathy bit her lip and tried not to react. Kilbride fondled her breasts as he probed. After a minute, he let her go. Then he pointed to a corner of the room.

"Why don't you wait over there until the game is over? Then we'll talk. Eyes to the wall."

Kathy did as she was told, standing in the corner like a chastened schoolgirl. There were five minutes left in regulation, which meant twenty minutes or more in basketball time. Kilbride made her wait until the buzzer. Then he turned off the set and called over his shoulder.

"Come."

Kathy was near tears but she bit them back and walked in front of Kilbride.

"Kneel down," he said, pointing to a spot on the hardwood floor that he knew would hurt Kathy's knees.

When she was on the floor in front of him, Kilbride let his eyes run over her. She wobbled a little as the wood cut into the bone. Kilbride smiled.

"So, Kathy, what did you want to talk about?"

"I need some coke but I'm a little short."

"Kathy, Kathy, you still owe me from the last time."

"I know but I . . . I really need it, and I have an idea I know you'll like."

Kilbride gave her an understanding nod and her words came out in a rush.

"Once, a while back, you said I could help you by selling a little. So I thought about that. There are these lawyers I know. One guy I slept with and his buddies. Most of them are recreational users. I think I could make a connection with them. I mean, I know I could because one of the guys I used with at a party, his connection was busted and he asked me who I used."

Kilbride's face clouded over and Kathy saw rage building.

"I didn't give him your name, Gary," she said quickly to avoid a beating. "I would never do that."

Kilbride's rage subsided as quickly as it had risen.

"He's in a bad way," Kathy babbled. "I told him I could fix him up. So, if you could front me a kilo, I could sell him some and sell the rest to these other lawyers and work off my debt."

Kilbride considered Kathy's proposition. He liked it. Lawyers had money and they couldn't risk exposure. If he could cultivate a group of attorneys . . .

"When would you need this kilo?" Kilbride asked.

"Right away. Like tonight. This guy is hurting. The one whose dealer was busted. He'll pay top dollar, but it's got to be tonight. I think he may have a lead on another dealer, but I said I'd try to get him some stuff right away."

"I don't have a kilo here," Kilbride said.

Kathy got on all fours and crawled over to Kilbride. She put her hands on his knees and leaned in.

"Can't you get it for me, Gary? I'd do anything if you helped me."

Kilbride's blood ran into his groin and he stroked Kathy's hair.

"Please, Gary. Make a call. I can keep you entertained until it gets here."

Kilbride hesitated. He never liked to do business at his house but . . . He picked up an untraceable phone.

"Richard, my shirts are dirty and I need a new shirt right away."

Kathy pulled down his zipper.

"At my house, right now," Kilbride said as he elevated his hips. Kathy slid his pants and underwear down to his ankles. Then she lowered her lips toward his crotch. She felt sick, she felt lower than an animal. Only one thing kept her going.

Kilbride had been right about the technology. The micro-transmitter that had been sewn into the hem of her jeans had picked up everything she and Kilbride had said and sent it to a van that was parked down the block from Kilbride's house.

"Police, open up!" Oscar Llewellyn shouted a moment before the SWAT team smashed open Gary Kilbride's front door.

Kilbride jumped up from the couch, his eyes wide with panic. A plastic-wrapped kilo of cocaine rested on a coffee table between him and Kathy.

"Hands in the air! Hands in the air!" Llewellyn shouted. Kilbride looked at the guns pointed his way and raised his hands above his head. Kathy did the same. Thankfully, Kilbride had let her get dressed, but her face was still a portrait of shame.

"What have we here?" Llewellyn said as he motioned one of the officers toward the cocaine. Kilbride didn't answer.

Llewellyn read Kilbride and Kathy their rights while they were being handcuffed. Then Jack stepped over to Kilbride.

"This is a warrant to search your house, Mr. Kilbride. You'll be escorted downtown while we execute it."

Kilbride glared at Jack. Then he turned toward Kathy.

"You did this, you bitch."

Kathy was too frightened to answer or look Kilbride in the eye. A vein throbbed in Kilbride's temple.

"I won't forget this," he said. "Ever."

As soon as Kilbride was led out, Kathy's knees sagged. "I'm going to be sick," she said.

Jack grabbed her elbow. He led her to the couch and eased her down. "You'll be okay," he assured her. "We'll protect you."

Kathy was terrified. "You don't know him like I do," she sobbed. "He's evil. He doesn't understand mercy or forgiveness."

Jack put his hands on Kathy's shoulders. "Gary Kilbride is going to prison for a long time and you are going to put all this behind you and start your life over. You're tough and you're smart and you're going to be okay."

Kathy looked deep into Jack's eyes, searching for reassurance, searching for hope. Then she took a deep breath and squared her shoulders.

"Thank you, Jack. Thank you for believing in me."

"I do believe in you. You're a survivor. You're going to get through this."

Oscar Llewellyn drove Kathy back to the police station and Jack drove home. When he got back to his sterile apartment he had trouble sleeping. Would Kathy really be okay? Had they sacrificed her in order to get Gary Kilbride? Jack didn't think Kilbride would escape punishment this time. He had checked and double-checked the legality of the wire and the search and he was convinced that there were no legal loopholes through which Kilbride could squeeze. Kilbride was going to prison. But he would get out someday. Kathy was right. Kilbride was not like other men. He didn't know the meaning of mercy, and Jack was worried that he would not forget that Kathy Moran was the reason he was in prison.

Part Four

THE *CAHILL* CASE

2005

CHAPTER FOURTEEN

The Seafarer was at the far south end of Ocean Avenue, a block from the divide between commercial and residential real estate. The exterior was wood that had been weathered by the salt spray and ferocious winter rains that had swept in from the Pacific since the day the bar opened. But it was summer now, the tourists were in town, the sky was clear, and it was still light at seven.

Jack had changed into a short-sleeve, sky-blue shirt that hung out over tan chinos. When he walked into the Seafarer's dark interior he was welcomed by a din that was a mix of raucous laughter, the music of a local band, and the hum of conversation. A hostess in tight jeans and a black T-shirt flashed a smile and asked him how many were in his party. When he told her that he was meeting Kathy Moran, the hostess pointed to a booth near the far wall.

A low ceiling was hung with ship lanterns, and the timbered walls were decorated with a nautical theme. Jack inched his way through the narrow gaps between the tight-packed tables and across a beer-stained and sawdust-covered hardwood floor until he reached the booth. Kathy smiled when she saw him. She was wearing pressed jeans and a blue work shirt with rolled-up sleeves that showed off her tanned forearms. She looked rested. Her hair shone even in the dim light in the bar, and her face had a fresh scrubbed look.

"So, you're vouching for the chowder?" Jack said as he sat opposite her in the booth.

"It's the best in Palisades Heights. The fish and chips are good, too."

A waitress came over and Jack took Kathy's suggestions and also ordered a pitcher of beer.

"Are you're doing okay?" Jack asked. "I don't mean tonight. I mean with life."

"I can't complain now, but it was rough at first. Rehab was hell. There were times when I wanted to run. Then I'd remember what I'd lost."

Kathy shuddered. "You have no idea how low I'd fallen, what Kilbride forced me to do. And remembering gave me the strength to stick it out."

"No relapses?"

"Once, soon after I moved here, but Grady . . ." Kathy nodded toward a meaty bartender with a sweaty, bald head and Popeye forearms. "He got me through it, and I've been squeaky clean ever since."

"Tell me about the photography," Jack said to change the subject to something pleasant.

Kathy beamed. "I love it, Jack. I've always done it. It started as a hobby when I was a teenager. In a way, getting disbarred was a blessing. I was never enamored with the law but I love painting pictures on film. And the coast with those massive rock formations and the sunsets and the storms . . ."

Kathy blushed. "Sorry, it's just . . ."

"Don't apologize. I think it's great that you have such passion for what you do. I wish I had something like that."

Kathy sobered. "You sound like someone who's burning out."

"No, it isn't like that. I still get pumped when I have a big case. But it's more about the winning. I don't know if I love any other part of it."

"Well, you did have a reputation as someone who would do anything to win."

"Oh?"

Kathy cocked her head to one side. She looked thoughtful.

"I don't know if I should tell you this."

"Go ahead. I'm a big boy. I can take it. This is about *Kilbride*, right?"

She nodded. "You had a reputation for wanting to win at all costs, but you also had a reputation for playing around. So I set you up. I dressed provocatively to distract you."

"You saw the flaw in the case from the beginning?"

"The minute I read the indictment."

Jack threw his head back and laughed. "I was a first-class fool."

"Don't be so hard on yourself."

Jack grinned ruefully. "I deserved to get clobbered."

"I'm glad you're taking it so well. I was worried that you'd harbor a grudge."

"No, actually I'm grateful to you. You taught me a good lesson. That was the last time I got caught with my pants down like that."

The waitress brought their food and they ate in silence for a while. Then Kathy said, "So, tell me what you've been doing. You left the DA's office . . ."

"Yeah. After *Kilbride* my reputation dropped several notches. It went up a bit when I put him away with your help, but the writing was on the wall. So, when this spot opened with the Department of Justice, I decided it was time for a change."

"And you like the new position?"

"I travel a lot, but the cases are usually challenging."

"Are you still single?"

Jack grinned. "That's certainly forward."

Now it was Kathy's turn to laugh. "I'm not hitting on you. I'm just curious to see if your reputation as a ladies' man is still intact."

Jack stopped smiling. "I'm not seeing anyone right now. That's okay, because I'm rarely around. What about you?"

Kathy shook her head. "I've been pretty celibate since I got out of rehab."

Jack looked around the tavern. "Now that I think about it, this is an odd place for someone who's been in rehab to work."

Kathy shrugged. "It was the only place I could get a job. And I'm not now and have never been an alcoholic. That thing with the cocaine was pure stupidity. I was full of myself and I was certain I could take it or leave it. Then it was too late and I was hooked."

Kathy shook her head ruefully. "It's hard once you've been addicted but—except for that one backslide—I've been able to control myself. Also, Grady watches me like a hawk. It's like having a guardian angel—or mother hen—around twenty-four/seven."

Jack was about to say something when someone at the front door of the tavern caught his eye. A man was standing half in shadow, but the half Jack could make out looked a lot like Gary Kilbride. Kathy saw where Jack was looking and she looked there, too, but the man had already left. She stared at Jack quizzically, but he didn't want to alarm her.

"I thought I saw someone I knew but I was wrong," he said. "So, you beat your addiction. That's great."

"You never beat an addiction. I learned that in rehab. You just learn how to keep from giving in to it."

"Have you thought about reapplying to the bar?"

"I'm not ready for that, yet. And, frankly, I don't know if I'd want to go back to being a lawyer, even if I knew I was a lock to be readmitted."

When Kathy smiled she looked serene. "I like it here. I like knowing everyone and knowing they care about me. And I love my photography. I'm not making the big bucks anymore but I'm at peace and you can't put a price on that."

"I envy you," Jack said. And he did. He couldn't remember a time when he was really content.

Kathy cocked her head to the side and grinned. "You could move to the coast, take up a hobby and find inner peace."

Jack laughed. Then he looked at his watch.

"I'm glad we did this," he said, "but I'm out on my feet."

He started to pull out his wallet but Kathy shook her head. "This is on me, Jack. And I enjoyed it, too."

They said good-bye and Jack left. The chowder had been as good as advertised, the beers he'd finished had mellowed him, and the night was balmy. As he walked to his car Jack thought about how much Kathy had changed. She seemed happy and so motivated about her photography. He'd told her the truth when he said he didn't hold a grudge anymore. But, if he had, he thought he would not hold one, now that they'd talked.

Jack was still in a good mood when he got into his car and checked his rear-view mirror for traffic. Then his mood changed. A man was standing in a doorway halfway down the block where he could watch the tavern. Jack couldn't see his face, but he was willing to bet that it was the man he'd seen in the tavern—the man who looked like Gary Kilbride.

Jack made a U-turn and drove back toward the Seafarer. The

man looked his way. Jack tried to see his face but it was in shadow. Jack floored the accelerator and the man sprinted into an alley between a bakery and a store that sold swimwear. Jack pulled to the curb and leaned across the passenger seat just in time to see the man disappear around the back of the bakery.

Jack sat back and thought about his next move. After a moment, he pulled out his cell phone and dialed Oscar Llewellyn. Oscar had retired from the Portland Police and tried retirement. After six months of golf, fishing, and drinking by himself he had called Jack when he read about an opening for an investigator at the DOJ.

"It's Jack."

"What's up?" Oscar asked.

"I'm in Palisades Heights working a new homicide and I've got a few things for you."

"Shoot."

"First, I want you to call the corrections division and find out if Gary Kilbride is still a prisoner at the state penitentiary."

There was dead air for a second. "That fucker's doing hard time. No way they'd let him out."

"Just check, okay, and call me as soon as you know. It's very important."

"Will do. What's next?"

Jack filled him in on what he'd learned so far. Then he asked him to check with his contacts in California to see if Frank Janowitz was having an affair with Megan Cahill.

"Anything else?"

"Yeah."

CHAPTER FIFTEEN

When Jack walked into Teddy Winston's office the next morning, the district attorney stopped talking to a man in a tan police uniform that looked like it had been cleaned and pressed moments before Booth entered the room.

"Jack, this is George Melendez, our chief of police," Winston said. "George was in Portland at a conference. That's why you haven't met him."

Melendez was a little over six feet, wore his hair in a buzz cut, and had the physique of someone who pumped serious iron. Jack guessed that he was ex-military and he learned later that Melendez had been a decorated Marine. When the men shook hands, Melendez did not apply any pressure, which Jack took as a sign of self-confidence.

"Teddy says you think we may have a problem," the police chief said.

"I'm pretty sure we do. That's why I wanted to meet this morning. Last night, I had dinner with Kathy Moran."

Winston frowned, and Jack held up his hand. "We didn't

discuss the case. We hadn't seen each other in five years. It was just two old acquaintances catching up."

Jack turned to Melendez. "I don't know how much Ted told you about Raymond Cahill's murder."

"He was just starting to bring me up to speed when you walked in," the police chief said.

"Do you know Kathy Moran?" Jack asked.

"Sure, the bartender at the Seafarer."

"Do you know she's a photographer?"

Melendez nodded. "I've seen her stuff at Ellen Devereaux's gallery."

"The night Raymond Cahill was murdered, Kathy finished her shift around one thirty and went down to the beach to take photographs for a proposed exhibition. That's when she saw Megan Cahill standing on the beach beneath her home, holding a gun. Kathy brought Megan into the house and discovered the body."

Jack looked across the desk at the district attorney. "I didn't want you to sit in on my interview with Kathy because I knew we'd bring up something that happened in Portland the last time we met. You'll learn momentarily why I'm telling you about it now but I want you to promise to keep what we say confidential because it could hurt Kathy's reputation."

"Tell us what you've got to say," Melendez said.

Jack looked at Winston and Winston nodded.

"Kathy practiced law in Portland for several years. We met when she represented a drug dealer named Gary Kilbride in a murder case. She won the case but Kilbride hooked her on cocaine. Kathy went downhill fast and embezzled money from her law firm to pay for her habit. Her partners came to me and we worked out a deal with Kathy: no prosecution if she set up

Kilbride and resigned from the bar. She kept her part of the bargain, Kilbride was sentenced to prison, and she went into rehab. It sounds like she's gotten her life back on track and I don't want anything to derail her."

"What's the problem, Mr. Booth?" Melendez asked.

"Gary Kilbride is a violent psychopath. The key witness in his murder trial was tortured and killed shortly after Kilbride was acquitted. There's no evidence connecting Kilbride to the murder, but I would be shocked if he wasn't responsible. Last night, when I was eating with Kathy, I thought I saw Kilbride in the Seafarer. When I left, I thought I saw him watching the front of the tavern. I drove back but the man I saw ran away. This morning I learned that Kilbride was given an early parole. I have no idea how he managed that but he's very bright and he has the money to hire very good lawyers."

"Do you think Miss Moran is in danger?" Melendez asked.

"He threatened to get Kathy when he was arrested and I can't think of a reason for Kilbride to be here that doesn't involve getting revenge on her. And I was the prosecutor in the murder and drug cases, so he could be after me, too."

"What do you want us to do?" Winston asked.

"Provide protection for Kathy."

"Are you certain the man you saw was Kilbride?" Melendez asked.

"No. He was half in shadow across a dark room so I can't swear it was him and he was over a block away when I saw him from my car. But it's too much of a coincidence that he's out on parole and someone who looks like him is in Palisades Heights."

Melendez thought for a moment. Then he made a decision.

"We don't have a big enough force to babysit Miss Moran but

I think we should tell her that Kilbride is out and you think you saw him last night. I can order a patrol officer to cruise by her place at night and I'll have someone escort her home while we see if we can find Kilbride. If we do, I'll have a talk with him. That's the best I can do."

CHAPTER SIXTEEN

Beachfront property in Palisades Heights was impressive to look at and cost a fortune. As you moved back from the Pacific, the houses decreased in size and value. The blue, weather-beaten bungalow with the white trim that Kathy rented from Grady Cox was six blocks east of Ocean Avenue and wouldn't impress anyone.

It took several minutes of hard knocking before Kathy unlocked her front door. She was barefoot and dressed in a rumpled T-shirt and shorts. She looked bleary-eyed and her hair was sleep-tousled. But she came awake instantly when she saw Chief Melendez and the worried look on Jack Booth's face.

"Sorry to wake you, Kathy," Jack said, "but something's come up."

Kathy looked back and forth between the two men.

"What's this about?" she demanded.

"Can we come in?" Chief Melendez asked.

Kathy hesitated before stepping aside. Jack walked into Kathy's living room. He was surprised at how messy it looked.

There were newspapers and books strewn over a dumpy couch and dirty plates and glasses on the coffee table in front of it. Kathy saw where Jack was looking.

"Excuse the mess."

"Not a problem," Jack said. "My place will never make *House Beautiful*."

Kathy cleared the literary debris off the couch and the two men sat down. Kathy moved to a rocking chair and folded her hands in her lap. She looked anxious.

"What's happened?" she asked.

"Do you remember when we were eating and I said I saw someone I knew?"

"Yes."

"I didn't want to alarm you but I thought I saw Gary Kilbride inside the Seafarer and I thought I saw him watching the front door of the tavern when I left."

Kathy's eyes went wide.

"My investigator called the penitentiary," Jack continued. "Kilbride was released on early parole."

"How could that happen?" Kathy asked.

"I don't know. I'm checking into it. But Chief Melendez is going to have someone escort you home until we clear this up. He'll also have a patrol car cruise by your house."

"I'm going to find Kilbride and I'm going to have a heart-to-heart with him," the police chief assured her. "He's not going to hurt you."

"You have to be very careful," Kathy said, her fear evident. "Gary isn't normal. He enjoys hurting people, and he thinks he's so smart that he can outwit everyone."

"I've dealt with people like that before, Miss Moran."

Kathy leaned forward. Her shoulders were hunched and she

was clasping her hands so tightly that the knuckles were white. She looked Melendez in the eye.

"Promise me that you won't underestimate Gary. He's different. He's not afraid of the police. He'll seem friendly. You'll think you've persuaded him to your way of thinking. But he'll be manipulating you. He can lie to your face and you'll never see it."

"I know exactly the type of person you're describing and I can assure you that I know how to deal with them. I spent many years in the Marines. Some were as an MP. There's not too much I haven't seen."

Jack thought Kathy was going to say something else but she changed her mind.

Jack pulled something out of his pocket. Kathy stared at it. Then she looked really frightened. There was a .38 police special in Jack's hand.

"This is my gun. Do you know how to use it?"

"I . . . I've done some shooting." Kathy licked her lips. "Yes."

"The chief is going to get you a permit and I'm going to lend this to you. It's strictly a safety precaution. But we'll both feel better knowing you're armed."

"Jesus," Kathy whispered.

"Look, this is probably an overreaction on my part, but we want to keep you safe and the chief doesn't have the manpower to provide a bodyguard. Will you take the gun?"

Kathy hesitated. She stared at the weapon. Then she nodded and held out her hand. Jack gave her the .38.

Melendez handed Kathy his card. "These are the numbers of my home and cell phones. Call immediately, any time of the day or night, if something happens."

"Thank you, both of you," Kathy said as she escorted the

men to the door. "You can't imagine how much I appreciate this."

"We just want you safe," Jack said.

Jack and the police chief walked out of the house. When he got to his car, Jack turned. Kathy was still in the doorway. She smiled at him and Jack smiled back.

CHAPTER SEVENTEEN

Fewer than twelve hours after Jack Booth's call, Oscar Llewellyn had discovered the identity of Parnell Crouse's California divorce attorney and had an appointment to meet him. His flight landed early, and Oscar had thirty minutes to spare when his cab dropped him off on the sidewalk in front of the glass-and-steel building in San Francisco's financial district where Lucius Jackson practiced law.

Oscar recognized Jackson the minute his secretary ushered him into Jackson's spacious corner office. Only a few of the pictures and decorations on the attorney's office walls hinted at his life before he began practicing law, but one look at the man and there was no question about how he had earned his law school tuition.

The African-American attorney was in his forties but he could still pass for the five-foot-eleven, 220-pound cannonball who had wreaked havoc on defenses during seven years as a San Francisco Forty-niner. Jackson's round, squat head featured a nose that had been flattened more than once by vicious defensive backs and massive linemen. His thick shoulders, biceps, and forearms seemed to want to break free from the constraints of his suit jacket in much the same way he had broken free from would-be tacklers. To the dismay of sports writers and fans, the Pro Bowler had walked away from professional football after winning his second rushing title so he could attend law school while his brain was still free of the effects of concussion. After graduation, Jackson had joined a prestigious San Francisco law firm and developed a lucrative practice representing past and present NFL players.

"Thanks for seeing me on such short notice," Llewellyn said.

"You got my imagination working overtime when my secretary told me that you're with a district attorney's office in Oregon and you wanted to talk to me about a murder investigation."

"Actually, I'm with the Oregon Department of Justice's District Attorney Assistance Program. We've been called in by a prosecutor in a small town on the Oregon coast to assist him in a murder investigation."

"Where do I fit in?"

"We're trying to get some background on Parnell Crouse's ex-wife, Megan. Since you handled Mr. Crouse's divorce, we thought that you probably learned a lot about her."

"Why do you want to know about Megan Cahill?"

"She's a person of interest in the murder of Raymond Cahill."

"Raymond Cahill is dead?"

"You didn't know?"

"I've been spending twenty-four/seven on a brutal divorce case that settled late yesterday afternoon. No TV, no radio, and I only had enough energy for the sports page this morning."

"Mr. Cahill and Megan were married Sunday and he was shot to death on their wedding night."

"You're kidding!"

"Unfortunately, I'm not."

"And Megan is a suspect," Jackson said.

"You don't seem surprised."

"The ex–Mrs. Crouse is not a nice person, so, no, I'm not surprised."

"What can you tell me about her?"

Jackson leaned back in his chair. "Have you met Megan?"

"No, but I looked her up on the Internet."

"Any pictures you've seen do not do her justice. She is every teenage boy's wet dream and she also has a very high IQ. That's a perfect combination for a gold digger. I assume you know what a leech is, Mr. Llewellyn? It's a parasite that attaches itself to a living organism, then sucks out all of the organism's blood. That description also fits Megan."

Oscar laughed. "Why don't you tell me how you really feel?"

"To know Megan is to despise her. Look, Parnell Crouse is a dumb farm boy. He and Megan were dirt-poor when they grew up in the same backwater in Texas. Parnell had the hots for Megan from day one, but she played hard to get in high school until it became evident that Parnell was going to get a full ride to some Division I powerhouse if he could meet the academic requirements. Megan tutored him and wrote a lot of his high school papers. Then she coached him for his SATs and he scored the bare minimum to get into Texas. Once he was accepted, she followed him and kept him on a string until it was clear he'd make a pro team.

"Parnell, thick as he was, finally figured out that Megan was only interested in the millions he was going to make in pro ball, so he tried to break up with her. But, like I said, Megan has a genius IQ and is excellent at problem solving. She told Parnell that she was pregnant. When he balked at marrying her, she threatened to go public and cause a scandal, which could have affected where he was drafted. They were married in Las Vegas the week before Oakland drafted him. Once they were married, Megan told him that she'd miscarried. The miscarriage supposedly happened when he was in training camp. Personally, I think she faked the pregnancy.

"Parnell never started and he was mostly used in short-yardage situations. He was never a finesse runner. It was always headfirst and brute force. There were several injuries, a torn ACL, concussions. He had terrible headaches and became addicted to pain pills. A few years ago he was cut and no team picked him up. That's when Megan filed for divorce and walked away with most of the money Parnell had earned."

"Couldn't you protect him?" Oscar asked.

Jackson shook his head. He looked sad. "He came to me when it was too late. Megan handled the finances from the get-go, and she siphoned money into her own accounts as fast as it came in. When she left Parnell, Megan took his manhood and his money and left him with debts and an addiction."

"What happened to him?"

"I helped him get into rehab and he called me once or twice after he got out. But I haven't heard from him in more than a year."

"Do you have any idea how I can contact him?"

"I can give you his last address. I don't know if he's still there."

"Thanks for your time," Oscar said as he stood to leave.

"I hope I've been of some help."

"You've definitely given me food for thought."

"If you do find Parnell," Jackson said, "tell him I said hello."

CHAPTER EIGHTEEN

Gary Kilbride was neither nervous nor irate. George Melendez found that interesting. The police chief had let Kilbride stew in the interrogation room for forty-five minutes without food or water while he observed him through a two-way mirror. The air-conditioning unit had been turned off, so the small, windowless room had to be uncomfortably hot, but Melendez never saw Kilbride wipe away the sweat that trickled down his brow or show any other sign of discomfort.

Melendez tried to imagine how he would feel if he'd just gotten a taste of freedom after five years in prison, and a small-town cop hauled his ass down to the police station without giving him the slightest idea why he was being rousted. He sure as hell wouldn't be sitting quietly with a smirk on his face.

When Melendez opened the door to the interrogation room, Kilbride was slouched on an uncomfortable wooden chair with his hands folded on the room's only table. A sea blue aloha shirt with red and yellow orchids hung over his jeans.

"Good morning," the police chief said as he took the chair on the other side of the table.

"Good morning, sheriff."

"Actually, I'm the chief of police."

"Sorry, *Chief*," Kilbride said, sitting up and flashing an amiable smile.

"Do you know why you're here?"

"Honestly, I have no idea. I'm hoping you'll tell me."

"Why are you visiting Palisades Heights, Gary?"

Kilbride looked confused. "I assume you know I was just paroled from the Oregon State Penitentiary a few weeks ago, right?"

Melendez nodded.

"I was locked up in a small cell for five years and you don't get outside much. So I came to Palisades Heights to see the ocean and breathe some fresh air. "

"Why were you at the Seafarer last night?"

"Everyone said it's a great bar with good food."

"And you had no idea that Kathy Moran was working there?"

"Is that what this is about?" Kilbride asked.

"You knew that Miss Moran lived in Palisades Heights and was tending bar at the Seafarer, didn't you, Gary?"

"Honestly, I didn't."

"So, you want me to believe that showing up in Palisades Heights and the Seafarer was just some sort of weird coincidence?"

"That's exactly what it was. I was shocked when I saw Kathy and Jack Booth in the bar. That's why I left so fast. I knew they'd get upset if they saw me."

Melendez smiled. "You must think I'm an idiot, Gary."

"I don't. I think you're a conscientious officer of the law who's worried about one of your citizens."

"Mr. Booth saw you outside watching the tavern when he left. Why did you stake it out?"

"I didn't. Mr. Booth is mistaken. As soon as I saw them I left and went back to my motel."

"So you skipped supper?"

Kilbride's facade slipped for a second. Then the bland look was back.

"I was upset so I went to my room to think. Later, I went to a fast-food place and got a burger to go."

"Do you have your receipt?"

"Unfortunately, no. I didn't realize I'd need it so I chucked it with the bag when I was through.

"Look, Chief, I can assure you that I have no feelings of ill will toward Kathy. I did after I was arrested. I won't deny that. But I had a lot of time to think in prison and I decided to let go of my anger and try to become a better person."

"The key witness in your murder trial was tortured to death. Don't you think I have good reason to be concerned?"

"Hey, I had nothing to do with that. Bernie was a good friend and I felt terrible when I heard what happened."

Kilbride stared at the tabletop and appeared to be lost in thought for a moment. When he looked up, his face was a picture of deep concern.

"I don't know if I should be telling you this, Chief Melendez. I don't want to ruin Kathy's reputation. But Kathy was a junkie when I knew her. I was responsible for her condition and I feel very bad about that. When she cut her deal with the DA she was strung out. When you're strung out you can't think straight. After I got over my initial anger I realized that I couldn't hold her responsible for what she did."

"That's very magnanimous, Gary. It's not everyone who can forgive someone who's responsible for sending them to prison."

Kilbride shrugged. "Like I said, I had a lot of time to think when I was locked up."

Melendez nodded. "Several people have told me that you're a clever liar who's really good at manipulating people, but I'm a trusting guy, so I'm going to give you the benefit of the doubt and accept your assurance that you've changed."

"Thank you."

"One thing, though. I'm not as evolved as you are. I don't forgive and forget. If you have any intentions of harming Miss Moran—or anyone else in my town for that matter—remember that there are a lot of places on the coast where a lawbreaker can disappear and never be heard of again."

Kilbride's eyebrows went up. He cocked his head and studied Melendez. Then he smiled.

"You're not threatening me, are you, Chief Melendez?"

Melendez returned the smile. "No. I don't do that. It's illegal."

The chief stood up. "You're free to go. Have a nice day."

CHAPTER NINETEEN

The address Lucius Jackson had given Oscar Llewellyn for Parnell Crouse was in a gang-infested section of Oakland that looked like it had never seen better days. The two-story apartment building was next to a body shop and appeared to have been built by a Mafia construction company with substandard materials. The second-floor balcony was a cracked, concrete slab bordered by a low, rusted railing on which Oscar was afraid to lean.

Crouse's apartment did not have a doorbell, so Oscar knocked. There was no response and he didn't hear any noise from the interior, so he knocked again, louder this time.

"He ain't in."

Oscar turned and saw a man sitting at the end of the balcony on a lawn chair, holding a paperback book. He was dressed in a wife beater T-shirt and stained blue jeans.

"You're lookin' for the football player, right?"

"Parnell Crouse," Oscar answered.

"Ain't been around for over a week."

Oscar walked along the balcony. When he got closer he saw that the man's chest was concave and his arms were thin and stringy. His pale cheeks were covered by gray-black stubble and he did not look well. From Crouse's apartment, he appeared to be in his sixties. Now Oscar realized that he was much younger.

"Do you know when Mr. Crouse will be back?" Oscar asked.

"I got no idea. What you want to know for?"

The man was holding his book on his lap and Oscar could see the title. The pages were yellowed and the book was clearly used.

Oscar smiled. "John D. MacDonald, huh? He's one of my favorites."

The man looked confused for a second. Then he looked down at the cover.

"I got it at the library at a book sale—three for a dollar."

"I don't think I've read this one," Oscar said.

"It's pretty good. I like the detective ones. Lots of action."

Oscar took out his ID. "I'm Oscar Llewellyn and I'm an investigator with the Oregon Department of Justice."

The man studied the ID. "You're a real detective?"

"I am."

"You don't look much like the guy in the book," he said with a grin.

"I have to admit that I haven't been in any car chases lately, and no one has knocked me out."

The man stopped smiling. "Then you're lucky the football player ain't in."

"Oh?"

"He is one mean son of a bitch. You ever seen him play?"

Oscar nodded. "When he was with Oakland."

"He wasn't much of a runner. Good for a few yards on third and one or down by the goal line. But he didn't have any moves.

Reason they kept him on was he liked to hurt people. And he still likes it that way. If you come to see Crouse again, make sure you got backup and make sure they're big. And don't bring no lady cops. He really gets off on hurting women."

"How do you know?"

"I got the apartment next door and these walls are thin. He's had a few women up, hookers I'm guessing. I hear the screams." The man shook his head. "I seen a few when they left, too, and they didn't look so good."

Oscar didn't bother to ask the man if he had called the police.

"So why do you want to talk to Crouse?" the man asked.

"I'm working on a murder investigation in Oregon."

The man perked up. "Murder, huh. Now that is more like this book. You think Crouse killed someone?"

"Mr. Crouse isn't involved, but he can give us some background information about a person of interest."

"Who's that?"

"I'm afraid I can't discuss the details because it's an ongoing investigation, but you could do me a real favor, Mister . . . ?"

"Zack Ivers. It's short for Zachariah from the Bible. My folks were real religious."

Oscar handed Ivers his card. "If Mr. Crouse comes back, can you give me a call?"

Ivers looked concerned. "I don't know."

"I promise I won't tell anyone. You'll be an anonymous informant."

Ivers smiled. " 'Anonymous,' " he repeated. "I like that."

CHAPTER TWENTY

George Melendez found Kathy at the Seafarer. It was early. Many of the tables were empty, and there were only a few people sitting at the bar. Grady Cox saw the police chief talking to Kathy and walked over.

"What's up, George?" Cox asked the policeman.

Melendez hesitated.

"It's okay, Chief," Kathy said. "Grady knows all about my problems in Portland. You can speak freely when he's around."

Cox looked puzzled. "What's this about?"

The police chief took a mug shot out of his pocket and put it on the bar.

"This is Gary Kilbride. He was just paroled from OSP. The reason he was in prison is because Kathy set him up for the Portland police. She was the key witness in his case. I've been told by Kathy and the DA who put Kilbride away that he is a sadist and extremely dangerous."

Melendez turned to Kathy. "We found Kilbride at the Sea View Motel and I had him brought to the police station. He was everything you said he would be, noncombative, very cooperative. He said he had no hard feelings against you or Mr. Booth."

"Then why does he say he's visiting Palisades Heights?" Kathy asked.

"He claims he wanted to see the ocean and breathe fresh air after five years in lockup. He also said that he had no idea you were here. That it's all a big coincidence."

"And you believe him?" Kathy asked.

"Not for one second."

Melendez pushed the mug shot toward Cox. "Keep this. If you see Mr. Kilbride in your bar, call me or one of my men immediately."

Cox looked angry. "If this asshole sets one foot in the Seafarer I'll take care of him personally."

"No, Grady," Melendez said emphatically. "I know you're a hard-ass but this is one guy you don't want to mess with. I called the penitentiary. Kathy said he was crazy and the warden backed her up. He's the type of guy who'll take a few punches and give up. Then he'll set your house on fire. The warden thinks he did torch an inmate who tried to intimidate him."

"Jesus!" Cox swore. "And they paroled him?"

"The warden said that there was no way to prove the assault. The victim wouldn't identify his assailant."

Kathy put a hand on Cox's forearm. "The chief is right, Grady. I know you want to protect me but you have no idea how sick Gary is. Please don't do anything foolish."

"Okay, but I'm not going to let him hurt you."

"That's why I'm giving you the number of my cell phone and a bunch of other numbers to call if you see him in here or nearby."

"Can't you just run him out of town?" Cox asked.

"On what grounds?" Melendez answered. "He hasn't done anything illegal. He hasn't threatened anyone."

"So there's nothing you can do?" Kathy asked.

"I don't have enough manpower to watch him around the clock. The best I can do is make sure you get home safe every night, and I'll send a patrol car by your house. Hopefully, Kilbride will get the hint and leave you alone."

CHAPTER TWENTY-ONE

Advantage Investments owned a two-story building a few blocks from Rodeo Drive. If the location was any indication, Oscar Llewellyn thought, Raymond Cahill had been doing okay. That impression was reinforced when Kevin Mercer walked into the waiting area sporting a country club tan and wearing a hand-tailored suit that fit perfectly. The investigator knew from his Internet search that Mercer was fifty-seven but his sculpted black hair showed no gray and his skin was wrinkle free.

Raymond Cahill's partner looked somber when he crossed to the investigator. Oscar stood and met him halfway.

"Thank you for seeing me on such short notice, Mr. Mercer."

"This is terrible." Mercer shook his head. "I still can't believe Ray's dead. Come on back to my office and we can talk."

Mercer's office was decorated with sports memorabilia. A stack of baseballs signed by famous Yankees encased in plastic stood on a credenza next to a football signed by every member of the 1994 San Francisco Forty-niners Super Bowl team. A signed Joe Montana jersey, framed and protected by glass, hung on one wall.

Oscar pointed at the jersey. "If you said he was the best who ever played I wouldn't be able to argue."

Mercer smiled. "I don't know, Peyton Manning is awfully good, but it's hard to say. You've got Elway, Brady, and don't forget Johnny Unitas." Suddenly, Mercer stopped smiling. "But you're not here to talk about football."

"No, I'm not. We're trying to get some insight into Raymond Cahill's personal and professional life to see if we can figure out whether this was a burglary gone bad or something more sinister."

"What do you want to know?"

"Let's start with his personal life. He'd been married before, hadn't he?"

Mercer nodded. "His first two marriages were disasters but his ex-wives wouldn't have wanted him dead."

"Why is that?"

"Dead men can't pay alimony."

"What about his new wife, Megan?"

"I didn't see marriage number three turning out any better than the first two."

"Oh?"

"From what I've heard about her marriage to Parnell Crouse, Megan is a gold digger, and Ray's murder is certainly convenient. The new Mrs. Cahill is going to be a very rich woman overnight. Is she a suspect?"

"Everyone is at this point in the investigation. Is there any reason other than your gut feeling that we should take a hard look at Mrs. Cahill?"

"No. To tell the truth, I don't know her very well. Ray jumped right in after Megan's divorce, but I only met her a few times."

"Can you think of anyone other than Mrs. Cahill who had a

motive to hurt Mr. Cahill? For instance, did he make any enemies in his business or personal dealings that you know about? We believe that robbery may have been the motive for the crime; the killer stole several items from Mr. Cahill's collection. Was Mr. Cahill worried about someone who was interested in his coins, stamps?"

"I'm not much of a collector except for sports memorabilia. I don't have an interest in stamps or coins like Ray. So I didn't have much interest in his collection, and Ray never said anything about someone who was showing an unhealthy interest in it."

"What about business?"

Mercer hesitated. "There are always people who are upset when our investment advice doesn't pan out."

"I understand there was an incident at the wedding reception."

Mercer hesitated again.

"We need to follow every possible lead if we're going to catch Mr. Cahill's killer, and we do act with discretion."

Mercer sighed. "Armand Tuttle crashed the party."

"Who is Armand Tuttle?"

"He's a client who made his money franchising the Healthy Hearts Athletic Clubs and products. He's a die-hard Raiders fan and he met Ray at a Raiders function. You know Ray was a minority stockholder?"

Oscar nodded.

"Anyway, he switched his investments to Advantage and we did very well with them. The problem is that Armand is very thickheaded and it's very difficult to get him to accept advice. Ray kept telling him to diversify. He did and things were humming along for a while. Then one of his investments went sour and he blamed Ray. He insisted that the investment made a profit but it didn't. That's what the argument was about at the reception. Armand demanded an accounting. Ray told him his wedding wasn't the appropriate place for the discussion. Armand got belligerent and security had to throw him out."

"And that's all there was to it?" Oscar asked, sensing that Mercer might be holding back some information.

Mercer sighed. "You'll find out anyway if you talk to the guests at the reception. Armand demanded the money he claimed we owed him. Ray said we didn't owe him anything and, well, Armand threatened Ray. He said he'd be sorry if he didn't get his money immediately. But I'm certain he just meant he'd sue or something like that. I can't imagine he was threatening to kill Ray."

"Did Tuttle know about Mr. Cahill's collection?"

"I imagine he did. Ray talked about it all the time. If memory serves me, Ray had Tuttle out to his house in Palisades Heights a few years ago."

"Did you stay in Palisades Heights the night of the wedding?"

"No, I flew in on the company jet. I had to get back here for a meeting, so I left for the airport shortly after Armand was thrown out."

"Can you think of anyone else we should look at?"

"Offhand, no, but I'll give it some thought. And now, if you'll excuse me, Ray's death has created chaos and I have to get back to my attempts to create order."

Oscar stood up. "Thanks for taking the time to see me."

"No problem. I want to see the person who did this behind bars."

Oscar turned to leave when he realized that he had forgotten to ask Mercer about Frank Janowitz.

CHAPTER TWENTY-TWO

Jack Booth ate dinner at Teddy Winston's house. He didn't really want to, but politics demanded that he accept the invitation. After dinner, he returned to his motel room and wrote a report about the case because he wasn't tired enough to turn in. He was halfway through when Oscar Llewellyn called and updated him on his investigation.

"I checked out Frank Janowitz," he said, after telling him about the interview with Kevin Mercer.

Jack perked up.

"You're barking up the wrong tree."

"Oh?"

"Your theory about Janowitz being Megan Cahill's lover, forget it. The guy is gay and he's never made a secret about his sexual preferences. He's also in a long-term relationship."

"He could still be Megan's accomplice. He'd have the contacts to sell the rare items from Cahill's collection."

"That's true, but my contacts in the LAPD say he's clean as a whistle."

"Oh, well, it was just a thought. What about Parnell Crouse?"

"I went to his apartment and a neighbor told me that he hasn't been around for a while. I asked my friends in the SFPD to try to run him down, but that's a real low priority, since he's not suspected of committing a crime."

"So what's your plan?"

"I'll interview Armand Tuttle next."

"Okay. Work on Tuttle and try to find Crouse."

They talked a little while longer before Jack hung up and returned to his report. It was eleven thirty by the time he finished and he still wasn't tired. But he was hungry. Teddy Winston's wife wasn't much of a cook, and he'd only picked at his meal. It occurred to him that Kathy Moran would be wrapping up her shift at the Seafarer in an hour or so.

Jack thought about going to the bar. They did have good chowder. He laughed. He was hungry but—if he was going to be honest with himself—the real reason he wanted to go to the Seafarer was to see Kathy.

Jack hesitated. This was not a good idea. She was a key witness in his case. Still . . . He thought some more and decided to go. George Melendez had given him a gun the police had confiscated from a drug dealer. He could tell Kathy that he wanted to walk her home in case Gary Kilbride made a move. She would probably see right through him. If she turned him down that would be that. But he hoped she wouldn't.

The Seafarer was noisy and crowded. Kathy was busy with a customer. Jack walked behind him and into her line of sight. Kathy broke into a wide smile, a good sign.

"I've got something to tell you." She sounded excited. Then she pointed to an empty stool at one end of the bar. "I'll come over as soon as I can."

Jack took the stool and watched Kathy mix drinks. He was impressed by the smooth way she poured from an array of bottles with hand movements that made him think of a Balinese dancer. After a few minutes, Kathy was able to break away. A manila envelope lay next to the cash register. She grabbed it and walked over to Jack.

"So what's the big news?" he asked.

"You'll never believe it."

Kathy opened the envelope and pulled out the photograph she'd taken of Megan Cahill standing with the revolver on the edge of the sea. Jack was stunned.

"That's amazing," he managed.

"Teddy asked me to develop it. He said he needed it for evidence. So I made a bunch of prints. I gave one to Teddy and I came to work with the rest."

She paused, too excited to continue, and grinned.

"Don't keep me in suspense," Jack said.

"The picture is going to be on the front page of *The Oregonian*!"

"How did that happen?"

"They sent a reporter to cover the murder and he heard that I was a witness. So he came here and interviewed me and I told him about the photograph and he saw it and he asked for a print to show his editor."

"Wow, that is great," Jack said with real enthusiasm. "The front page, huh?"

"The reporter called me from Portland. He said the editor flipped over the photo."

"I'm really happy for you," Jack said. "When is the picture going to be in the paper?"

"Tomorrow. I can hardly wait."

"I'll have to buy a few copies."

"Not a chance," Kathy said. "I'm buying up every single one."

"Now that you're famous, I hope you're not going to quit work, because I'm starving."

Kathy laughed. "What can I get you?"

"I couldn't stop thinking about the chowder."

"I'll get you a bowl and a beer to go with it, on me."

"You don't have to treat me."

"Hey, I just got paid a hundred and fifty bucks for that photo. The price of a bowl of chowder and a mug of beer are chump change for someone in my tax bracket."

Jack laughed. Kathy cocked her head and studied him. "Did you only come here for the chowder?"

"Actually, no. You must be near the end of your shift and I didn't want you walking home alone."

Kathy sobered and covered the back of Jack's hand with hers.

"That's really nice of you," she said. "I'm off in an hour. Chief Melendez has a man escorting me home, but with Kilbride out there I'll feel a lot safer with two men watching my back."

The night sky was blanketed by clouds. That was not a problem on Ocean Avenue where there were plenty of streetlights, but the lights were few and far between when they walked into the low-rent part of town. As the streets grew darker, Kathy moved closer to Jack until they were walking shoulder to shoulder.

"Worrying about Gary is making me sick," Kathy confided. "I'm having trouble sleeping and I'm jumping at every creak and rattle when I'm alone at home."

The idea of offering to stay with her flashed through Jack's mind but he shook it off.

"I don't blame you," he said, "but Kilbride would have to be crazy to try anything with everyone on alert."

She turned her head and looked him in the eye. "He is crazy, Jack. That's why I'm scared."

"Good point, but he's also someone who won't make a move if it would put him in danger."

"What about next month or next year?" She shivered. "I hate having to live like this."

Jack fought the urge to put his arm around Kathy's shoulder and pull her to him but he exercised self-restraint. A patrol car was following them, driven by a police officer who could see everything they did.

"I don't know what to say. I never thought about something like this happening when I asked you to help us get Kilbride. I was certain he'd be locked away for a long time."

"It's not your fault. I got myself into this mess and you did what any prosecutor would have done—use a junkie to get to her supplier. I just wish I'd been smarter."

Jack couldn't think of anything to say to that so he said nothing and they walked along in silence for a while.

"Are you making any progress with Raymond Cahill's murder?" Kathy asked.

"Not really. Mrs. Cahill can't remember what happened between getting in her car at the wedding reception and you finding her on the beach."

"Is she going to remember?"

"The doctors say she will eventually, but they don't know when her memory will return."

"So you have no suspects?"

In his mind, Megan Cahill was suspect number one but he said, "Not right now."

They were a block from Kathy's house when Jack stopped and put his hand on his gun. Kathy felt him tense.

"What's wrong?" she asked, alarmed.

"I thought I saw someone in the shadows by that telephone pole."

Kathy peered into the darkness. "I don't see anyone."

"It must have been my imagination," he said after a few seconds.

"Now you see what I've been going through."

Jack didn't relax until they arrived at Kathy's front door. The patrol car parked and the officer went into the house to check each room.

"I appreciate this a lot, Jack," Kathy said while they waited outside for the officer. "I know you didn't have to walk me home."

Jack reached out and took Kathy's hand. He squeezed it lightly and smiled. "I can't let anything happen to my key witness, can I? Especially now that you're going to be famous."

Before Kathy could answer, the officer came out. "All clear in there, Miss Moran. Lock all your doors after I leave. I'll be swinging by several times tonight."

"Thanks, Henry. Next time you're at the Seafarer, there'll be a free beer for you."

The officer laughed. "I'll take you up on that. Just don't tell the chief." He turned to Jack. "Can I give you a ride back to your car?"

"Thanks," Jack said. Then he turned to Kathy. "Sleep tight. I think you'll be okay."

Kathy went inside. Jack and the officer waited until they heard the lock on the front door snap into place before they walked to the patrol car.

CHAPTER TWENTY-THREE

The headquarters of the Healthy Hearts Fitness Centers was on the top floor of one of their gyms in a suburb of San Francisco. Oscar Llewellyn walked through the entrance and into a sea of spandex, bare midriffs, and bulging biceps. The receptionist, who had perfect, pearly white teeth and a body to die for, directed the investigator to an elevator at the end of a hallway. On the way to the elevator, Oscar walked by glass partitions behind which men and women sweated on stationary bikes and elliptical machines or pumped iron.

The elevator went to the third floor and opened into a stereotypical corporate office where not a bead of perspiration or a hint of skin could be seen. An attractive redhead dressed in a severe business suit greeted Oscar when he walked out of the elevator.

"I'm Sandra DiPaola, Mr. Tuttle's administrative assistant. I'll take you back."

DiPaola led Oscar to a spacious corner office by following a narrow carpeted path that was bounded on both sides by cubicles where Healthy Hearts employees toiled. The outer walls of Armand Tuttle's office were all glass and looked out on the mall in which the gym was located. The decor of the rest of the office was silver and black, the colors of the Oakland Raiders, and the office was a shrine to Tuttle's favorite team, with every square inch taken up by Raiders paraphernalia and memorabilia.

Seated behind an aircraft carrier–size desk was an oversize male who looked like he walked the walk when it came to the products he was promoting. When Tuttle stood, it looked like a chiseled granite mountain rising.

Oscar had run a background check on Tuttle. He had been born and raised in Oakland and had been a fanatic Raiders fan since he was old enough to understand football. Tuttle had played on the offensive line at USC and was good enough to be drafted by the Raiders. A catastrophic knee injury had ended Tuttle's pro career halfway through his second year but it had not dimmed his ardor for the team.

Tuttle had married Marie Stewart, a Raiders cheerleader. When his days as a player ended, he opened a gym in Oakland. Marie, who had studied nutrition, convinced him to sell health food products at the gym, and her idea had spawned the Healthy Hearts empire.

"Come on in and have a seat," Tuttle said, gesturing to a comfortable chair on the other side of his desk.

"On the phone, you said you're looking into Ray Cahill's murder," Tuttle said when Oscar was seated. "I hope you're also looking into that crook's Ponzi scheme."

"You don't seem too upset about Mr. Cahill's death."

"Don't get me wrong. Me and Ray were friends right up until I found out he was stealing from me. After my accountant told me what was going on I didn't want anything to do with him, but that doesn't mean I wanted someone to kill him on his wedding night." Tuttle shook his massive head. "That's cold."

"I understand that you crashed the Cahills' wedding reception and threatened him."

"That is one hundred percent correct. Cahill wouldn't take my calls or return them. Every time I went to his office he'd have his secretary say he wasn't in. But I figured he'd be at his own wedding."

"You admit you threatened Mr. Cahill?"

"Sure. There were plenty of witnesses so I can't deny it. Not that I would. But I didn't threaten to kill him. I threatened to sue his ass for every penny he owned. My lawyers are filing the papers this week. If his partner doesn't own up to what that crook was doing I'll drag Mercer through the courts—then I'll get the Feds after him."

"How did Mr. Cahill swindle you?" Oscar asked.

"He had me invest in these IPOs he said were sure things but he never bought the stocks. A couple of them did okay so I figured I'd made a killing and I wanted to cash out. He kept stalling. That's when I figured out he was counting on the stocks to tank and had pocketed my money. When they didn't, he was caught in a bind and had to shuffle money from the investors whose companies went downhill to the ones like me who made a profit; only too many of the companies were successful."

"Do you know any of the other investors?"

"Nah. Most of them were in L.A. and I didn't hang with that crowd."

"Where did you go after you were tossed from the party?"

Tuttle laughed. "Don't you mean, did I lurk around Palisades Heights and pounce on old Ray when he got home?" He laughed again. "You're barking up the wrong tree if you think I killed Ray. I wanted him alive so he could pay me my money.

But in case you think I'm lying, you can talk to my chauffeur or the people at the airfield where my company jet was parked. That's where I went from the party—straight to the airfield, then home."

"Was Kevin Mercer's jet at the same airfield?"

"If he flew in on a private jet it would be."

"Did you see him at the airfield?"

"No, but I wasn't looking for him. I checked in and went straight to my ride. He could have been there without me seeing him."

CHAPTER TWENTY-FOUR

Jack Booth was having a smoke on the balcony of his motel room when Teddy Winston called to tell him that Megan Cahill had remembered something about the night her husband was killed and he would pick Jack up in ten minutes.

Archie Denning pulled into the driveway of the Cahills' house seconds after Winston parked. Henry Baker had been waiting for them, and he opened the front door as soon as he heard Winston's car.

"Thanks for coming to the house," Henry said. "Mrs. Cahill is too upset to go to your office."

"No problem," the DA answered.

Baker led the three men down to the living room. Megan was sitting on an armchair dressed in a floor-length, dark blue caftan embroidered with gold thread.

"The doctor just left," Baker said as they descended the stairs. "He prescribed some sedatives but she's going to wait to take them until after you've talked to her."

Jack sat facing Megan. He leaned forward, his hands folded and his forearms resting on his thighs.

"How are you doing?" he asked, his voice heavy with concern.

"It was Parnell," she answered in a monotone.

"Your ex-husband, Parnell Crouse?"

Behind Jack, Denning and Winston looked at each other for a moment before turning back to Megan Cahill.

"He . . . he was wearing a ski mask and gloves and he tried to disguise his voice but he's no actor. I know it was him."

"You're certain?" Jack asked.

When Megan answered she sounded angry. "Have you ever seen Parnell in person?"

"No."

"His body is freakish. Even now, after being out of the league for a few years, he's still built like one of those Greek statues. It's the steroids. He kept thinking he'd get back with a team, so he pumped iron obsessively and he used that shit like it was candy. That's why our marriage fell apart."

She paused. Before she looked down, Jack saw her eyes tear.

"I loved him," she whispered, "but he'd fly into these rages and beat me. I wouldn't stand for that. It was the 'roids. They made him crazy."

She paused again. Then she began to sob. "Did you know I was pregnant? It was right before he was drafted. He said he was happy about the baby. He proposed and we were married. I always hoped we would be. We'd been going together since high school. Everything was so great. Parnell had always dreamed about the NFL and his dream was going to come true. And we were going to be a family. Then there was trouble in training camp. I can't remember what happened, but he took it out on me and . . ." She gulped down some tears.

"He hit me in the stomach," she said when she could talk, "and I miscarried. I should have left him then. I was so stupid."

While they waited for Megan to regain her composure, Jack remembered the very different version of Megan's pregnancy that Lucius Jackson had told Oscar Llewellyn.

"What happened the night Mr. Cahill died?" Jack asked.

"We came home and Parnell was waiting for us. He must have been hiding in the bushes near the front door. Ray drove into the garage. As soon as we got out of the car Parnell ran in and hit Ray with the butt of a gun. Then he put the gun to Ray's temple and told me to open the door to the house and disable the alarm. After that he marched us into the den where the collection is. He was behind me. That must be when he hit me."

"Can you remember what happened when you came to? Was anyone still in the den?"

"I don't know. The next thing I remember is standing on the beach."

"How did you get the gun?"

"I don't remember. The gun must have been in the den but I'm just guessing."

"How certain are you that the man who hit you was your ex-husband? Would you swear under oath at a trial?" Teddy Winston asked.

"Yes."

"Well, this certainly helps, Mrs. Cahill," Archie Denning said. "I'll put out an APB for Crouse."

"My investigator went to his apartment and a neighbor told him that he hasn't been there for some time," Jack said.

"Which makes sense if he was in Palisades Heights pulling this job," Winston said.

Jack looked at the DA and Denning. "Do either of you want to ask any more questions?"

They shook their heads.

"I did have something else I wanted to ask you," Jack said. "It's about Mr. Crouse."

"Yes?"

"I hate to ask about this but I'd like to get it cleared up."

"What is this?" Henry Baker asked.

"My understanding is that Mr. Crouse was almost broke after the divorce because you drained his bank accounts. Is there any truth to that?"

"Jesus, Jack," Baker exploded. "Can't you see how upset Mrs. Cahill is? What are you suggesting?"

"I'm not suggesting anything. I'm just following up on information my investigator uncovered."

"Who's spreading these rumors?" Baker demanded.

"I'm afraid I can't answer that."

"Then I'm afraid I'll have to instruct my client not to answer."

"No, Henry," Megan said. "I know where this bullshit comes from. Lucius Jackson, right? That pig of a lawyer Parnell hired."

"Our sources are confidential, Mrs. Cahill," Jack said.

Megan shook her head. "He's a real piece of work."

"You don't have to say anything else," Baker cautioned his client.

"But I want to. If you're looking for someone who cleaned out Parnell you should talk to Jackson. That bastard took most of what Parnell had left. And yes, I emptied out *our* accounts. But I did it for us. He was spending *our* money as fast as it came in, on cars and parties. I tried to explain that the money might not last forever and we had to save. But he just kept spending on the drugs and steroids and I'm sure he was fucking one or more women on the side, so I protected myself by setting up accounts he couldn't touch and shifting the money as fast as it came in. It was for his own good."

"Why didn't you split it with him when you divorced?"

"After he killed our baby I figured I'd earned it," she said defiantly.

"I think this is enough questioning," Winston said.

Jack looked like he wanted to follow up, but he decided that he'd gotten enough.

"We'll let you get some rest, Mrs. Cahill," the DA continued.

Henry Baker turned to Denning. "Can you assign a man to watch this house in case Crouse decides to come back?"

"I'll get right on it."

Baker didn't look happy when he walked the three men to the front door. When they were far enough from Megan so she couldn't hear them, Baker turned on Jack.

"Why did you go after Mrs. Cahill like that? Can't you see how fragile she is?"

"This is a murder investigation, Mr. Baker. Your client was holding the murder weapon and she had a million motives to kill her husband. At this point, everyone is a suspect and I wouldn't be doing my duty if I didn't ask the type of questions I did."

"Well, this may be the last time you get to ask any questions of my client," Baker said before he stomped off.

"That was a mistake," Winston said.

"Maybe, maybe not," Jack said as they walked to Winston's car. "Are you discounting the possibility that she killed Cahill?"

"I don't know. She doesn't seem to be acting," the DA replied. "What about you, Archie?"

"I'm not sure. It's awfully convenient that her ex just happens to be the killer."

"So you think she's faking?" Winston asked.

Denning shrugged. "If we talk to Crouse and he has a solid

alibi for the time of the killing, it's going to look bad for her. I'm going to wait and see what happens."

"My investigator talked to Cahill's partner, Kevin Mercer, and Lucius Jackson, Crouse's divorce attorney," Jack said. "Neither one had anything nice to say about Mrs. Cahill. They both thought she was marrying Cahill for his money.

"Something else. One reason Crouse had to quit playing football was because he suffered a number of concussions. That means that Megan Cahill would know how a person who has suffered a concussion would act. Crouse's divorce attorney told my investigator that Mrs. Cahill has a genius IQ. Someone with a genius IQ could probably figure out how to fake the symptoms of a concussion if they wanted to."

"That's a stretch," Winston said.

"You asked for my opinion. Like I told Henry Baker, shortly after he was killed, Megan Cahill was holding the gun that was used to murder Raymond Cahill. She had several million reasons to off her spouse. And now she's blaming for the crime a person who she claims used to beat her up."

Jack shrugged. "Call me crazy but Mrs. Cahill is at the top of my list of suspects."

"Archie?" Winston asked.

"I'm not sure. Finding Parnell Crouse is my number one priority. When we find him we may be able to clear this case."

Jack turned to Winston. "I can't think of anything more I can do right now, so I'm going to drive back to Salem tomorrow. If you get to the point where you think there's enough for an indictment, or if you just want to talk, give me a call. And, both of you, please keep me in the loop."

Winston talked about the case while he drove Jack back to his motel, but Jack was only half listening. Mostly, he was thinking about Kathy Moran. From the first moment he'd seen her in the Multnomah County district attorney's office, he had been drawn to her. He was certain that he could think up an excuse to stay in Palisades Heights so he could continue to see her, but for once, he was thinking with his brain and not his penis. Any relationship that developed now could seriously impact the *Cahill* case, so he was going to drive back to Salem. After the case was over, there would be plenty of time to see if anything could develop between them.

CHAPTER TWENTY-FIVE

The call came at three in the morning. It was George Melendez on the phone, so Jack knew something bad had happened.

"I'm at Kathy Moran's house," the police chief said.

"She's not . . . ?" Jack started.

"No, it's the other way around. Kilbride broke in and she shot him."

"Is she okay?"

"She's shaken up but she isn't hurt."

"And Kilbride?"

"He's dead. She asked me to call you."

"I'll be right over."

Jack's chest swelled. He felt as high as if he'd taken a drug. He knew it wasn't right to rejoice over the death of another human being but he couldn't help himself. When the police chief told him that Kathy was okay and Kilbride was dead he'd felt giddy with relief.

If Jack hadn't been there before, he still would have been able to pick out Kathy's house as soon as he turned into her block. Several police cars and an ambulance were parked in front, and every light in the house had been turned on. Even though it was the middle of the night a crowd had formed on the sidewalk. Jack parked down the block, then worked his way past the rubberneckers and the deputy who was trying to keep them out of the way of the lab techs collecting evidence around the perimeter of the cottage.

Jack flashed his ID at the cop who was guarding the door and asked for Melendez. He was directed to the kitchen in the back of the house, but he ran into Teddy Winston before he got there. Winston was standing at the spot where a hall led from the living room to Kathy's bedroom. There was a body sprawled on the floor and a lot of blood.

"Hell of a thing," Winston said to Jack.

Jack paused to look at Gary Kilbride. He was on his back, eyes wide, mouth open. Blood spread through the pattern on his aloha shirt.

"Is Kathy okay?"

"George is with her in the kitchen."

Kathy was sitting at a Formica-topped table, cradling a cup of tea. She was wrapped in a blanket even though it wasn't that cold and she was staring at the tabletop. George Melendez was sitting opposite Kathy and a female officer was sitting next to her. Jack could see Kathy's lips move but she was speaking so softly that he had no idea what she was saying.

The back door that opened into the kitchen was ajar, and two techs were kneeling next to it, carefully collecting shards of glass, while another forensic expert photographed their every move.

"Jack," Melendez said as he beckoned the lawyer over to the table.

Kathy raised her head. She looked exhausted. Her hair was uncombed, her eyes were bloodshot, and her complexion was ashen.

"Are you okay?" Jack asked.

She nodded, but it looked like the motion had taken an effort to make.

"Kathy was just going to tell us what happened," the police chief said. "I asked her to wait until you got here."

Melendez turned to Kathy. "Do you feel up to it?"

"Let's get this over with," she said.

"Okay. Go ahead, and take your time. If you want to stop, just tell us."

Kathy kept her eyes on the tabletop as she spoke. "I went to sleep after my shift but I haven't been sleeping well since you told me Gary was here."

She nodded toward the kitchen door. "He broke in through there. That's what woke me up, the glass breaking. I came out of my bedroom with the gun you gave me. He was in the living room. I shot him as soon as I saw him."

"Did Kilbride say anything?" Melendez asked. "Did he threaten you?"

Kathy stared at Melendez hard enough to make him break eye contact. She looked furious.

"He broke into my house, George. I didn't wait for him to threaten me. The second I saw him, I emptied my gun."

"Hey, you did the right thing. I'm just asking to get a clear picture of what happened. So did he say anything?"

"I don't know. He may have. He was in the living room and I just kept shooting."

"Okay. I think this is enough for now, unless you have some questions, Jack."

Jack shook his head.

"We'll get a statement from you tomorrow after you've gotten some sleep. Is there someplace you can stay tonight? You won't get any rest here. There'll be cops, guys from the crime lab here all evening."

"I can call Ellen Devereaux or Grady."

"Do you want me to call for you?" Melendez asked.

Kathy nodded. Melendez got the numbers and walked to a corner of the kitchen. Jack took his place at the table. He covered her hand.

"You did the right thing, Kathy. We both know what would have happened to you if you hadn't stopped him. Kilbride was a monster. Everyone is better off without him."

Kathy didn't answer.

Melendez came back to the table. "Ellen Devereaux says you can stay with her. Get dressed and I'll have someone drive you over."

Kathy stood up. She looked shaky.

"I'm going to Kilbride's motel," Melendez told Jack. "Do you want to come with me?"

"Yeah, that's a good idea," Jack said.

The policewoman walked Kathy out of the room. Jack waited until Kathy was out of earshot.

"Was he armed?" Jack asked.

"He had a knife."

"This looks like a classic case of self-defense," Jack said.

"That's how I see it."

Jack nodded toward the living room where Teddy Winston was talking to a police officer.

"What about Winston?"

"He'll be happy to write this one off, and he should be. The world's better off without that piece of shit."

"Amen," Jack said.

The Sea View Motel was a squat, one-story affair several blocks from the ocean. None of its rooms had a view of the sea. Booth and Melendez parked next to the office. Two lab techs had followed in a van and they pulled in beside the chief's car and waited while Booth and Melendez went into the office.

A young man in a short-sleeve shirt and chinos greeted Melendez when he walked in.

"Hey, Chief."

"Hi, Ronnie."

"You here about Mr. Kilbride again?"

"I am."

Melendez turned to Jack. "Ronnie is working the desk until school starts at Oregon State. He was our star tailback at Palisades Heights High."

Ronnie handed the chief of police the key to Kilbride's room.

"Thanks. And a heads-up. Mr. Kilbride is dead."

"No shit!"

"So you can rent the room after my guys are through with it."

"How did . . . ?"

"Sorry, but I can't talk about the details. You understand."

"Yeah." Ronnie paused. "I don't know if this is important but he got a call from someone around midnight."

"Oh? Do you know who it was?"

"No. The voice was muffled. I couldn't even tell if it was a man or a woman. They just asked to be connected to his room."

"Thanks. If you remember anything else about the call, let me know."

"Will do."

"He's a good kid," Melendez told Jack as they walked to

Kilbride's room. "He's walking on at OSU. I think he's got a chance to make the team."

"He seems like a good kid. About the phone call. I'll have my people check the phone records to find out who made it."

"I was going to suggest that. We found Kilbride's cell phone and the tech guys are going to go through it. Maybe they'll come up with something."

Kilbride's room was neat and clean. His clothing was in the room's chest of drawers or hung in the only closet. Kilbride had placed his toiletries next to the sink in the bathroom in orderly rows.

A paperback novel sat on the night table next to a queen-size bed. The blankets had been thrown back, suggesting that Kilbride had been in the bed since the maids had cleaned his room. A large duffel bag sat on a luggage stand in a corner of the room. Melendez had a lab tech photograph it before he opened it. Then he pulled out two more paperbacks and a crumpled newspaper. He paid no attention to the novels but he showed great interest in the newspaper. He thumbed through it, then stopped to read something.

"Well, well," Melendez said. "This answers a question that's been nagging at me since you told me that Kilbride was in town."

"What question is that?" Jack asked.

"Haven't you wondered how Kilbride knew Kathy was living in Palisades Heights?"

"Huh, I never thought about that."

"Well, I have, and here's the answer," the police chief said as he held up the newspaper. It was an old issue of the *Palisades Heights Gazette*, the weekly newspaper.

"Peter Fleischer is a reporter for the *Gazette* and he wrote an article about Raymond Cahill because Cahill was getting married at the country club."

"Kathy took the pictures for the article!" Jack said. "She told me about it."

"And the *Gazette* gave her a credit for them."

"Kilbride must have read the article and discovered that Kathy was living here."

Melendez frowned. "This article has a section about Cahill's collection."

"Do you think . . . ?"

"I don't know what to think."

"Was Kilbride in town when Cahill was killed?" Jack asked.

Melendez nodded. "He checked in the day before the wedding."

"Could he have been involved in the robbery and murder?"

"I have no idea," the police chief said. "But I'm definitely going to look into that possibility."

"Can I get a copy of the article?" Jack asked.

"They have a copying machine in the motel office. I'll have Ron run one off for you before we leave."

Jack frowned. "That newspaper tells us how Kilbride found out Kathy was living in Palisades Heights but it raises another question."

"Oh?"

"How did Kilbride get the paper? The *Palisades Heights Gazette* doesn't exactly have national distribution."

"I hadn't thought of that," Melendez said.

"Do you think someone sent Kilbride the paper?"

"That's an interesting possibility."

Jack stayed at the Sea View a little while longer before driving back to his motel. During the drive a thought nagged at him. Gary Kilbride was very smart. He had to know that everyone would focus on him if a burglar broke into Kathy's house and killed her. Kathy had told him that her greatest fear was that Kilbride would wait for months or years to take his revenge. Jack had talked to people about Kilbride when he was prosecuting him. Kilbride knew how to be patient. So why would he try to kill Kathy now? The answer to that question was that he wouldn't—he was too clever. And that thought caused Jack to pose several very unsettling questions. What if Kathy was the person who called Kilbride around midnight? What if she didn't want to live in fear and decided to take matters into her own hands? What if Kathy lured Kilbride to her house, killed him, then faked the break-in?

Jack decided that he didn't want to know the answers to these questions. Kilbride was an animal and the world was better off without him. If someone else wanted to investigate Kathy he couldn't stop him. But he'd be damned if he would help him. Kathy had gone through hell five years ago and she'd straightened out her life. Jack had been asked to help Teddy Winston with Raymond Cahill's murder. The Kilbride shooting was none of his business.

Jack was exhausted when he got back to his motel room but he was too wound up to sleep. He switched on the lamp next to an armchair and started reading the article in the *Gazette*. The headline was RAYMOND CAHILL'S LOVE AFFAIR WITH PALISADES HEIGHTS. Above the headline was a photograph of Cahill's house and another of the man himself standing on the beach with his arm draped over Megan Cahill's shoulder. The couple were smiling. Raymond's black hair was windblown. His jaw was square, his nose was straight, and his eyes were sky blue. Cahill looked trim and fit and easily ten years younger than fifty-two, a sharp contrast to the way he appeared on a slab in the autopsy photo Jack had looked at earlier.

Raymond Cahill is in love with his bride-to-be, Megan Crouse. The couple will tie the knot at the Palisades Heights Country Club on June 12. But Ray has also had a love affair with Palisades Heights since his first visit to his grandparents' rustic, seaside cabin, which Jordan and Evelyn Cahill built on a bluff overlooking the Pacific Ocean. Ray's parents moved to California when Ray was a toddler, but summer vacation at the cabin was always a special time for the family and especially little Ray.

"I have wonderful memories of playing on the beach, Grandma's pies, fishing with my granddad, or just sitting with him while he told me stories. Naturally, when I made enough money to build my own second home, Palisades Heights was the first place I thought of."

Ray dropped out of college in his sophomore year and started investing in real estate with money he'd made in the stock market. Both ventures were so successful that he was a millionaire by the time most of his classmates were job hunting. He has lived his adult life on an estate in Arlington, an upscale, seaside community in California, but he still tried to spend at least a week a year at his grandparents' cabin. When they passed away, Ray inherited their land and bought the lots on either side of the property. He had some regrets when he tore down the cabin, but the house that world-renowned architect Russell Salas designed blends seamlessly into the dunes and sky and is a showpiece in our community. Ray graciously gave us a tour, and the highlight was a peek at his collections, which he moves to Palisades Heights in the summer.

"I've always been a serious collector," Ray said as he showed us through his private museum. "I started with baseball cards, stamps, and coins when I was in elementary school and I was a fanatic about completing any collection I started. When I was old enough to buy guns I added historic firearms to my collection."

The highlight of Ray's stamp collection is an Inverted Jenny, a twenty-four-cent stamp that was issued in 1918 as the first stamp for air delivery. One sheet was printed with the Jenny plane upside down. There are only 100 of these stamps known to still exist.

Ray's rarest coin is a 1913 Liberty Head nickel. The mint stopped making the coin in 1912 but five of the nickels with the Liberty Head design were issued in 1913 and are considered to be among the world's rarest coins.

Ray positively beamed when he showed us the pride and joy of his historic firearm collection, a Schofield .44 Smith & Wesson six-shooter that Ray believes was wielded by Wyatt Earp in the Gunfight at the OK Corral. But I'll bet his smile will be even broader when he kisses his lovely bride this summer.

Photographs of the stamp, the coin, and the revolver illustrated the story. Jack noticed the photo credits for Kathy Moran.

The next section of the article described a guided tour of the house. Jack's eyes started to close and it took a real effort to finish. When the article ended, Jack shed his clothes and crawled into bed. There were only a couple of hours before sunrise and Jack hoped he could still the thoughts that were swirling around in his head and get some sleep before the new day dawned.

CHAPTER TWENTY-SIX

When Jack woke up a few hours later he felt like he had not slept at all. He took a cold shower, packed for the trip back to Salem, and drove to Ellen Devereaux's house to say good-bye to Kathy Moran.

The art gallery owner lived in a bungalow on a narrow lane a block from the beach. A low picket fence surrounded a sandy yard. Jack knocked and Devereaux opened the door. The gallery owner was in her early forties. She had curly brown hair and skin with the hard, tanned look of someone who spent a lot of time outdoors in the sun and wind, and she appraised Jack with sharp blue eyes.

"I'm Jack Booth, an assistant attorney general working on the Cahill murder," he told her. "I wanted to see how Kathy is doing."

"She just got up. I'll tell her you're here."

Devereaux ushered Jack into a living room cluttered with art. Every inch of wall space was covered by photographs and paintings. Sculptures in an array of mediums and handblown glass bowls and vases stood on bookshelves and end tables.

Devereaux walked into the kitchen, which was close enough to the living room so Jack could hear her announce his presence. A minute later, Kathy appeared. Jack was holding several copies of the *Oregonian* featuring Kathy's photograph of Megan Cahill on the front page. He held them out to her.

"With all the excitement, I wasn't sure if you'd gotten any of these."

Kathy smiled. "Thanks, Jack. This is really nice of you."

"I'm on my way back to Salem but I wanted to see how you're doing before I left."

"Do you have time for a walk on the beach? I was just going to go outside and try to clear my head."

Kathy was wearing jeans and a sweater and she grabbed a windbreaker that was hanging on a hook next to the door. A cold wind was whipping inland from the Pacific, and Jack turned up the collar of his coat, hunched his shoulders, and stuffed his hands in his pockets.

"Did you get any sleep?" Jack asked.

"Not really."

"How are you feeling?" Jack asked.

"Besides exhausted?"

Jack nodded.

Kathy stopped and looked directly at Jack. "I've read articles about policemen who suffer psychologically even when a shooting is justified, but I don't feel the least bit guilty." She paused. "I know this is going to sound cold but I feel great. Gary was a horrible person, and the world is better off with him out of it."

"Amen," Jack said.

Kathy expelled a deep breath. "Thank you for that, Jack. I was afraid you'd think less of me."

Jack put a hand on her shoulder. "When I heard that Kilbride was dead I felt euphoric."

"I'm so glad you understand," Kathy said.

Jack studied her for some sign that would tell him whether Kathy had lured Gary Kilbride to her house and executed him, but he didn't see any evidence of guilt or dissembling.

Kathy reached up and squeezed Jack's hand. Then she started walking toward the water's edge. Storm clouds were hanging off the coast but they were drifting south and the sun was starting to burn through.

"Can I ask you something?" Jack said.

Kathy nodded.

"Now that you've had a few days to think about it, what's your impression of Megan Cahill?"

"What do you mean?"

"Do you think she was faking when you found her?"

"You think she killed her husband?"

"I don't know. That's what I'm trying to figure out. She was holding the murder weapon and she'll be a rich widow if we can't prove she was involved in her husband's death. The doctors say she was suffering from a concussion, but Parnell Crouse suffered from concussions so she'd know how to fake them. And now she's claiming that her ex-husband robbed and murdered Mr. Cahill."

"She remembered what happened?"

"Some of it. She claims that Parnell Crouse was waiting for them when they got back from the wedding reception and forced her and Mr. Cahill to go into the den. The next thing she remembers is seeing you on the beach."

"Have the police talked to Crouse?"

"They're looking for him."

"And you think Megan may be lying?"

"I don't know. I'm just trying to sort things out."

Kathy walked along the beach, head down, lost in thought. Jack walked alongside her.

"I don't know what to tell you," Kathy answered after a while. "I didn't think she was faking when I found her, but I'm not a doctor. She seemed dazed and very confused. Does that help?"

"Yeah, thanks. One other thing. When we searched Kilbride's motel room we found a copy of the *Palisades Heights Gazette* with the story about Raymond Cahill and your photos. We think that's how Gary knew you were living here, but it raised another interesting question: How did Kilbride get the paper? That's been bothering me and I can see two possible answers: someone who knew Kilbride and was traveling through Palisades Heights saw the story and sent it to him or someone who lives in Palisades Heights sent it to him."

"What are you getting at?"

"Do you have any enemies in town who know about your past and your relationship with Kilbride?"

Kathy looked worried. "Only a few people know about my problems in Portland. Grady and Ellen know, but I can't think of any reason they'd sic Gary on me. It's got to be a coincidence. Maybe one of Gary's crime partners or someone he met in prison saw the article while they were vacationing here and told Gary where I was living."

"That's probably it."

They walked side by side for a while without speaking. Then Kathy laughed.

"What?" Jack asked.

"You may be overthinking this newspaper thing."

"Oh?"

"I sell my photographs in galleries on the Oregon coast, in

Washington, and there's a gallery in California. What if Gary did a Web search for my name when he got out? There could be a search result for my photography credit. He could have gotten in touch with the *Gazette* and asked for a back issue."

"I never thought of that."

"That's why we photographers make the big bucks."

Jack laughed. "I'll go online and check out your theory when I get back to Salem." He glanced at his watch. "Which I really should be doing now."

They turned around and walked without speaking until they arrived at the beach access.

"Thanks again for checking on me," Kathy said.

Jack stopped and looked down at the sand. Then he took a deep breath.

"Actually, I just wanted to see you again before I left." Jack hesitated. "Look, I probably shouldn't be saying this, since you're a witness, but we got off on the wrong foot five years ago . . ."

"Completely my fault."

"When the case is over, would you mind if I visited you?"

"No, Jack. I think that would be nice."

"Okay, then. And I'll probably see you anyway if Teddy decides he has the evidence to indict someone."

They walked side by side until they got to Jack's car. He opened the door and looked at Kathy again.

"I'm glad you've got your life back," he said.

Kathy smiled. "Me, too."

"So I'll see you," Jack said with a smile.

"Definitely," Kathy answered.

Jack drove off but he checked his rearview mirror before he made the turn off Devereaux's street. As he hoped, Kathy was standing in the road, watching him drive away.

Jack was back in his office just after noon. The first thing he did was run a Web search for "Kathy Moran." There were several hits. Most of the results were connected to galleries that sold her photographs. A few were old references to her cases. But there was a mention of her photo credit in the *Palisades Heights Gazette* story about Raymond Cahill.

Jack organized his file for the *Cahill* case. Then he went through his mail and caught up on developments in some of his other cases. He quit at five and ate dinner at a restaurant near his apartment. While he ate, he thought about Megan Cahill, Gary Kilbride, Parnell Crouse, and, most of all, Kathy Moran.

CHAPTER TWENTY-SEVEN

The beginning of the end of Jack's involvement in the *Cahill* case started with a call from Teddy Winston four days after Jack left Palisades Heights.

"They found Parnell Crouse," the Siletz County DA said.

"Where?" Jack asked.

"In his car on a logging road twenty miles east of Palisades Heights. He's dead. He'd been shot in the temple."

Jack remembered that Bernie Chartres had been found on a logging road.

"And that's not all. When the state police searched the trunk they found a gold coin from Cahill's collection. When can you come down? We need to talk about the case."

Jack walked into the Siletz County district attorney's office at five forty-five and found Teddy Winston, Archie Denning, and George Melendez waiting for him in the conference room. Jack took a seat next to Winston.

Pictures from the Crouse crime scene were spread out on

the conference room table. Jack watched a lot of football and he had vague memories of Crouse being interviewed on ESPN after a game. Jack remembered a clean-shaven man with a high forehead and jutting jaw. He also remembered the menace the running back projected. There had been something about his eyes and the way he stood that convinced Jack that he would not want to be alone with Crouse in a dark alley.

Death had sapped Crouse of all his violent energy. In the crime scene photographs the muscles in his face were placid, the jaw slack. Jack's eyes were drawn to a close-up of the left side of Crouse's head where a hole and a halo of blood gave him a graphic explanation of how the ex-Raider had died.

"How long has he been dead?" Jack asked.

"The ME thinks he was killed on Monday evening."

"So the evening of the day that Cahill was murdered," Jack said.

Winston nodded. "The way I figure it, Crouse robs Cahill and leaves with the loot in the trunk of his car. His accomplice meets him. The driver's window was down when they found Crouse, so he wasn't worried when his killer came up to the car." Winston made a gun out of his fingers. "Bang! One shot in the head. The blood-splatter pattern confirms that Crouse was seated behind the wheel when he was shot.

"The keys to Crouse's car were on the seat next to him but there's no blood on top of the keys, just the bottom, where they lay in Crouse's blood. So the theory is that the murderer takes the keys out of the ignition, opens the trunk, and takes out the coins, stamps, et cetera, but one coin accidentally drops into the trunk. Then he tosses the keys back in the car and leaves."

"That makes sense," Jack said.

"One thing is clear," Winston said. "Megan Cahill is innocent.

She couldn't have killed Crouse. She was with Kathy Moran, police, or in the hospital during the time Crouse was murdered."

Jack thought about that. "There could be a third person. Megan and this third person get Crouse involved. Then the third person kills Crouse while Megan is in the hospital, giving her an alibi."

"Why are you so set on Megan being involved?" Winston asked.

"There's just something about her," Jack said. "She knew all about Cahill's collection, she profits financially from the murder, she was caught with the murder weapon . . ."

"About the murder weapon," Winston said. "You said you thought she would have thrown it in the ocean if Kathy Moran hadn't found her on the beach before she could get rid of it."

"Yes?" Jack said.

"Why didn't she kill Kathy? Here's a witness who catches her red-handed with the murder weapon right after she's killed her husband. It's the middle of the night with no witnesses to see her do the deed. Why didn't Megan just shoot Kathy?"

Jack had to think about that. Everyone waited to hear what he would say but he couldn't think of anything.

"I don't know."

"Well, I do. She didn't shoot Kathy because she's not a killer. And who is this mysterious third person?" Winston asked.

"Gary Kilbride," Jack answered. "He was in town when the robbery and Crouse's murder took place, he had a copy of the *Palisades Heights Gazette* that ran a story about Cahill's collection, and he is an ultraviolent psycho who'd have no compunctions about killing Crouse."

"That won't wash, Jack," Winston said. "How would Megan

or Crouse know about Kilbride, or vice versa? Crouse and Mrs. Cahill were raised in Texas, then they were in Oakland, California, when Crouse played for the Raiders. Kilbride was incarcerated in an Oregon prison for five years and he wasn't released until shortly before the robbery-murder."

"And even if Mrs. Cahill is guilty as sin," Melendez said, "we can't prove it. Crouse lost everything in a vicious divorce. He would have every reason to do her and her new husband harm. And there's no getting around the fact that she was hit on the head with a lot of violence. Plus, as Teddy said, there's no way she could have killed Crouse. If she's in this we certainly don't have anywhere near the evidence we'd need to get an indictment."

Jack sighed. "You're definitely right about the indictment. I don't believe in going for one unless I feel that the person I'm after is guilty beyond a reasonable doubt. My gut tells me Megan may be guilty, but I can't say I'd convict her based on the evidence we have if I was on her jury.

"By the way, did you find anything on Kilbride's cell phone that links him to someone in Palisades Heights?" Jack asked.

"No," Melendez answered. "And we had no luck with that midnight call. It was made from a disposable cell. So the call is a dead end."

Jack was relieved that the call had not been traced to Kathy.

"So what do we do now?" the police chief asked.

"I've got people watching for any sign of the stolen property," Archie Denning said, "but, from what Frank Janowitz said, that's a long shot."

"As things stand," Winston said, "I don't think we can do anything. Crouse is dead, there's not enough evidence against Megan Cahill to take to a grand jury, and we have no idea who killed Crouse. We're at a standstill unless some new evidence is uncovered."

The meeting didn't break up until after six and Jack didn't feel like driving back to Salem. It occurred to him that Kathy would be tending bar at the Seafarer. He was disappointed in the way the case was going but the thought of seeing Kathy brought a smile to his face.

The tavern was only half full when he walked in the door and there were plenty of seats at the bar. During the four days since they had walked on the beach he had thought about calling Kathy but he had restrained himself because she was still a witness.

Kathy smiled when she spotted Jack. "Did you drive all the way from Salem for the clam chowder?"

"No, but that would certainly be a valid reason."

"Then was it to see me?"

"Another good reason for the trek, but that's not it, either. Teddy called me. They found Parnell Crouse. Someone shot him to death on a logging road about twenty miles from here."

"My God! Do they know who did it?"

"No, but his death creates a problem. There was evidence in Crouse's car linking him to the robbery. If we'd arrested him he could have told us what happened, but we're at a dead end now. Megan Cahill couldn't have killed Crouse because she was in the hospital when he was shot and we have no evidence that tells us who did kill him."

"What happens now?" Kathy asked.

"Nothing unless we catch a break."

"So everything just stops?"

"That's about it."

"What do I do?"

"Nothing. Teddy has your statement. If they do make an arrest you'll probably testify at the grand jury. Which reminds me, what is Teddy doing about Gary Kilbride?"

"He told me I don't have to worry. They're treating it as self-defense."

"As they should."

"I don't think they're even convening a grand jury. Teddy said it would be a waste of taxpayer money."

"I agree."

"I've got some news of my own," Kathy said.

"Oh?"

"After the *Oregonian* printed my photograph of Megan Cahill I received requests from several other papers, including the *New York Times*, the *Chicago Tribune*, and the *Los Angeles Times*. So the picture was published all over, and a New York gallery asked to see my portfolio. They called this morning. They want me to do a show and they're going to fly me to New York.

"And that's not all. I show in a gallery in L.A. and they want me to do a show, too."

"That's fantastic."

"I'm really excited."

"You should be. So you'll be doing a lot of traveling?"

"It looks like it."

"Well, I'm really glad for you."

A customer took a seat at the bar and Kathy had to break away to fill his drink order. Jack tried the oyster stew for a change, and he wasn't disappointed. When she wasn't busy with other customers, Kathy spent time with Jack. He thought about asking her if she wanted to spend the night, but the case was still open and making a move didn't seem right.

A little after eleven Jack's eyes got heavy. He was too tired to drive back to Salem so he said good-bye and found a motel near the beach.

The next morning, a misty drizzle lowered the temperature and forced Jack to use his windshield wipers when he started back to the capital. The depressing weather fit his mood. He was frustrated about the case and unsure of what to do about Kathy Moran.

Part Five

PALISADES HEIGHTS

2015

CHAPTER TWENTY-EIGHT

It was in the low nineties and the humidity had gotten worse by quitting time, but Stacey Kim was so excited by her idea of writing a novel inspired by *Woman with a Gun* that she hardly noticed the weather. Stacey rode the subway to her stop, then bought a take-out chicken Caesar salad and a cold drink at a neighborhood grocery store before walking the three blocks to her apartment.

The price of housing in Manhattan had shocked Stacey and all she had been able to afford was a third-floor walk-up in Chelsea that was so small that her foldout sofa almost touched all four walls when she converted it into a bed. There was a window air conditioner that rattled when it ran, the heat only worked intermittently in winter, there was a constant drip in the bathroom sink, and her "kitchen" was a microwave oven. When she moved in, the apartment had seemed romantic. Now, it just felt claustrophobic.

A folding card table served as Stacey's desk and dining room table. When she made her sofa into a bed at night the table had to be folded up and moved into the narrow hall that led from the front door to her living room. Stacey set her food down on the table and ate her salad while she looked through the catalogue of the Museum of Modern Art exhibit. According to a brief biography in the introduction, Kathy Moran had practiced law in Oregon for five years before moving to Palisades Heights, a beach community on the Oregon coast, to pursue her true passion, photography.

Moran supported herself by tending bar and selling her photographs for small sums at galleries in Oregon, Washington, and California. The work was exceptional, but Moran's career did not take off until her photograph of Megan Cahill won the Pulitzer Prize and catapulted her work into public prominence.

According to the introduction, Moran's enigmatic photograph had been compared to Leonardo da Vinci's *Mona Lisa*. Stacey could see why some people would make that comparison. People wondered what had prompted the enigmatic smile on the lips of the woman in Leonardo's masterpiece. Moran's photograph made Stacey wonder what had brought the woman in it to the edge of the sea, armed with an ancient six-shooter. The rest of the introduction focused on Moran's photography, and Stacey learned that the MoMA exhibition was comprised of works, some early, some more recent, that had been donated by private collectors.

After Stacey finished eating, she booted up her laptop and ran an Internet search on Kathy Moran and her famous photograph. She learned that the woman with the gun was Megan Cahill and the photograph had been taken on her wedding night minutes before the body of her husband, multimillionaire Raymond Cahill, had been discovered in their beach house in Palisades Heights, Oregon.

As she read, Stacey thought about the plot of her novel. What would have to happen to cause a bride to murder her groom on their wedding night? That question would be at the heart of her novel, if she made the bride the killer. In her novel, the wife might be guilty or innocent. Her fictional wife's fate would depend on the way Stacey decided the plot would twist.

Stacey wasn't going to write a true crime book. The real case would only be the inspiration for her novel. But to make the world she created in her novel seem real, Stacey knew she would have to interview the people who had been part of the *Cahill* case and see the locations that figured in it firsthand. Stacey had grown up in the Midwest, far from the ocean, and she had never seen the Pacific. What did the wind off the ocean feel like when Megan Cahill stood on the shore, looking out to sea? What did the sand feel like as she walked across the beach from her house? If the descriptions in her novel and her characters were going to come alive, Stacey would have to visit Palisades Heights and the Cahill beach house.

Stacey opened her purse and took out her checkbook. After looking at her balance, she made a decision. Moving across the country to Oregon would be easy. She had no ties to New York, she had no social life here, and she hated her job and her apartment. She was renting by the month and she would give notice at her job. Meanwhile, she would learn as much as she could about the *Cahill* case and make a list of people who could help with her research.

Stacey felt like a runner at the start of a race as she brought up a fresh page on her laptop. Her heart beat fast and she could barely stay seated as she typed MEGAN CAHILL and KATHY MORAN on it. It would be terrific if she could interview them. But how would she get them to talk to her?

Stacey got an idea. She added HENRY BAKER to the list. He had been Megan's defense attorney. Ten years had passed since the murder, but he might know how to contact Megan and he would be a great person to talk to. He could tell her how to investigate a murder case in addition to helping her develop her characters.

A moment later, Stacey added JACK BOOTH to the list. He was a special prosecutor with the Oregon Department of Justice who had been assigned to assist the local district attorney. He would be able to tell her how a prosecutor prepares for trial. Maybe he would put her in touch with forensic experts and detectives who would tell her about preserving a crime scene and how a crime lab processes evidence.

Stacey thought of something. She looked at the clock. It was six forty-five in New York but it would be three forty-five in Oregon. She did a Web search for Jack Booth and found a number in Portland for his law office. She felt a tingling in her stomach as she punched in the number on her cell phone.

CHAPTER TWENTY-NINE

Seconds before he came, Jack Booth caught sight of the clock on Mildred Downey's end table. It was almost six and he had to be in court at nine so he pumped harder, came quickly, then rolled onto his back and took a few deep breaths before heading for the bathroom to shower and shave.

Jack had been seeing Mildred for two months. They'd met when he deposed one of her clients and there had been an immediate attraction on both their parts. Like Jack, Mildred was a hard drinker and a dynamo in the sack. More important, she was not into "relationships" and "commitment," which made her a perfect companion for Jack, whose alimony payments had eaten up a good part of his sizable income.

Mildred was sitting up against the headboard, naked, with the sheets at her waist when Jack walked out of the bathroom and crossed to the chair where he'd carefully arranged his clothes the evening before. Mildred didn't say a word while he dressed.

"Got to go," Jack said when he was done.

Jack had his hand on the doorknob when Mildred spoke.

"Don't I even get a kiss good-bye?"

Jack hesitated before walking back to the bed. He kissed Mildred and fondled one of her breasts. Mildred ran her fingers lightly across Jack's earlobe. He savored the sensation for a moment before pulling away.

"You're tempting me, Millie, but I have to be in Judge Farrell's court at nine, and you know how cranky he can get if you're late."

"I could tell you had a trial this morning. You were thinking about your case the whole time we were screwing."

"That's not true," Jack protested.

"Save the bullshit, Jack. Look, this isn't working."

"Hey, Millie, when we're making love I'm only thinking about you."

Mildred smiled. "You're a bad liar, and you're not even a good lay anymore. I can tell when a man loses interest."

Jack frowned. "I thought you didn't want a commitment. I thought we both wanted to have fun without any ties."

"That's absolutely true. Two bad marriages were enough."

"Amen to that."

"But I do expect a little enthusiasm in bed, and it's obvious that you've just been going through the motions lately. So I think it's time we called it quits. No hard feelings. You're a great guy."

Jack snuck a quick look at the clock. "Can we talk about this later over drinks?"

"There's nothing to talk about. You'll realize that, when you have the time to think about something other than your case."

Jack wanted to say something nice but he couldn't think of what to say. He wasn't mad or even hurt. And that told him that Mildred was right to end it.

"I'll call you," was the best he could come up with as he left. On the way down in the elevator he wasn't angry, embarrassed, or the least bit upset about being dumped. If he was experiencing any emotion it was relief. He wondered about that.

Jack loved to win. He got a thrill out of crushing an opposing lawyer. But aside from that, what gave him an emotional high? There was the thrill of a sexual conquest but that didn't last long, and the older he got, the more effort it took to form even a temporary attachment.

What did he do when he wasn't trying cases or preparing for trial? Drink and smoke. Where had the zest for life gone? Hell, he was only forty-three. He was rich, successful. He had a fabulous condo with a terrific view. He should be happy, but his work was the only thing in his life that brought him joy.

Jack walked out of Mildred's building into the sunlight. It was a perfect day. He had a case to try and he couldn't wait to get to court because he had a delightful surprise planned for opposing counsel. So Jack walled off his emotions—something he was very good at—got in his car, and headed for court.

When Jack stepped out of the elevator on the fifth floor of the courthouse a female deputy district attorney he'd seen around smiled at him. Jack smiled back. As he rounded the corner he spotted Ronald Kinsey conferring with his client on a bench next to the door to the courtroom. This time Jack's smile wasn't a pleasant smile like the one he'd flashed at the deputy DA. It was the smile you would see on a cat, if cats could smile, as it was creeping up on a helpless bird that had no idea it was being stalked.

Kinsey's client was Irene Plessey, a drop-dead gorgeous fashion model who had done some acting. She'd been arrested for driving under the influence of intoxicants and had been found "not guilty" after testifying that she was completely sober. She explained the ticket by claiming that the arresting officer had hit on her and had gotten angry when she refused to give him her phone number. Her passenger, Tammy Longwell, another model, had backed up Plessey's story. There were six men on the jury. The verdict had been a unanimous "not guilty." After her criminal case, Irene hired Kinsey's firm to sue the police department for false arrest. Jack was representing the company that insured the city.

Jack had talked to the arresting officer and the prosecutor. Officer Howell swore that Plessey had been intoxicated and had offered to have sex with him if he didn't write her up. When he turned her down, she had been furious and she'd sworn to make his life hell. The officer and the DA both said that Plessey had turned on tears while testifying but was cold as ice whenever the jury was out of the room.

Yesterday Booth and Kinsey had picked a jury and had given their opening statements. Then Plessey had testified about her ordeal and even had Jack believing her. Court recessed after Jack's cross-examination, during which he had scored no points.

"Hey, Ron, can I talk to you for a minute?" Jack said.

"What do you want?" Kinsey asked. "Court's gonna start soon."

"This will only take a minute," Jack answered. He walked far enough down the hall so Kinsey's client wouldn't be able to overhear them. As Kinsey walked away, he sighed to give his client the impression that having to converse with opposing counsel was a major imposition on his time on earth. Jack thought that Kinsey might have a crush on his sexy client and was acting tough to impress her.

Jack didn't like Kinsey one bit. The twit had only been out of law school for two years but he was an associate at one of Portland's prestigious law firms and he thought that endowed him with some kind of magical power. He was overweight and overconfident and he had treated Jack disrespectfully every time they met. Jack found it especially annoying that Kinsey acted like the verdict was a foregone conclusion.

"I talked to my client," Jack said when Kinsey waddled over. "If Miss Plessey will settle we'll give her fifteen hundred dollars."

Kinsey threw his head back and laughed. "Why don't you ask us to pay you, Booth? Fifteen hundred is an insult. We'll settle for one hundred and fifty thousand plus attorney fees. That's a lot less than what the jury is going to award."

"Last chance, Ron," Jack said.

Kinsey snickered and walked back to his client. Jack waited a minute before following. When he passed their bench he heard Kinsey tell his client that he and Jack hadn't discussed anything important. Jack smiled and entered the courtroom.

"The plaintiff calls Miss Tammy Longwell, Your Honor," Kinsey said as soon as court convened. Longwell was a knockout with wide blue eyes, silky blond hair, full red lips, and long legs. Jack was certain that every male on his jury had gotten a hard-on when she walked to the witness stand. He was equally certain that Kinsey believed that Longwell's testimony would cement the verdict. Jack agreed.

"Miss Longwell, were you a passenger in Miss Plessey's car when Officer Howell pulled her over?" Kinsey asked after a few preliminary questions.

"I was."

"Now, the officer cited Miss Plessey for driving under the influence of intoxicants. Do you have an opinion about Miss Plessey's state of sobriety at the time of her arrest?"

"I do."

"And what is your opinion?"

Tammy Longwell turned her head and stared across the room at Irene Plessey. Jack also turned his head so he could watch Kinsey's reaction to the answer.

"Irene was drunk," Longwell said.

Irene Plessey turned bright red and glared at Longwell. Kinsey's mouth gaped open and he was robbed of the power of speech for a moment.

"You mean sober?" he managed.

"I do not," Longwell insisted.

Kinsey riffled through his papers until he found a copy of the witness's trial testimony.

"Do you remember testifying at Miss Plessey's trial?"

"I do."

"And isn't it true that you testified under oath that Miss Plessey was completely sober when Officer Howell pulled her over?"

"Yes. Irene begged me to lie. She had another DUII pending and she was afraid she'd go to jail if she got two convictions. I'm not proud of what I did, but I feel bad about getting that nice officer in trouble. He was very professional even after Irene offered to sleep with him if he'd drop the charge. Then she threatened him. He was only doing his duty. I wouldn't have said anything if she'd stopped after she was acquitted, but I don't think it's right for her to get rich after she lied in court."

Officer Howell thanked Jack profusely as soon as the jury found in his favor. When the policeman left, Jack packed up his papers. He didn't know that his opponent had reentered the courtroom until he spoke.

"You knew Longwell was going to turn, didn't you?" Kinsey said. "That's why you made that lowball offer."

"Miss Longwell had a crisis of conscience and called me last night," Jack said.

"And you didn't tell me? That's . . . that's unethical."

Jack's features hardened and he took a step toward Kinsey. Kinsey grew pale and took a step back.

"I don't like being called names, Ron. Longwell was your witness. I didn't have to tell you jack shit about her call. And you should be careful before accusing me of being unethical. I bet you didn't tell your client about my offer. What do you think the rules of ethics say about that?"

"You're not going to get away with this, and neither is Longwell. I'll see that she's prosecuted for perjury."

"Not gonna happen, Ron. Tammy got immunity this morning. It's Miss Plessey who should start worrying about whether she's going to end up as Miss June in next year's Department of Corrections calendar. Now, why don't you run along and explain to the partner who trusted you with this sure winner how you fucked up."

Kinsey made a comment to save face that Jack didn't catch because he had turned away from the lawyer. On the way back to his office he had a big smile on his face. He loved to win, but that wasn't why he was smiling. He was remembering Longwell's phone call. Longwell had not come clean about what happened during Plessey's arrest because she felt sorry for Officer Howell. She had turned on Irene Plessey after discovering that the woman she had always considered to be her closest friend had been screwing her boyfriend.

Jack was in a great mood when he got back to his office at six. It lasted only as long as it took him to answer Stacey Kim's voice mail message. She said she was calling from New York but she didn't say why. Jack had never heard of Stacey Kim but she'd phoned from the Big Apple and that made him curious.

"Thank you so much for getting back to me," Stacey said.

"No problem. But your message didn't mention why you wanted me to call."

"I'm a writer and I'm working on a novel. I'm flying to Portland in a few weeks and I was hoping you could spare some time for me."

"I'm confused. I don't know anything about writing a novel. I'm an attorney."

"I know. That's why I want to talk to you. I'm interested in learning about a case you prosecuted."

"What case is that?"

"I just saw *Woman with a Gun* at the Museum of Modern Art. I was blown away by it and did some research to find out what inspired the photograph. That's how I learned about the *Cahill* case."

"There's nothing much to talk about, Miss Kim. The *Cahill* case was never solved."

"I'm not writing a true crime book," she said quickly. "*Cahill* is just the inspiration for the novel. The book is going to be a heavily fictionalized version of the case. For instance, I'm making the prosecutor a woman. I just wanted to talk to you for background."

"Look, I don't want to be rude, but I've got a very busy practice."

"I'll meet you anytime, anywhere. We can have breakfast, lunch, on me."

The line went quiet.

"I don't want to be a pest, Mr. Booth. I know you're busy. I'll accommodate your schedule."

"Call me when you get in and we'll see."

"Thank you so much," Stacey said.

As soon as he hung up, Booth walked to the wet bar he'd had installed in his corner office when he made partner. He poured a shot of very good scotch and carried his glass to the floor-to-ceiling window that faced east. Across the river, the snow-covered slopes of Mount Hood loomed over the foothills, but nothing in the picture postcard scene registered. Jack's thoughts were elsewhere.

It had been a while since Jack had thought about what had happened between him and Kathy Moran after his involvement in the *Cahill* case ended. Or, more accurately, what hadn't happened. The *Woman with a Gun* photograph sparked interest in the murder case, which already had legs because the cast of characters included a stunningly gorgeous wife, a multimillionaire husband who had been murdered on his wedding night, and an ex-professional football player. Kathy became an instant celebrity. Galleries in Los Angeles, New York, and Chicago started showing her work and selling it for thousands of dollars. It didn't hurt that she was beautiful and photogenic. National television shows wanted her as a guest; she was interviewed in national magazines and prominent newspapers and was hired to do photo shoots all over the world.

Jack had called once or twice but Kathy was always traveling and had not returned his calls. When they finally spoke, she was in a hotel in New York, dressing for a gallery opening. The conversation had lasted fewer than five minutes, and Kathy had politely explained that she liked Jack but her life was so hectic that she didn't have time for a serious relationship. When the phone call ended, it was crystal clear that Kathy Moran was now part of a world of A-list celebrities in which an assistant state attorney general who lived in Salem, Oregon, on a government salary would never fit.

Jack had moved on but sometimes late at night, when he was

alone, thoughts of Kathy Moran would slip in unbidden and leave him sad and wanting. Jack had been with women as beautiful and as intelligent as Kathy Moran, but he didn't think about them after the affairs ended. What was it about Kathy that kept him unsettled and longing after all these years? Was he frustrated by his inability to conquer her? Had she evoked some emotion that drove him to try to save her after her fall from grace? Was it some unexplainable chemical reaction that scrambled his emotions without affecting her? He could not pin it down but there was still something deep inside that tied him in knots whenever he thought about her.

CHAPTER THIRTY

The light of a summer sun seeped through the thin shades that covered the bedroom window of Stacey Kim's apartment in Portland, Oregon, and woke her from a deep, peaceful sleep. Stacey opened her eyes and smiled as she did every time she thought about the lucky break that had led her to Portland. If she had not read about the Dalí exhibit, if it had been bigger and it had taken all of her lunch hour to see it . . . If, if, if. One break in the chain and she would still be spending endless hours suffering behind the reception desk in Wilde, Levine and Barstow instead of forging forward with her novel in this jewel of a city in the Pacific Northwest.

Stacey had fallen in love with Portland even before her plane touched down. One glance out her window at the snow-covered peak of majestic Mount Hood and the lush forests that surrounded it and she was sold. Growing up in the flatlands of the Midwest had not prepared her for the verdant splendor of the hills that towered over Portland's west side or the massive mountains of the Cascade Range that dominated the scenery to the east. Portland was a city of varied and colorful architecture; a city of bridges that spanned the Columbia and Willamette rivers, which met in the city and divided it; a city without humidity or annoying bugs in summer but with an overabundance of bright, multicolored flowers.

After a few days of living in a hotel, Stacey found a one-bedroom apartment on the second floor of an early-twentieth-century Victorian that had been turned into a triplex. The apartment had high ceilings and spacious rooms and it was only a few blocks from Northwest Twenty-third, a delightful street lined with boutiques and restaurants. After her claustrophobic dump in Chelsea, the flat seemed like Versailles.

In Manhattan, it had taken real effort to get out of bed in the morning, but Stacey couldn't wait to start her days in Portland. Transferring to the West Coast had reinvigorated her and restored her belief that she was capable of crafting the novel Professor DeFord had been confident she would write. There was a coffeehouse two blocks from her apartment where she spent part of each day sipping caffe lattes while working on her laptop. Ideas were tumbling out now and Stacey had filled several pages with rough character sketches and notes for scenes and plotlines. She had some idea who her murderer would be, but she had only vague ideas about how her book would end, and she hadn't settled on the clue that would let her hero or heroine figure out whodunit. This didn't worry her. She had shed the negative feelings that had crippled her in New York and she was confident that she would conquer any obstacle placed before her.

Stacey sat up and stretched. Waking in a real bed instead of a foldout sofa was so nice. She showered and dressed quickly before going to the kitchen to rustle up some breakfast. After breakfast, she checked the clock. It was a little before nine. She hoped that Jack Booth would be at work.

Booth had been so negative during their first conversation that Stacey worried that he would refuse to meet with her. Of course, she could still write her novel without his help. On the first day of class, Professor DeFord had said that novelists were basically liars who made up stories about things that never happened. Stacey could always invent a prosecutor. Her DA was going to be a woman anyway. And there were many ways she could learn about trying a murder case. But it would be a lot easier if she could find out what happened in the *Cahill* case from the prosecutor who investigated it.

Stacey took a deep breath, gathered up her courage, and punched in the number for Jack Booth's law office.

Stacey experienced déjà vu when she walked out of the elevator on the twenty-eighth floor of the office building that housed Jack Booth's law firm. Through floor-to-ceiling glass doors that were almost identical to the doors to Wilde, Levine and Barstow she could see a clone of the reception desk behind which she had spent so many excruciating hours. When Stacey told the receptionist that she had an appointment with Jack Booth she was greeted with the same phony cheer Stacey had exuded every day for almost one year.

After a hushed exchange, the receptionist told Stacey that Mr. Booth would see her in a few minutes. Stacey took a seat on a very comfortable couch. On the coffee table in front of her were that day's edition of the *Wall Street Journal* and a selection of business and news magazines. Stacey was halfway through an article about a new development in neuroscience that had implications for selecting stocks for investment when a tall man dressed in a navy blue, pinstripe suit came into view.

"Miss Kim?" Jack Booth said.

Stacey thought that the lawyer looked stern and humorless.

This impression jibed with the mental image Stacey had constructed after both of their phone conversations. When she had called two days ago he had agreed to see her but he hadn't sounded happy.

"Thank you for meeting with me, Mr. Booth," Stacey said as she stood up.

Jack nodded, then turned without making a comment and led the way down a long corridor to a corner office with breathtaking mountain views. He gestured toward a sofa and took an armchair catty-corner to it. As Stacey seated herself, she looked around the room. It was sterile. The paintings on the walls were unexciting abstracts that had probably been selected by an interior decorator. College and law school diplomas and certificates attesting to Jack's admission to state and federal bar associations hung on the walls. A few golf trophies stood on a credenza, but there were no family photographs or anything else in the room that gave Stacey a glimpse into Jack's personal life.

Stacey booted up her laptop. "Do you mind if I make notes while we talk?"

"No, that's fine." Jack looked at his watch. "Why don't you start?"

Stacey noticed that Jack had not engaged in any small talk. He hadn't asked her how she was enjoying Portland or where she'd gone to school and it was clear that he was uncomfortable. Stacey wasn't sure how long Jack would tolerate her so she decided to get to the point.

"Do you still think Megan Cahill was part of a conspiracy to kill her husband?" Stacey Kim asked an hour later when Jack finished telling her about the *Cahill* case.

"I don't know. I've thought about the case off and on over the years. At one point I wondered if Crouse and Megan faked their differences when it became obvious that Raymond Cahill had a romantic interest in her."

"You think their divorce was a sham and they planned to kill and rob Mr. Cahill all along?"

Jack shrugged. "It was just an idea, and even if Megan was involved in a plot to kill her husband there still had to be a third person, because Megan couldn't have killed Crouse. I always figured Gary Kilbride for that role, but he's dead so we'll probably never know."

"Did any of the items stolen from Mr. Cahill's collection ever turn up?"

"Not a one. I've always been surprised by that. Frank Janowitz did say that the stamps and coins would probably be sold to private collectors who weren't bothered by the fact that they were stolen goods, so I could see how they might simply disappear."

"You'd think some item would have surfaced by now," Stacey said.

"Maybe not. Kathy Moran shot Gary Kilbride soon after the robbery. If he and Crouse were crime partners and Kilbride killed Crouse and took the stolen items, Kilbride might not have had a chance to get rid of the loot before he was killed. The stolen stamps, coins, and antique firearms could be languishing in a storage locker or another cache no one has been able to discover."

"That makes sense."

Stacey made some notes. "Have you kept track of Megan Cahill and Kathy Moran?" she asked when she was done.

"I did try to keep tabs on everyone who was involved in the case for a while but I lost interest when it became obvious that there were no new leads. I do know that Kathy Moran still lives in Palisades Heights."

"Didn't she have problems with drugs?"

Jack nodded. "She became famous overnight because of the *Woman with a Gun* photograph and got caught up in the celebrity lifestyle. She was in and out of rehab before moving back to the coast."

"What about Megan Cahill?"

"Her life was pretty hectic, too. Advantage Investments was sued by Armand Tuttle. An investigation showed that Raymond Cahill had cheated several investors. Kevin Mercer claimed he knew nothing about it. There were lawsuits, and the investors were paid back. Settling the lawsuits drained away a lot of the money Raymond had accumulated and his other wives and children tied up the estate in litigation, so Megan didn't come away with much."

"Didn't she have her fifteen minutes of fame, too?" Stacey asked.

"The publicity from the case landed her a spot on a reality TV show but it only lasted one season."

"Do you know where she's living now?"

"She still owns the Palisades Heights house, but she married Kevin Mercer and she was living in L.A. most of the year."

"She married Cahill's partner?" Stacey said.

"They got to know each other during the litigation over the stock fraud."

"What happened to Mercer?"

"Advantage went bankrupt, but I read that Mercer started a new company that's doing well."

"Are Megan and Mercer still together?"

"I think they are, but I've also heard that they're separated."

"Did you ever think Kevin Mercer was the third man?" Stacey asked. "He could have hired Crouse to kill Cahill and he knew about Cahill's collection."

"That's an interesting idea. You have a good imagination. I think your book is going to be pretty good."

Jack looked at his watch. "I hope I've been helpful but I'm going to have to kick you out now. I have to be in court this afternoon and I need some time to prepare."

Stacey closed her laptop and stood up. She smiled at Jack. "You've been a terrific help. Thanks for taking so much time to talk with me."

Jack returned the smile. "Good luck with the writing."

CHAPTER THIRTY-ONE

Two days after her interview with Jack Booth, Stacey tossed a suitcase into the trunk of a rental car, pushed a CD into the player on the dashboard, and set off for the coast. During the drive to Palisades Heights she felt like she was cruising through an art gallery that specialized in landscape paintings. Above her, puffy white clouds drifted through an azure sky. On both sides of the highway, farmland, divided into squares of yellow, green, and brown, stretched out until it met rolling green hills. This pastoral scene soon gave way to towering evergreen forests, and bends in the road suddenly revealed white water bouncing along fast-moving rivers. Then the highway wound out of a low mountain range and joined a coastal highway giving Stacey her first glimpse of the rocky shores of the Pacific Ocean through the veil of a low-hanging fog.

Stacey was in a great mood when she parked at the Oceanside Motel. As soon as she unpacked, she walked onto her balcony. Stacey had seen the Atlantic during a weekend excursion to the Hamptons with some of the women from Wilde, Levine and

Barstow. The Pacific's rocky coastline seemed more violent and untamed.

Stacey's stomach began to growl. She was going to ask at the motel office for a restaurant suggestion when she thought of the perfect place to eat. Ocean Avenue was mobbed with raucous children, harried parents, and happy, hand-holding couples. Almost everyone was dressed in jeans or shorts and T-shirts and Stacey felt overdressed in the tan suit and sky blue, man-tailored shirt she'd chosen for her interview.

Stacey found the Seafarer at the end of a block populated by art galleries, clothing boutiques, coffee shops, and a bookstore. Her pulse quickened as she walked into the tavern where Kathy Moran had tended bar before fate sent her to the beach beneath Raymond Cahill's vacation home. The hostess showed her to a table near a large fieldstone fireplace. As she walked across the dimly lit room, her eye was drawn to photographs of ocean scenes that hung on the wall among the nautical paraphernalia. She didn't need to read the captions to know who had taken them. Stacey ordered a cup of clam chowder, a plate of fried oysters, and a Coke. While she waited for her food, she jotted down a description of the Seafarer.

By the time Stacey finished lunch, the morning fog had burned off and the sun was shining on the crowds on Ocean Avenue. There was no breeze to cool the air and she was perspiring by the time she found the address for Baker and Kraft. Stacey had called from Portland to set up an appointment with Henry Baker, but Mr. Baker's secretary had informed her that Mr. Baker had suffered a stroke and only came to the office infrequently. When Stacey explained why she was calling, the secretary had suggested that she talk to Mr. Kraft, who had also worked on the case.

The law firm was on the second floor of a building three

blocks north of the tavern. A narrow entryway opened into a stairwell between a store that sold fudge and a store that sold kites. Stacey walked up to the second floor and into a waiting room. A middle-aged woman looked up from her computer and smiled.

"Can I help you?" she asked.

"My name is Stacey Kim and I have an appointment with Mr. Kraft."

The smile widened. "Oh, yes, the writer. He's expecting you. I'll tell him you're here."

Stacey sat on a couch across from the reception desk and looked down a hallway that stretched along the length of the second floor. A few minutes later, a door in the middle of the hall opened and a young man in jeans and a faded Amherst T-shirt walked into the corridor. He had wavy brown hair, kind brown eyes, and a welcoming smile. From a distance, Stacey took him for a twenty something. When he drew closer she saw a few gray hairs and some lines on his tanned face and upped her guess by ten years.

"Hi, Stacey. I'm Glen Kraft. Henry wasn't well enough today to come to the office, so you'll have to make do with me."

"Thanks for seeing me," Stacey said as she got to her feet.

"Your project has me intrigued. Come on back."

Kraft's office looked out on Ocean Avenue. The walls were decorated with Kraft's law and undergraduate degrees and certificates attesting to his admission to federal and state bar associations, but the thing that drew Stacey's eye was a photograph of Kraft standing next to a huge fish. The attorney saw where she was looking and smiled.

"That's a blue marlin I snagged in Australia. Do you fish?"

Stacey was tempted to say, Not if I can help it, but she thought it was more politic to simply say, "No. Is it dangerous?"

"Not if you know what you're doing and have the right equipment. But it sure is exciting. You should try it sometime. If you're here for a while you should go out on a sports fishing boat and try to catch some salmon."

"Thanks, that sounds like fun," Stacey said, trying her hardest to seem excited.

Glen laughed. "You're not much of an outdoors type, are you?"

"How did you guess?"

"Well, you turned green when I mentioned deep sea fishing. That was a clue. And you're not exactly dressed for the beach."

Stacey blushed. "I grew up in the Midwest. We don't have a lot of beaches where I come from."

"I don't usually dress like this at work but I thought I'd take you on a walk along the shore to the Cahills' house so you can see where Kathy Moran shot her famous photo."

"That would be great."

"Did you pack shorts or jeans and sneakers?"

"I did. I was planning to go to the beach after we talked, but I'd appreciate a tour."

"Where are you staying?"

Stacey told him.

"That's only a few blocks from here. Let's go to your motel so you can change and I'll tell you what I remember about the case while we walk."

Glen told his receptionist that he would be out for a while and they went down the staircase to the street.

"So, how did you get interested in the *Cahill* case?" Glen asked as they headed toward Stacey's motel.

"I moved to New York from the Midwest after I got an MFA. My plan was to expand a short story I'd written into a novel, but I ran into a brick wall. Then I went to MoMA and saw *Woman with a Gun* and it was . . ."

Stacey stopped talking. Her brow furrowed and she shook her head. "I don't know how to explain it. But I just knew I had to find out the story behind the photograph, and that I was meant to write a novel inspired by it. So I quit my job and moved to Oregon, and here I am."

Stacey stopped, embarrassed. "I'm sorry, but I get excited just thinking about the book. It's hard to explain."

"I've never had the urge to write a novel but I get it. You don't have a book deal, right? You're writing the book on spec?"

Stacey nodded.

"I admire your guts, just packing up and leaving everything behind to follow a dream. It's very romantic. Although you should be in Paris, France, instead of Palisades Heights, Oregon."

Stacey laughed.

"So what can I do to help?" Glen asked.

"I guess the best thing would be for you to just talk about the case—how you got involved, what you remember about it and the people who were mixed up in it."

Glen waited on the landing outside Stacey's second-floor room while she changed. There was a beach access behind the motel and Glen told Stacey about his and Henry Baker's involvement in the *Cahill* case while they walked along the shore.

"Then Mrs. Cahill claimed that some of her memory had returned," Glen concluded. "She told the police that her ex-husband, Parnell Crouse, was the man who attacked her and Raymond Cahill."

"Why did you say that 'she claimed that some of her memory had returned'?" Stacey asked. "Did you doubt her?"

"Not really."

"You didn't have any second thoughts?"

"Personally, no, but it was convenient for Crouse to be the killer."

"Why do you say that?" Stacey asked.

"Shortly after Megan accused Crouse, he was found in his car on a logging road. He'd been shot to death and a coin from Mr. Cahill's collection was found in his car. With Crouse dead, there was no one to contradict Megan when she said that Crouse had killed her husband. And Megan was in the hospital when the ME said Crouse had been killed so she was off the hook for her ex-husband's murder."

"Jack Booth told me that Mrs. Cahill could still have been involved in both murders if she had an accomplice who gave her an alibi by killing Crouse while she was in the hospital."

"That was one possibility," Glen conceded. "But there was another. While Raymond Cahill's murder was being investigated, a paroled convict named Gary Kilbride was shot and killed when he broke into Kathy Moran's house."

"Mr. Booth told me all about Kilbride."

"Okay. Then you know one theory the police had was that Kilbride had learned about Raymond Cahill's collection by reading an article in the *Gazette* and hooked up with Crouse to pull off the job."

"I'd love to read that article. Do you know where I can get a copy?"

"I had our file in Megan's case brought up from storage when you told me you were coming. I'm pretty certain that there's a copy in it. You can read the article when we get back to the office."

"Thanks. What did Mrs. Cahill do once she was in the clear?"

"She flew back to L.A."

"Did she ever regain all of her memory?"

"I couldn't tell you."

"Do you think Mrs. Cahill is innocent?"

"She insisted that she was, but being objective about the facts you could go both ways based on what the investigation uncovered."

Glen stopped and turned toward the sea.

"This is it," he said.

Stacey was confused for a few seconds. Then she understood that Glen was telling her that she was staring at the same eternal ebb and flow that had hypnotized the woman with a gun. Stacey's heart beat faster. This was the moment she had been waiting for ever since her fateful visit to the museum. She took a deep breath to calm herself and let her imagination take her back in time until she was Megan Cahill standing in the moonlight, holding the Smith & Wesson revolver that had been used to kill her husband.

Stacey turned her back to the ocean. The Cahill house loomed above her. Weathered gray wooden stairs led up to a deck. She could see part of a picture window, a chair, and an umbrella. Stacey had brought a steno pad in case she needed to take notes. She jotted down her impressions of the house, the way the sun felt and the way the sea looked.

Finally, Stacey looked down the beach in the direction of the Seafarer and tried to imagine that she was Kathy Moran, searching for a shot she could use in her one-woman show and stumbling on the opportunity of a lifetime.

CHAPTER THIRTY-TWO

Glen brought the Bankers Boxes containing the *Cahill* files to an empty office at the end of the hall and left Stacey with her treasure trove. Stacey rifled through each box quickly to get a feel for the contents, making notes as she went. The edition of the *Palisades Heights Gazette* with the article about Raymond Cahill was in a box with miscellaneous items. She set it aside and read the police and autopsy reports of the Cahill murder, Crouse's murder, and the Kilbride shooting.

The sun was starting to set when she finally opened the *Gazette* to the society page and the article about Raymond Cahill and she was almost finished reading it when Glen walked into the office.

"How are you doing?" he asked.

"Great! The stuff in the files is going to help me make my book very realistic. I was worried about writing a scene with a medical examiner, but I can take the autopsy report and rewrite it as a conversation."

"I'm glad the stuff is useful."

"You have no idea."

"Look, I'm done for the day and I was going to get something to eat. Do you want to join me?"

Stacey looked at her watch. "Seven o'clock! How did that happen?"

Glen smiled. "So?"

"Just let me straighten up."

"I'll meet you in the reception area. Do you like seafood?"

"You sort of have to in Palisades Heights, don't you?"

Glen drove to a restaurant overlooking the ocean and made sure they were seated next to a picture window so Stacey could see the sunset.

"The view is so beautiful," Stacey said when the waiter left with their order for cocktails.

"That's one of the perks of living in Palisades Heights," Glen answered.

"Do you like practicing law here?"

"I do. I didn't at first. When I graduated from law school I wanted to work for one of the big Portland firms, but the market for lawyers was really bad and I was having trouble getting any kind of job. My dad knew Henry and he mentioned my dilemma. By a lucky coincidence, Henry's associate had just quit.

"I wasn't very enthusiastic about coming back to my hometown and I definitely didn't look forward to a small-town practice. But a funny thing happened. After a while I started enjoying representing real people instead of faceless corporations. I don't make the money I'd make in a big Portland firm but I do okay and it feels good when you can help someone out of a jam or ease them through a tough divorce. Now I consider myself lucky to have my job."

"You are lucky. When I moved to New York to write my book

I got a job as a receptionist at a big firm in Manhattan. No one seemed very excited about what they were doing and the hours the attorneys worked were deadly, twelve- to sixteen-hour days. I was there less than a year but there were serious drinking problems, one suicide, and several divorces."

"We aren't immune from stress in Palisades Heights."

"Oh?" Stacey said, wondering if Glen was divorced.

Glen shrugged. "We're like anyplace else. People in small towns get divorced and drink too much. In Palisades Heights we just feel bad in a beautiful setting."

Stacey laughed just as the waiter arrived with their drinks. She took a sip of her cocktail and watched the sun complete its voyage below the horizon. She wanted to forget why she was in Palisades Heights for a few moments, but thoughts about the *Cahill* case kept intruding.

"Do you think Raymond Cahill's murder will ever be solved to everyone's satisfaction?" she asked Glen.

"You can solve it while you're working on your book. Think of the publicity you'd get if you figure out whodunit."

Stacey smiled and Glen raised his glass.

"To your best seller."

"From your lips to God's ears."

"You know, if you ever get a movie deal, Megan could play herself," Glen said. "She looks like a movie star."

"Do you ever see her?" Stacey asked.

"Once in a while. She still owns the house."

"Jack Booth told me that. Isn't it odd that she held on to it? You'd think she would have sold it because of the bad memories."

"It is a little surprising."

"I would love to interview Kathy Moran and Megan Cahill," Stacey said wistfully.

"Ms. Kim, your timing could not be better," Glen said, breaking into a grin. "I was going to save this for later but since you brought it up . . ."

"Save what for later?"

"Kathy's exhibit is going to move to the Portland Art Museum now that its run at MoMA is over, but Kathy insisted that a local gallery here in Palisades Heights get the opportunity to show her work for a week in between. The exhibit is opening at Ellen Devereaux's gallery tomorrow, and Kathy Moran and Megan Cahill are the guests of honor."

"Oh, my God!"

Stacey's energy delighted Glen. "I'm glad I could make your day."

"You've just made my century." Then Stacey sobered. "Do you think they'll talk to me? I'd love to get inside the Cahill house to see what it looks like."

"You'll have to ask Megan. As for Kathy, she's been a bit of a recluse. She was a real celebrity for a while and her career took off. But she crashed when she started using drugs. She almost died from an overdose. When she got out of rehab she moved back to Palisades Heights, and she pretty much keeps to herself.

"From what I hear, the people at MoMA wanted her to be at the opening in New York but she wouldn't go. There was an article in the *Gazette* that said she had no involvement in the exhibit at all except for giving her permission to MoMA to show her work."

"Do you know her?"

"Not well. But you can turn on your charm at the gallery and see what happens."

"I don't know how to thank you."

"You can use my name for a character in your novel when it's published."

"Deal," Stacey said as she held out her hand.

Glen shook and Stacey held his hand a moment more than was necessary. She noticed that he wasn't wearing a wedding ring and wondered if he was seeing anyone. She didn't remember any pictures of Glen with a woman in his office. Then she chided herself for being silly for thinking about a relationship when she wasn't going to be in Palisades Heights, or Oregon for that matter, for very long. Still, she was curious.

CHAPTER THIRTY-THREE

Ellen Devereaux's gallery occupied a large space on the corner of Ocean Avenue and Third Street. When Stacey and Glen arrived, a crowd was milling around on the sidewalk and the interior of the gallery was packed. Some people clustered in groups, talking and nibbling on hors d'oeuvres. Others walked around the gallery, sipping wine while they looked at the exhibit. Stacey squeezed inside and scanned the crowd for Kathy Moran or Megan Cahill, but she didn't see them.

"Do you want some wine?" Glen asked.

"Thanks, red, please."

"I'll see if they're pouring some of our famous Oregon pinots and I'll be right back."

Glen headed for the bar Devereaux had set up along the rear wall just as Jack Booth entered the gallery.

"Mr. Booth."

Jack looked surprised.

"Good evening, Stacey."

"What are you doing here?"

"I came to see the exhibit. Other than *Woman with a Gun*, I've only seen a few of Kathy's photographs. I assume you're here doing research."

"I am. I'm with Glen Kraft. He's let me set up in his office and he's given me his files on the *Cahill* case. Do you remember him?"

"Sure. He was Henry Baker's associate when I was investigating *Cahill*."

"He's his partner now."

"I know. We were on opposite sides of a case two or three years ago," Booth said just as Glen walked up with two glasses of wine.

"Jack," Glen said as he handed a glass to Stacey. "It's good seeing you again. What brings you to Palisades Heights?"

"I was just explaining to Stacey that I haven't seen a lot of Kathy Moran's work. An article in the *Oregonian* said that the exhibit was showing here before it moved to the Portland Art Museum. I have a lengthy trial that's supposed to start the day the exhibit moves. If the case doesn't settle this will be my only chance to catch Kathy's show."

"You're going to enjoy it," Stacey said. "Ms. Moran is a terrific photographer."

"It was nice bumping into you two," Jack said. "I'm going to grab a glass of wine before I look at Kathy's photographs."

Stacey watched Booth stop on his way to the bar to say hello to a tall, muscular man with salt-and-pepper hair he wore in a Marine cut.

"Is that George Melendez?" Stacey asked.

"Yeah, he's still our police chief and he still does a great job."

"Is Teddy Winston still the DA?"

"No, he's a judge. Gayle Sutcliff is the DA now. Shall we?"

The photographs were mounted on the walls of the gallery.

All of the pictures Stacey had seen in New York were on display, along with several photographs from Ellen Devereaux's private collection of Kathy Moran's work.

"Life is funny," Stacey mused when they had seen the entire exhibit.

"Why do you say that?"

"Think about it. If Raymond Cahill hadn't been murdered, Kathy Moran would probably be an unknown artist showing her work in a couple of West Coast galleries."

"Too true," Glen agreed just as Ellen Devereaux shouted to get the room's attention.

Stacey sized up Devereaux as a vigorous woman somewhere in her fifties. Her curly brown hair had gone mostly gray but her blue eyes had lost none of their luster.

"Thank you for coming to honor a local artist who has achieved international fame," Devereaux said when she had everyone's attention. "Ten years ago a terrible tragedy occurred on the evening Raymond Cahill married Megan Cahill at the Palisades Heights Country Club. When the newlyweds returned to their home a burglar murdered the new groom.

"Now there is no way to put a good spin on an event that awful, but a great work of art was produced because of that tragedy. Kathy Moran was wandering along the beach after midnight, looking for scenes to shoot for a one-woman show she was organizing for this gallery when she saw Megan Cahill standing at the edge of the sea. The haunting photograph she took became a cause célèbre and Kathy's talent was validated when *Woman with a Gun* was awarded a Pulitzer Prize.

"The exhibit you are viewing tonight was recently shown at the Museum of Modern Art in New York to commemorate the tenth anniversary of Kathy's Pulitzer and it will be displayed at the Portland Art Museum. But Kathy insisted that the citizens of her adopted town get a chance to see *Woman with a Gun* and her other exceptional work in this limited engagement.

"Kathy has been out of town, taking photographs in Zion National Park in Utah, but she came back to Palisades Heights this morning. So, it is with great pleasure that I introduce a master photographer and the subject of her greatest work, Kathy Moran and Megan Cahill."

Kathy and Megan walked out of Devereaux's office, and the crowd in the gallery burst into applause. Kathy stood next to Devereaux and waited for the applause to die down. Stacey thought that Moran was still beautiful, but she was definitely showing the ravages of a life lived hard. And, as Glen had said, Megan Cahill still looked like she could star in a movie based on Stacey's novel.

"Ellen Devereaux supported me and my work when I was a complete unknown. She has always believed in me, and this exhibition is my way of thanking her for the trust she put in me. I want to thank every one of you for coming to support me and Ellen's wonderful gallery, and I am especially grateful to Megan Cahill for traveling from California to be here tonight."

The crowd applauded Megan, who blushed and looked down for a moment before stepping forward.

"It took me a while to decide if I was going to come to Palisades Heights for this exhibition. For obvious reasons, Kathy's photograph, which has amazed so many people, brings back very dark memories for me. But I decided to come because *Woman with a Gun* proves that good can come out of the most terrible circumstances. I arrived only a short time ago and I will have my first chance to view the exhibit at the same time you are seeing Kathy's amazing photographs. I believe we're all in for a treat."

"And now," Ellen Devereaux said, "please enjoy the wonderful photography of Kathy Moran."

Most of the crowd flowed toward the exhibition, the table with the food, or the bar, but some guests moved in to talk to Devereaux, Kathy Moran, and Megan Cahill.

"Go ahead," Glen urged Stacey. "This is your chance."

Stacey gathered her nerve and hovered on the fringe of the crowd around the guests of honor. When the crowd around Megan Cahill thinned, Stacey moved in.

"Mrs. Cahill, my name is Stacey Kim and I'm in Palisades Heights doing research for a novel that was inspired by *Woman with a Gun*. I know you're very busy now but I'm staying in Palisades Heights for a few days and I'd be very grateful if you could spare some time to meet with me. I'll meet anytime that's convenient for you."

Megan seemed annoyed. "I don't like to think about what happened on my wedding night."

"I appreciate that, but it's not a true crime story, so this would just be for background. It would mean so much to me."

Megan looked over Stacey's shoulder, saw someone approaching, and made a quick decision.

"Do you know where I live when I'm in Palisades Heights?" Megan asked.

"Yes."

"Come over tomorrow morning around ten and we can talk."

"Thank you," Stacey said. "I promise I won't take up too much of your time."

Megan flashed an impatient smile. "We'll talk tomorrow."

Stacey could tell that Megan wanted to end the conversation so she backed away and almost ran into a solidly built older man who was standing behind her.

"What are you doing here, Kevin?" Stacey heard Megan say.

"Trying to talk to you. You've been avoiding me, and this was the only place I knew I could find you."

Stacey turned around to see if Kathy Moran was free but she was talking to Jack Booth. As Stacey walked back to Glen, she wondered if Booth was in Palisades Heights to see Kathy Moran's photographs or Kathy Moran.

"Guess what!" Stacey said excitedly.

"Megan is going to let you interview her."

"Yes! At her house, so I'll get to see the scene of the crime. I'm going over tomorrow morning."

Kevin Mercer and Megan Cahill had moved to a corner of the gallery near the far end of the exhibit. Mercer stood with his back to several of the photographs. He was gesturing angrily and Megan was shaking her head. Then a big man hobbled up and stood next to Mercer. The man was using a cane and the left side of his face was twisted, indicating that he had been the victim of a stroke. Glen saw the man, too.

"That's Henry," Kraft said. He sounded surprised.

"Your partner?" Stacey asked.

"Yes."

Megan turned toward Baker and stared at him. Then her hand flew to her mouth and she wheeled away and ran out of the gallery.

"Megan," Mercer yelled after her. Megan didn't slow down.

Stacey saw Kathy Moran and Jack Booth turn toward the fleeing woman. Then Kathy walked over to Mercer with Booth a few steps behind her. She stopped in the space Megan had just vacated.

"What did you say to her?" Kathy demanded.

"Nothing. I have no idea what caused Megan to run off."

"You must have done something."

"Honestly, I don't know what brought that on. Henry walked up and Megan got this terrified look on her face. Then she ran out."

Kathy turned to Henry Baker. "Do you know why Megan ran?" she asked.

Baker shook his head. "I just wanted to say hello." His words were slurred and it took an effort for him to speak.

Kathy started to say something but she stopped and frowned. Then she looked angry again.

"Thanks for fucking up the opening, Kevin."

Kathy turned on her heel and walked off with Jack Booth in tow before Mercer could respond.

"That was really strange," Glen said to Stacey.

"What?" Stacey asked. She'd been watching Jack Booth and Kathy Moran walk off and she hadn't heard what Glen had said.

"The way Megan ran off," Glen said. "I thought it was strange."

"No kidding," Stacey agreed. Then she frowned. "I want to ask Miss Moran if I can interview her, but I don't think this is the right time. Do you know Ellen Devereaux well enough to ask her to act as an intermediary?"

"Actually, I do. Our firm's done some legal work for her. I'll call her tomorrow."

"Thanks, Glen. You're definitely going to be a character in the book, an important one!"

Glen laughed. "Come on. I'll introduce you to Henry."

Glen led Stacey across the room.

"How are you doing, Henry?"

Baker pivoted on his cane and turned toward Glen.

"I thought the doctors didn't want you taxing yourself," Glen asked with concern.

"They don't but I didn't want to miss the exhibit, and I heard Megan was going to be here. I haven't seen her in a long time."

"Do you want me to get you a chair? Are you okay?"

"Stop fussing. Helen Dooley, my neighbor, drove me over."

Henry pointed his cane at a middle-aged woman who was looking at the photos at the end of the room near the door. "She's going to take me home when I've seen the exhibit. Now introduce me to your friend."

"Sorry. Henry, this is Stacey Kim. I told you she was going to come here to do some research."

"You're writing a novel that's a fictional version of the *Cahill* case, right?" Baker said.

"Yes."

"That's a book I'll have to read. Have you figured out who killed Ray and Parnell Crouse yet?"

"No, but I'm not trying to solve the case. I'm just using the facts as a skeleton for my book."

"Too bad. I'd sure like to know whodunit."

"I told her solving the case would be great publicity," Glen said.

"That it would. Some pretty smart people have tried to get a handle on what happened and no one has succeeded so far."

"I thought Crouse killed Raymond Cahill," Stacey said.

"Maybe he did and maybe he didn't. What if Crouse was completely innocent and the real killer set him up and planted that coin so it would look like Crouse was in on the robbery?"

Stacey thought about that possibility. Then she frowned. "If Crouse wasn't at the Cahills' house, Megan Cahill lied when she said he was the robber."

"That would be the conclusion you would have to draw," Baker agreed. "And she was holding the murder weapon when Kathy found her on the beach."

"You think Megan murdered her husband?" Stacey asked.

"No. I believe her story. I was just trying to help you plot your book."

"Oh."

Baker tried to smile but his attempt to twist his lips just made him look more grotesque.

"It was nice meeting you, Miss Kim. I'm getting tired so I want to look at Kathy's photographs while I still have the energy. Let Glen know if you want to pick my brain."

Baker limped over to the photographs and Glen looked at his watch.

"It's still early. Do you want to grab a bite to eat or a drink?"

Spending more time with Glen sounded way more appealing than returning to her motel room.

"Sure. I didn't get a chance to eat any of the hors d'oeuvres and I'm starving."

"Then let's go."

"What do you think that was all about?" Jack asked Kathy moments after Megan Cahill ran out of the gallery.

"Megan and I had dinner this evening. She told me that she and Kevin are in the middle of a drawn-out and nasty divorce, so I assume it has something to do with that."

"So, how have you been?" Jack asked.

"Great, actually. I've never stopped taking photographs, but my career has been in the doldrums for a while, what with the drugs and my self-imposed exile in Palisades Heights after rehab. Then MoMA announced the exhibit and I'm suddenly hot again."

"So you're back exhibiting?"

"I've got shows in New York and L.A., and there's a gallery in Seattle that wants to talk about an exhibit. Plus I've had offers for commercial shoots."

"That's great."

Jack looked around. There had been a momentary lull when

Megan raced out of the gallery but everything seemed to be back to the way it had been before the argument.

"I don't think their spat affected the mood of the crowd. Everyone looks pretty happy."

"Why are you here, Jack?"

"My, you're blunt."

Kathy didn't respond.

"It's Stacey Kim's fault," Jack said with a grin.

"Who?"

Jack gestured toward Stacey. "The woman talking to Glen Kraft is writing a novel inspired by your photograph. She interviewed me in Portland about the *Cahill* case and I suspect she'll ask you to sit down with her. You should do it. She's a good kid, very enthusiastic. It would be a good deed."

"You still haven't answered my question."

Jack shrugged. "Reliving the *Cahill* case made me think about you. Then I saw an article about the exhibit moving from New York to the Portland Art Museum with a brief stop in Palisades Heights. I thought it would be nice to see you again."

Kathy smiled but she looked sad. "I know you wanted something to develop between us, Jack, and there was a time when that might have happened. But I'm really not interested in any kind of relationship at this point in my life. So I'm glad to see you, but if you came to Palisades Heights because of me, you shouldn't have."

Jack didn't try to hide his disappointment. "That's fair," he said. "Thanks for being up-front."

Kathy reached out and touched Jack's cheek. "You're a good guy and I'm flattered that you still harbor romantic feelings for me. At my age that's a real ego boost. I've got to go mingle now. I hope you enjoy my photographs."

CHAPTER THIRTY-FOUR

Stacey was in a great mood when she woke up the next morning. She ate breakfast in a mom-and-pop restaurant a few blocks from her motel. Then she walked on the beach and thought about the questions she would pose to Megan Cahill. At nine thirty, Stacey walked down Ocean Avenue to Megan's house and rang the doorbell. The house blocked the ocean breeze and she enjoyed the warm sun while she waited for Megan to let her in. After a few minutes, Stacey rang the bell again. There was still no response.

The weather was glorious and Stacey decided that Megan had not heard her because she was on the deck, basking in the sun. She tried the door. It was open, a good sign that she was expected.

"Hello," she shouted. "Mrs. Cahill, it's Stacey Kim."

There was no answer. Stacey stepped into the stone entryway, and a rank odor made her nostrils flare. Stacey remembered Jack Booth telling her that there had been an awful smell in the den where Raymond Cahill's body was found, and a queasy feeling started to grow in the pit of her stomach.

The foul odor seemed to be coming from the living room. Stacey stopped breathing to block the smell and forced herself to look over the banister. Her hand flew to her mouth. Megan Cahill lay on her back. Her white T-shirt had been dyed rust red and her head lay in a halo of blood. Megan's eyes were wide open and her arms were spread out. Her mouth formed a small circle. She looked as if death had come as a complete surprise.

Later, when she had time to think about what had happened, Stacey was proud of the fact that she didn't scream, but she'd definitely backed out of the house faster than she ever thought she could move. As soon as she was standing on Ocean Avenue, she dialed 911.

When Glen Kraft walked into George Melendez's office, Stacey was sitting across from the chief of police, sipping tea from a chipped mug. Glen's tie was pulled down, and the suit he'd worn in court looked rumpled, as did his hair. Stacey took that as a sign that he'd rushed to her aid and that made her feel good for the first time since she'd seen Megan Cahill splayed on the living room carpet.

"I'm sorry it took me so long to get here," Glen said. "I was in court when you called and I didn't retrieve your message until we recessed."

Glen turned to the police chief. "Is Stacey in trouble?"

"No, not at all," Melendez said. "She's a witness. You heard what happened?"

"Not really. Stacey's message just said that Megan Cahill was dead and she found the body."

Melendez nodded. "I brought her back here from the Cahills' house to get her away from the crime scene."

"Someone killed her?" Glen asked.

The police chief nodded.

Glen looked alarmed. "Are you okay?" he asked Stacey.

"I'm still shaken up but I'll be all right."

"The killer wasn't in the house, was he?" Glen asked.

"The medical examiner thinks that Mrs. Cahill was killed sometime late last night long before Miss Kim arrived."

"That's one thing to be thankful for," Glen said. "What happened?"

"Mrs. Cahill's body was found in the living room," Melendez said. "She'd been stabbed, but she fell over the balcony and snapped her neck. That's probably what killed her."

"God, that's awful. Was it a burglar? Did someone break in?"

"We don't think so. There were no signs of forced entry and the house doesn't look trashed. We're guessing Mrs. Cahill was sleeping when the killer rang the doorbell. She was probably stabbed when she opened the front door. Then she either fell over the banister into the living room or she was pushed."

Glen noticed that Stacey had lost color. "Do you need Stacey anymore?" he asked.

"No, I've got her statement."

"Can she leave?"

Melendez nodded.

"Thanks, George."

Stacey stood. The tea had helped calm her but she was a little unsteady. It was one thing to read or write about a dead body and another to see one.

"How are you really?" Glen asked when they were standing on the sidewalk outside the courthouse.

"Not great."

"Where's your car?"

"At the motel. I walked to Mrs. Cahill's house."

"Do you want me to take you to the motel?"

"Not really. I . . . I don't want to be alone right now."

Glen paused. He looked a little unsure of himself. "Do you want to go to my house? I've got a guest room. You can pick up some stuff from your motel and stay the night."

"Thanks. Let's do that." She flashed an exhausted smile. "You're a good guy, Glen."

Glen blushed. "Hey, it's no big deal. Helping damsels in distress is something I do at least once a week."

Glen lived in a modern box-shaped, two-story house a block from the beach. The front door opened into a living room with a sliding glass door that opened onto a deck that faced the sea. Glen led Stacey upstairs to the second floor and opened the bedroom door. When Stacey was inside, Glen put her suitcase on the queen-size bed and showed her the bathroom. A door opened onto a deck that provided a view of the ocean. Stacey walked outside. The fresh air felt good.

"This is nice," Stacey said.

"Why don't you change into something comfortable. Come down when you're ready."

Glen closed the door and Stacey collapsed on a deck chair. The house was close enough to the ocean for Stacey to hear waves crashing onto the shore. She hoped that the white noise would hypnotize her so she could forget what she'd seen earlier, but the moment she closed her eyes, a vision of Megan Cahill's bloodstained corpse overwhelmed her.

Stacey remembered how Megan's legs had twisted under her and the way the dead woman's head lay in a pool of blood. She imagined Megan answering the door and the killer rushing at her. Megan would have staggered backward to escape the blows until the balcony caught her at the waist and her momentum pitched her over the railing. Stacey shuddered as she imagined the poor woman's skull smashing against the living room floor. She hoped that death had been swift so Megan didn't suffer.

Stacey shook her head to clear it, but the image stayed with her. Suddenly she could not stand being alone, so she went into the bedroom and hurriedly traded her suit for jeans and a T-shirt.

Glen turned when Stacey walked into the living room. Something about the expression on her face alerted him.

"Are you okay?" he asked.

"I keep thinking about the body."

Glen hesitated for a moment. Then he took Stacey in his arms. Stacey let herself melt into Glen. She began to sob. It felt so good being held.

"It's okay," Glen said.

Stacey stepped back and wiped away her tears.

"Sorry," she said.

"Don't be. Do you want a drink? I've got some great single malt scotch."

Stacey sniffed and forced a smile. "That sounds like a fabulous idea."

"Why don't we go out on the deck," Glen said as he dropped some ice cubes into a glass and poured Stacey a stiff shot. Stacey went outside and sank onto a lounger. Glen followed with his drink. They sipped in silence and Stacey was grateful that Glen didn't ask her to talk about the murder. But several things were bothering her and she finally brought them up.

"Do you think what happened in the gallery had something to do with Megan's murder, and do you think the murder has anything to do with Raymond Cahill's death?"

"Both of those thoughts occurred to me, but I can't see how her death is linked to something that happened ten years ago."

"A lot of the people who were involved with the *Cahill* case were in the gallery. There was Jack Booth, your partner, Kathy Moran, and Kevin Mercer."

"Don't forget me," Glen said with a smile.

Stacey smiled back. "You've been my number one suspect all along but I thought it would be rude to mention it after you've been so nice."

"Aw."

Stacey got serious again. "Megan was shocked by something that happened right before she ran out. But what was it? She was arguing with Kevin Mercer but she didn't run off until Mr. Baker walked up. Could he have triggered her reaction? She freaked out right after she saw him?"

Glen frowned. "I don't see what Henry could have done to send her running off like that."

"Mr. Booth told me that he was surprised that Mr. Baker was representing Mrs. Cahill, even though he didn't have the expertise to handle a death penalty case. Why would he take a case this serious if he wasn't qualified and why did Mrs. Cahill want him to be her lawyer?"

Glen hesitated. Then he sighed. "If I tell you what I think will you promise to keep it to yourself? I really don't want to see this in your book."

"Okay."

"Henry's wife walked out on him shortly after Henry met Megan. The divorce devastated Henry. He was drinking. He let himself go completely. His work suffered. I was really worried about him. Then this case came along and it rejuvenated him. Megan is a very beautiful woman and she was even more stunning ten years ago. Henry never said anything to me, but I think he was infatuated with her. He did promise to represent her even though he didn't have the experience to handle a death case. And Megan couldn't pay him because the executor of Raymond

Cahill's estate wouldn't free up the funds until it was clear that she hadn't killed Ray. Then the case ended before Henry got in too deep, so I don't know if he would have come to his senses if Megan had been indicted."

"Do you think . . ." Stacey hesitated. "Is it possible that Henry and Megan . . ."

"Were they lovers? I don't think so. If she slept with him I didn't know about it."

Stacey's brow furrowed. "I just had a crazy thought. When did Mr. Baker meet Mrs. Cahill for the first time?"

"It was probably the night I met her. Henry and Alma and my parents and I were having dinner at the country club when Ray introduced Megan to us."

"So Henry knew her before the wedding night?"

Glen's mouth gaped open. Then he laughed. "You're not suggesting that Henry was the mysterious third man?"

Stacey shrugged. "It was just a thought."

"That might be a good twist in your book, but I can't imagine Henry murdering anyone. And, assuming he was Megan's accomplice, why would just seeing him freak her out? Also, there's a problem with Henry killing Megan. You saw him. The stroke has left him weak and unsteady on his feet. Where would he get the strength to stab her?"

Stacey sighed. "You're right. I'm not making sense. I guess I'm simply exhausted and my brain isn't working."

"I'm not surprised after what you just went through. Now why don't you relax and I'll see what I can whip up for lunch."

Glen went inside. Stacey looked out at the ocean and thought about her host. Last night, over dinner, Stacey had learned that Glen had not had a woman in his life since his fiancée had broken their engagement the year before to take a job in Chicago. Stacey thought Glen liked her because he'd gone out of his way to be with her during her short stay in Palisades Heights. Stacey had been attracted to Glen since the day she met him, but she had decided that they should just be friends. She was going to move on when her research in Palisades Heights was complete, and Glen, who had a law practice and a life in the coastal town, was not going to leave. But now, after the murder and the way Glen had helped her, she was wondering whether there was some way to make the relationship work, because she found that she was enjoying her time with Glen more than she'd enjoyed being with any man in recent memory.

"Lunch is ready," Glen said ten minutes later. He carried a large wooden bowl to a table on the deck. "I made a salad. I figured you wouldn't want anything too heavy."

"Thanks," Stacey told him.

Glen went back inside and returned with two ice teas, napkins, and silverware.

"So," Glen asked, hoping to distract Stacey from thinking about Megan's murder, "did you always know you wanted to be a writer?"

Stacey laughed. "That was never in my parents' agenda."

"Oh?"

"Everyone in my family is an overachiever. My sister is a partner in a three-hundred-person law firm and my brother is a neurosurgeon. I'm really good at science, so my parents decided I would go to medical school."

"What happened?"

"Everything was humming along. I had straight As in premed, an acceptance to Harvard Medical School, and a fiancé headed to Harvard Law when it dawned on me that I was going to hate medical school and my parents were more enamored of my boyfriend than I was. A month before graduation I gathered my courage and told my parents that the engagement was off and I was going to start teaching English in an inner-city high school in the fall."

"How did your parents take that?" Glen asked with a smile.

"Not well. I thought they might have a heart attack. They told me I'd be paid a pittance. And they were horrified by the kind of man I'd meet in a slum school. But I held my ground."

"How did you end up in New York with an MFA?"

"After four years of teaching, I burned out. Secretly, I'd always wanted to be a writer but I never had the courage or financial security to take a shot at a career as an author. In the middle of my last year teaching my grandmother passed away and left me a six-figure inheritance. I applied to the MFA program at the state university and got in, and the rest—as they say—is history."

"So, are you going back to Portland when you finish your research in Palisades Heights?" Glen asked. The look on his face told Stacey that he had not asked the question out of casual interest.

"A writer can write anywhere," Stacey answered cautiously. "I could stay in Palisades Heights while I work on a first draft."

"It would be expensive to stay in a motel *and* keep paying rent on your Portland apartment."

Stacey smiled. "Do you know a way I can save on rent?"

"I've been thinking, you could work in the spare office at Baker and Kraft like you're doing now and you could stay in my guest room."

"I am on a tight budget and that would certainly help," Stacey answered, fighting hard to keep her tone even. "I appreciate the offer. Let me think about it."

"Of course," Glen said in a businesslike manner. "You don't have to decide right now."

Stacey told him she'd give the offer serious thought, but actually she'd already made up her mind.

CHAPTER THIRTY-FIVE

When the idea of driving to the coast to see Kathy Moran's exhibit occurred to Jack Booth he had harbored a secret hope that they would end up together, so he'd gotten a room for the night. But Kathy had made it crystal clear that wasn't going to happen, so Jack spent part of the night alone in the motel's bar. When he woke up he took a run on the beach to clear his head. Then he ate a big breakfast before checking out a little after noon. On the way to the coast highway he passed Ellen Devereaux's gallery. Two police cars were parked in front and George Melendez was standing on the sidewalk, talking to an officer.

Jack pulled to the curb and walked over to the police chief.

"What happened?" he asked.

"A hell of a lot for a small town. Someone killed Megan Cahill last night."

"What?"

"That writer, Stacey Kim, went over to interview her around ten and found the body. Then Ellen Devereaux called and said there'd been a break-in."

"Do you think the two crimes are connected?"

"I have no idea at this point." Melendez paused. "Are you headed back to Portland?"

"Yeah, why?"

"I know you're a civilian now, but you really impressed me when you came down to help Teddy Winston with Raymond Cahill's murder. Now his wife is dead. There's probably no connection between the two crimes, but you know Ray's case backward and forward. I could use a second set of eyes in here if the new murder or the old murder have something to do with what went on in the gallery."

"I see what you mean."

"The break-in is probably just vandalism, but I'm not a big believer in coincidence. Could you stick around for a bit?"

"Sure, if you think I can help."

Inside the gallery, chairs had been tossed around, the table that had been used for the hors d'oeuvres had been overturned, and trash cans had been upended. As they passed the Moran exhibit, Jack saw a police photographer taking pictures of gaps on the wall where photographs had hung. Other photographs were strewn across the floor.

Ellen Devereaux was in her office, hunched over her desk, her face tight with anger. She looked up when Jack and the police chief walked in.

"What happened?" Melendez asked.

Devereaux pointed through the office door into the gallery. "I opened up at noon and found the gallery looking like this. Some son of a bitch broke in through the back door and wrecked the place."

"When did you lock up?"

"Around eleven thirty."

"Do you have any idea who did this or why? Someone with a grudge, someone who's had a run-in with you lately?"

"I don't have any enemies, George. I run a fucking art gallery."

"Okay, Ellen. I get that, but I have to ask."

Devereaux's shoulders sagged and she looked contrite. "Sorry. I didn't mean to bite your head off. I'm just upset."

"You've got every right to be. So, what's missing? Did you have any cash lying around?"

"I put the checks and cash in the safe, but some of Kathy's photographs are gone."

"Are you insured?" Melendez asked.

"The Portland Art Museum insisted on insurance before they'd let us take the photographs. Most of them belong to private collectors."

"Can the stolen photographs be replaced?"

"Some can. I called Kathy as soon as I saw what happened. She says she has the negatives for most of the missing shots. She's on her way over."

"Can you show me what you're missing so I'll know what photographs were stolen?" Melendez asked.

Devereaux opened a folder on her desk and pulled out a series of photographs she had taken of the exhibit. Then she led Jack and Melendez out of her office and into the desecrated gallery.

Devereaux stood in front of two blank spaces on the wall where the photographs had been displayed. Then she pointed at the photograph of the exhibit that she held in her hand.

"These shots hung here," Devereaux said.

Jack looked over Melendez's shoulder at a picture that had been taken of a bearded man who was staring into the mirror behind a bar, his sad and soulful face framed by bottles of liquor.

Another photograph showed waves breaking against a majestic rock formation under the light of a full moon.

"Kathy took the seascape shortly before she discovered Megan Cahill on the beach below her summer home," the gallery owner said.

Just before they moved down the wall, Jack realized that he was standing where Megan Cahill had stood just before she fled the gallery.

"This was one of my favorites," Devereaux said angrily as she pointed to a shot Kathy Moran had taken on Ocean Avenue during a flash downpour: people running for cover, arms thrown over their heads, newspapers whipping down the street, rain-caused chaos.

A section of the exhibit closer to the front of the gallery had more blank spaces. Devereaux pointed at several more pictures that had hung in the exhibition.

"Kathy took these four photos two years ago during a climb up Mount Jefferson."

Before anyone could say anything else, Kathy Moran rushed into the gallery, clutching a file.

"What's going on, George? First Megan is murdered. Now this. Is it the same person?"

"It's too early to say that the murder and the burglary are connected. There was a forced entry through the back door of the gallery. You can see the mess. It looks like the thief trashed the place and took pictures at random, so it could just be vandalism."

"I can't believe that," Kathy said.

"I'm not counting out any possibilities right now but it's a big mistake to go into any investigation with a theory. You tend to try to make the facts fit it and you can miss something."

"How many negatives did you find?" Devereaux asked Moran.

"I've got them for all but three of the photographs you told me were stolen."

"That's great. What are you missing?'

"I don't have the negative for the rainstorm on Ocean Avenue, the bearded guy in the bar, and the seascape, but I found the Mount Jefferson shots. Some of my earlier stuff, like the rainstorm and the man in the bar, was bought by individuals from galleries. The galleries that showed them may have the negatives. We can call later today."

Kathy handed Devereaux the file. While the gallery owner looked through it, Kathy looked at the exhibit.

"I'm sorry this happened," Jack said.

Kathy didn't turn toward him. Her jaw clenched. "I'd love to get my hands on the bastard who did this."

"It looks bad now, but I'll have the exhibit looking just fine as soon as the police leave," Devereaux assured Moran.

"We'll be out of your hair soon," Melendez told the women. "I'll send Frank in to take a statement. Call if you remember anything that might help."

Jack tried to think of something else he could say that might engage Kathy, but it was obvious she was in no mood for small talk so he followed the police chief outside.

"Well?" Melendez asked.

"I didn't see anything," Jack answered. "My gut says vandalism, kids."

"Yeah, you're probably right. But I can't help thinking about Megan rushing out of the gallery."

"I see what you mean," Jack said, "but, if there's a connection, I can't see it."

And he couldn't. Then, during the drive back to Portland, something started to nag at him, but he couldn't figure out what it was so he shrugged off the feeling and focused on a brief that had to be filed by the end of the week.

Part Six

THE SMOKING GUN

2015

CHAPTER THIRTY-SIX

Over the weekend, Glen helped Stacey move out of her Portland apartment and into his house. They made an effort to keep the relationship chaste for a few days, but their attraction for each other was too strong and before a week was out the only thing residing in Glen's guest room was Stacey's valise.

The emotions that Megan's murder had unleashed faded as Stacey experienced some of the happiest times of her life. During the week they worked at Glen's law firm, then they came home and watched television or read, and they made love a lot. On the weekends, they socialized with Glen's friends and went sightseeing along the coast. Glen even got Stacey out on a fishing boat and she had the time of her life.

Part of Glen's routine every morning was a run on the beach. Stacey was not much of an athlete but she had been on the cross-country team in high school. She had never placed in any championship, but she was a determined runner who finished high enough in a meet every once in a while to get points for her team. Stacey's college was Division I so she didn't even bother trying out for cross-country, but she did keep running for exercise until she moved to New York City. Now that she was living with a runner, Stacey vowed to get back in shape and she started joining Glen each morning.

With Kathy Moran's help, Ellen Devereaux was able to replace all but three of the stolen photographs. The publicity surrounding the murder and the break-in brought unexpected crowds to the gallery and made the exhibit a rousing success. Stacey had been tempted to ask Devereaux to intercede with Kathy Moran on her behalf but she decided to wait until the exhibition moved to the Portland Art Museum before renewing her efforts to interview the photographer. It turned out that it didn't matter. Glen talked to Devereaux who asked Kathy if she would be willing to let Stacey interview her. Kathy declined. This was a setback, but Kathy's only involvement in Raymond Cahill's murder was as the witness who found Megan on the beach and, of course, the person who'd taken the famous photograph. Stacey decided that she could use her imagination to flesh out the character of the photographer in her novel, which she had decided to call *Woman with a Gun*.

Energized by her love affair, Stacey made real progress on an outline of her book, but she was frustrated by her inability to figure out the big clue that would lead to the solution of the murder. Readers would be upset if her book had an unsatisfying ending but—as in the real case—no good solution presented itself.

One evening Stacey and Glen were sitting on the deck, sipping wine and watching the sunset.

"I was thinking about the *Cahill* case and I got an idea," Glen said.

"Oh?"

"In the police report of Frank Janowitz's conversation with

Teddy Winston and Jack Booth, Janowitz said that there are unscrupulous collectors who will buy stolen items for their secret collections. What if Crouse wasn't the killer? What if some of the items in Cahill's collection had previously been stolen and Cahill bought them from the thief? The article in the *Gazette* mentioned several items, like that rare stamp, that were later stolen when Cahill was murdered. What if the thief read the article and murdered Cahill because he was worried that Cahill would give the police his name?"

"Why would Cahill do that? The police might think he had hired the thief to steal the stuff. That would make him an accomplice."

Glen shrugged. "It was just an idea. And even if it didn't happen that way, I thought you could use it as a plot twist in your book."

Stacey laughed. "Thanks."

"Hey, I want this book to be a best seller so I can become a kept man, living in the lap of luxury in a huge mansion in Beverly Hills while you slave away for hours on end on your laptop."

"Dream on, bozo. Once I start making millions, I'm ditching you for a boy toy."

Glen laughed and squeezed Stacey's hand. "Before I forget, I'm representing one of the plaintiffs in a suit against the owner of several retirement homes. I'm going to be in Portland for a few days, taking depositions, and my client is putting me up at the Heathman. The hotel is pretty swanky and my room has a king-size bed. I asked several women if they wanted to share it but they're all busy, so what do you say?"

Stacey grinned. "I say you're a jackass but I'll put up with you if you throw in dinner at some very expensive Portland restaurant."

"Deal," Glen said.

Two days later, Stacey and Glen set off for Portland at noon and were in their hotel room a little after three. They ate out, then saw a movie and had a great time. Stacey was starting to give serious thought to what she would do when she finished writing *Woman with a Gun*. She liked everything about Oregon, Palisades Heights was growing on her, and she kept reminding herself that a writer could write anywhere. Then there was Glen. She'd only known him for a short time but she was beginning to think that he was special.

Their first morning in Portland, Glen got up early but Stacey stayed in bed until eight thirty. She ate breakfast in the hotel, then she carried a latte up to their room and got to work on her laptop. Stacey was toying with the idea of making the old Western revolver the big clue in her book, and that got her thinking about how Cahill had acquired the Schofield revolver. She wondered how she could find out and had the answer to her question almost as soon as she had formed it.

Stacey looked through her notes and found a phone number of a store in San Francisco. Stacey dialed and waited nervously as the phone rang.

"Antiques," a man said.

"Is this Frank Janowitz?"

"Yes."

"My name is Stacey Kim. I'm a writer and I'm living in Palisades Heights while I research a novel that was inspired by Kathy Moran's famous photograph of Megan Cahill."

"Does this have something to do with Megan?" Janowitz asked, his concern evident.

"Not directly, no. But I discovered her body."

"My God, that must have been awful for you."

"It was. I had an interview scheduled with her. When I went to her house . . ."

Stacey paused. "I really don't like talking about it."

"I'm sorry. I understand completely. But why are you phoning me?"

"I have a question I hope you can answer. It's about an item in Raymond Cahill's collection. You know that Mr. Cahill was shot with a Schofield .44 Smith and Wesson revolver that may have been owned by Wyatt Earp?"

"Yes."

"Do you know how Mr. Cahill acquired the gun?"

"Raymond already owned the Schofield when I started helping him with his collection, so I don't know how he got it."

"He never told you who owned it before he did?"

"No."

"I understand that Mr. Cahill believed that Wyatt Earp used the revolver during the Gunfight at the OK Corral but that might not have been true."

"That's correct."

"Did you ever try to authenticate Mr. Cahill's claim?"

"I offered to try shortly after he hired me, but he said that he didn't want to know." Janowitz laughed. "What he actually said was, 'What I don't know can't hurt me.' I think he was happy, believing he owned Wyatt Earp's gun, and he didn't want to know the truth if it was going to spoil his illusion."

After she hung up, Stacey remembered what Glen had said a few days before about Cahill's possibly getting some of his collection from a thief. That set her wondering why Cahill didn't want Janowitz to try to find out if Wyatt Earp had really used the revolver at the OK Corral. Was he afraid that Janowitz would discover that the gun he owned was never used by Wyatt Earp or was he afraid that Janowitz would discover that the gun had been stolen?

Stacey's latte had cooled by the time her conversation with Janowitz ended. She took a sip, then she dialed Jack Booth's office.

"Stacey, to what do I owe the pleasure?" Booth said when they were connected.

"I'm in Portland for a few days and I had a question for you."

"Shoot."

"I've been trying to figure out the big clue in my novel that will help catch the killer and that got me thinking about the real case, and I've concluded that the most intriguing aspect of the case is the gun."

"What about it?"

"Haven't you ever wondered why Parnell Crouse used the Schofield as his murder weapon? I mean, I could understand shooting Mr. Cahill with Wyatt Earp's gun if Crouse didn't have a gun, but Mrs. Cahill said that Crouse did have a gun. So why did he go to the trouble of breaking open the glass case and loading this old weapon, which might not even work?"

"We did talk about that at one time. Teddy Winston, the DA, thought that Crouse might have been afraid that the police would run a ballistics test and match the bullets that killed Cahill to his gun, but I didn't buy that explanation. The police searched Crouse's car and his apartment and they didn't find a gun. I think Crouse got rid of it. There are plenty of places on the coast where he could ditch his weapon. Hell, there was a great big ocean outside the back door of the Cahills' house. As soon as Crouse got rid of the gun he wouldn't have had to worry about a ballistics test tying him to it. And the gun was probably stolen anyway or had its serial numbers filed off, which means that there would be no way to connect Crouse to it."

"So why did he use the Schofield?" Stacey asked.

"We never came up with an explanation and I still don't have one. If you solve that mystery, let me know."

"One other thing, now that I have you on the line, I've been trying to find out about Kathy Moran's childhood, because I'm trying to flesh out the background of my fictional photographer. There's a lot of information about Miss Moran's adult years but not much about her childhood. You knew her in Portland and you spent time with her in Palisades Heights. Do you remember anything about her folks or where she grew up?"

"I think her parents died when she was young. If I remember correctly, she was in junior high."

"Do you know how they died?"

"No."

"Who raised her after her parents passed away?"

"An aunt on her mother's side."

"Do you remember her name?"

"No. I think she lived in Montana."

"Do you know where Miss Moran was living when her parents were alive?"

"No. I did know but . . . Wait, I do remember. I think it was Arlington, California. I remember thinking that it was like the Arlington Cemetery."

"Thanks." Stacey made a note. "You've been a big help. If you remember anything else, I'm staying at the Heathman."

CHAPTER THIRTY-SEVEN

Moments after Stacey hung up, Jack remembered that Kathy had pled guilty to a drug charge as part of her deal when she agreed to testify against Kilbride. The case had been dismissed when Kathy kept her part of the plea bargain, but the court had ordered a presentence report and the presentence writer had worked up a biography. Jack had read the report years ago and didn't remember a lot that was in it, but he had a friend who was pretty high up in the DA's office who could probably get it for him.

Jack started to dial the number for the Multnomah County district attorney's office but he stopped midway through. Information in a presentence report *was* confidential, and he shouldn't be sharing it with Stacey without Kathy Moran's approval. Jack found Kathy's number and dialed.

"Yes," Kathy answered.

"Hi, this is Jack Booth."

"Why are you calling me?" Kathy asked. She sounded suspicious.

"You know I told you about Stacey Kim, the woman who's writing a novel inspired by your photograph of Megan Cahill?"

"What about her?"

"She just called me. She's trying to work up your biography for background on one of her fictional characters who is a photographer."

"What did she want to know?"

"She was asking about your parents, where you grew up, your aunt."

"What did you tell her?"

"I didn't tell her anything. I was going to call Rex Baron at the DA's office to see if he'd let Stacey read your presentence report. There's a biography in it. Only it's confidential and I didn't want to do anything without getting your approval."

"Well, you don't have it," Kathy answered vehemently. "That woman is a pest. She's tried to interview me and now she's prying into my private life. I won't have it. And if you give her that report I'll sue you and the county. I do not want to read about my private life in some goddamn supermarket tabloid. I've had enough of that."

"This is why I called. I'd never do anything that would hurt you. I hope you know that."

The line was silent for a moment. Then Jack heard Kathy take a deep breath.

"I apologize, Jack. I shouldn't have gone off on you. I appreciate the call. I've just gone through too much. All I want now is my privacy. It's about the only thing I've got left."

Jack hung up and worked until noon. It was a nice day and he decided to buy a sandwich and a soft drink and eat outside on the Park Blocks, a strip of parks that ran with few interruptions through the city. The bench was opposite the Portland Art Museum. A banner advertised the Kathy Moran exhibit and a sudden thought occurred to Booth. Something had happened in the blink of an eye that had sent Megan Cahill running out of Ellen Devereaux's gallery on the evening she was murdered. There was no apparent connection between Megan's rapid exit, her murder, and the theft of the photographs from the gallery, but it was hard to believe that there was no connection between some—and maybe all—of those occurrences.

Booth had thought about the incident at the gallery a few times and he had concluded that Megan had been shocked by something Kevin Mercer said or something connected to Henry Baker, but one other possibility suddenly presented itself. In her short speech, Megan had said that this was her first opportunity to see the exhibition of Kathy's photographs. Before she ran out of the gallery, Megan was standing where she could see the photographs on the wall behind Mercer and Baker. Had something she saw in one of them upset Megan?

As soon as he finished lunch, Jack bought a ticket to the Portland Art Museum and walked through the Moran exhibit, paying close attention to each picture. He didn't see anything startling in any of the photographs.

When he had been in Ellen Devereaux's gallery after the break-in, Devereaux had told Jack and the police chief which photographs had been stolen and where they had hung in the exhibit. When she was telling them about some of the photographs it had occurred to Jack that he was standing where Megan had stood just before she fled the gallery. Jack closed his eyes and tried to remember which of the missing photos Megan would have been able to see. He smiled. The old brain was still functioning. Devereaux had told Jack about two photographs. One was the seascape Kathy had snapped shortly before she found Megan on the beach and the other showed a bearded man gazing into a mirror in a bar. Jack frowned. Why would either photo shock Megan so much that she would run out of the gallery? After thinking about the question for a few minutes, Jack decided they wouldn't.

CHAPTER THIRTY-EIGHT

Two days after their trip to Portland, Glen drove to Lane County for several days of pretrial hearings in a federal case. The first day he was gone, Stacey slept late, then went for a run. The morning was pleasant and there was almost no breeze, but there had been two murders in the now deserted Cahill beach house and Stacey shivered involuntarily when she ran by it. As far as she knew, the police were still stymied in their attempts to figure out who killed Megan. She assumed that there would be an article in the *Gazette* if something broke and she had not seen anything about the case in the paper in a while.

Kathy Moran had purchased a house on a cliff overlooking the ocean with the money she'd made after *Woman with a Gun* won the Pulitzer and her photographs started to sell for outrageous prices. Two miles past the Cahill place, Kathy's house appeared on the horizon. Whenever Stacey ran near it, she hoped that she would see the photographer walking on the beach. She was convinced that she could get Kathy to open up to her if she could just talk to her in person.

As she ran below the house Stacey thought she saw someone standing in the window. She pulled up and waved, hoping that it was Kathy Moran and she could attract her attention. The few steps Stacey had taken had shifted her perspective and she found her view obstructed by a reflection in the glass in Kathy's picture window. Stacey walked backward until she was at the spot where she thought she saw someone watching her but there was no one there. Stacey frowned. She was certain she'd seen someone in the window, but she'd been running and looking up at an odd angle so it might have been a mirage. Stacey waited below the house, hoping that Kathy would walk down to the beach to talk to her. After a few moments, she realized that this was wishful thinking and she continued on her run.

Once Stacey got into a rhythm, her mind would wander. She was still fascinated by the possibility of making Wyatt Earp's gun the big clue in her book, and that started her thinking about everything she knew about it. An Internet search had informed her that Major George Schofield had designed the revolver to be shot one-handed by United States cavalry soldiers, who could break open the pistol and reload it while riding. Jesse James and Wild Bill Hickok also used the weapon, and the Schofield Russian was a favorite sidearm of the Russian government. All of this was interesting, but it hadn't helped her develop the gun as a clue.

Stacey started thinking about information about the gun in the *Cahill* case file. There was the photograph of the gun in the article in the *Palisades Heights Gazette* and the discussion about the gun in the police report that recounted Jack Booth's and Teddy Winston's interview with Frank Janowitz . . .

Stacey stopped in midstride. Jack Booth had told her that Kathy Moran had grown up in Arlington, California, and it dawned on her that she had heard about Arlington, California, before. Stacey reversed course and headed to Glen's law office. Three-quarters of a mile past Kathy's house, Stacey happened to glance over her shoulder. Someone was running along the shore a quarter mile behind her. The runner was dressed in black and the cowl of a sweatshirt obscured the runner's face. At this distance, Stacey couldn't tell if she was being followed by a man or a woman.

Stacey turned her head forward and kept running, but she began to worry. She looked over her shoulder again. The runner was still there and seemed to be gaining. Stacey picked up her pace but she felt silly. No one was following her. This was just another person out for some exercise. People ran on the beach all the time. Still, on such a warm summer morning, it seemed odd that this runner was wearing a sweat suit.

Stacey spotted a beach access that would put her in a residential area a few blocks from Ocean Avenue. She turned quickly and cut across the sand. Her breathing was getting shallow and she gritted her teeth and raced onto the narrow sandy path that led off the beach to safety. When she turned onto Ocean Avenue she chanced a backward glance. No one was behind her. Her legs were starting to cramp and she was breathing heavily so she slowed to a jog. The hum of traffic was comforting and she was starting to make out the buildings on the edge of the business district. She looked around again and was certain she was alone but she didn't stop running until she was safely surrounded by people.

Once she was in her office at Baker and Kraft, it didn't take Stacey long to find the Banker Box containing the file she wanted. She pulled out the issue of the *Palisades Heights Gazette* with the Raymond Cahill interview and flipped through it. The sentence she was looking for said exactly what she thought it would.

He has lived his adult life on an estate in Arlington, an upscale, seaside community in California, but he still tried to spend at least a week a year at his grandparents' cabin. . . .

Stacey sat back in her chair. Raymond Cahill and Kathy Moran had both lived in Arlington, California. What did that mean? It provided a connection between the two that Stacey did not know existed, but what kind of connection? Cahill was many years older than Kathy. Did Cahill know Kathy's parents?

Stacey tried to remember what she knew about Raymond Cahill. He had dropped out of college, he was a millionaire by the time he was in his early twenties, and he'd bought his mansion in Arlington shortly after he struck it rich. Kathy's parents died when she was young and she had been raised by an aunt in Montana. So Kathy would have been young when she and Cahill lived in Arlington.

One implication of her discovery suddenly occurred to Stacey. Was it possible that Kathy Moran was not just a witness in the *Cahill* case? Could she be involved in Raymond Cahill's murder? If she was, then Megan Cahill was probably innocent. If Megan was innocent, then she was telling the truth when she said that Parnell Crouse killed her husband. There was certainly enough evidence that Crouse had been involved in the robbery-murder. The mere fact that Crouse was in Palisades Heights pointed to his involvement and there was the coin that had been found in the trunk of his car. But how would Kathy, who lived in Oregon, know Crouse, who was raised in Texas before living in Oakland, California? And what motive would Kathy have to kill Raymond Cahill?

After a while, Stacey gave up and decided to go home and shower. On the way back to Glen's house, she looked for any sign that she was being followed but she didn't see anything unusual. By the time she arrived home, she decided that finding Megan's body had spooked her and caused her to be on edge. After giving it some thought, Stacey was convinced that the person in black was just out for a morning run and not a threat.

CHAPTER THIRTY-NINE

After her shower and a quick bite for lunch, Stacey returned to the law office. She couldn't shake the idea that Kathy Moran was involved in Raymond Cahill's murder. On the evening that she snapped her famous picture, was she taking photographs for her one woman show or was that a cover? And who murdered Parnell Crouse? Crouse was killed on Monday night. Jack Booth questioned Kathy at the police station on Monday afternoon but Stacey didn't remember anyone mentioning Kathy after she left the police station. She'd told Booth that she was working Monday night. Did Kathy show up for her shift? Just as Stacey thought of someone who could answer that question, Henry Baker hobbled in and surprised her.

Baker was a big man but he seemed frail. He stooped over to rest on his cane, his skin had a sickly pallor, and the left side of his face sagged. Glen's partner had been in the office a few times since the gallery opening but he tired easily so he rarely stayed long. Other than saying hello, Stacey had not had much contact with him.

"How's your book coming?" Baker asked.

"I'm making progress."

"Good, good."

Baker hesitated. When he spoke Stacey sensed that he was tamping down his emotions.

"I understand you were the one who . . . that you found Megan Cahill."

"Yes."

"That must have been horrible for you."

"It was. Did you know the Cahills well?"

"Not well. I did some legal work for Ray. We played a few rounds of golf. And I was Megan's attorney for a short time after Ray was murdered. She moved back to California as soon as she could."

"But she kept Mr. Cahill's summer home. Did she use it often?"

"Every once in a while."

"Did you see her when she was in town?"

"We did meet at the country club. Why do you want to know?" Baker asked. He sounded suspicious.

"Just curiosity. Finding her . . . in that way. I'd just like to know what she was like when she was alive. I met her briefly at the gallery opening and that didn't give me much time to form an impression."

"She was a good person. Having her husband killed like that on their wedding night . . . It affected her."

"Do you have any idea why she ran out of the gallery?"

"No. It caught me completely by surprise."

Baker shut his eyes for a moment and leaned against the doorjamb.

"I'm sorry. I don't have a lot of energy these days. Best of luck with the book," he said. Then he walked down the hall toward his office.

Stacey watched him leave. Baker's reaction when the conversation turned to Megan Cahill hinted at strong, suppressed feelings.

Stacey turned her thoughts back to Kathy Moran and the person who might be able to tell her where Kathy had gone after she left the police station on the day Raymond Cahill was murdered.

There were only a few people in the Seafarer when Stacey walked into the tavern. A large, muscular man was tending bar. His head was shaved and his enormous arms were covered with tattoos. Stacey gathered her courage and took a seat at the end of the bar.

"Are you Grady Cox?" she asked when the bartender came for her order.

"I am," Cox answered with an easy smile.

"I'm Stacey Kim. I'm a writer."

Stacey paused to see if this statement elicited a reaction, but Grady's expression didn't change.

"I'm working on a book that was inspired by Kathy Moran's famous photograph of Megan Cahill, and a photographer is going to be a character in the book. Kathy Moran worked here when she took the famous photograph and I want to get your impressions of her."

"She was a hard worker and a pleasure to be around."

"Did you know that she was a talented photographer before she became famous?"

"She showed her stuff at Ellen Devereaux's gallery and I'd seen a few of her photos. Kathy even gave me a few for the bar," he said, nodding toward the wall where some of Moran's photographs were hanging.

"I understand you hired Miss Moran as your lawyer before she moved to Palisades Heights."

Cox nodded.

"Was she a good attorney?"

"She did a bang-up job for me."

"I imagine finding Raymond Cahill's body must have been very upsetting for her."

"I'm sure it was."

"Did she tell you about it when she came to work that night?"

"Probably, I don't remember. That was a long time ago."

"Did she come to work the evening she found Mr. Cahill's body?"

Cox stopped smiling. "If your book will be made up, why would you want to know that?"

"It's just background."

Cox took a hard look at Stacey. "I don't think so. If you're looking for dirt on Kathy, you're in the wrong place."

"That's not it. I want to learn what she's like. I won't write anything that will embarrass Miss Moran," Stacey said as she scrambled to win over the bartender.

"Look, Miss . . ."

"Kim. Stacey Kim."

"I'm a big fan of books, but you're going to have to write yours without any help from me. Kathy Moran is a good friend and I'm not going to do anything to hurt her."

Cox turned his back on Stacey and walked to the other end of the bar. When she left, he pulled out his phone and dialed Moran.

"There was a girl in here asking questions about you and Raymond Cahill's murder."

"Was it Stacey Kim?"

"Yeah, that's the name she gave me."

"What did you tell her?

"I told her to get lost."

"What did she want to know?"

"If I knew you were a good photographer, were you a good lawyer, if you were in the Seafarer the day you discovered Cahill's body, stuff like that. I cut her off pretty quick."

"Thanks for calling, Grady."

They talked for a little longer, then Cox hung up and started polishing shot glasses. Bartenders have a nose for bullshit. Grady didn't know why Kim wanted to know about Kathy but he knew it wasn't for any novel. Kathy had gone through enough and he wasn't going to do anything that would add to her troubles.

CHAPTER FORTY

Stacey bolted up in bed. Something had jerked her out of sleep. She strained to pick up the slightest sound but there was only the wind. Her heart was beating fast and she took deep breaths to calm herself. It was a dream. She felt foolish and was about to lie down when she heard a faint rattling, as if someone was moving a doorknob.

Stacey got out of bed. It was quiet now. Was someone trying to get into the house or was her imagination working overtime? Then she heard the sound again. She tried to remember if she'd locked all the doors as she grabbed her phone and dialed 911. While she waited for the operator, Stacey looked around the bedroom for a weapon. Glen's golf clubs were propped against the wall near the closet.

"My name is Stacey Kim and I'm calling from 67 Dune View Drive," she told the 911 operator as she pulled Glen's driver out of his golf bag. "I think someone is trying to break into my house."

Stacey inched into the hall.

"Why do you think someone is trying to break in?" the operator asked.

Stacey hesitated. How embarrassing would it be if the police came and this was a false alarm? Then she heard glass break.

"They just broke the glass in the kitchen door!" she yelled as she raced down the hall. "Please, send someone fast!"

Stacey ran into the kitchen in time to see a gloved hand reach through the broken pane in the back door. She screamed at the top of her lungs and smashed the club head down on the hand that grasped the doorknob. The intruder grunted and the hand retreated. Stacey looked through the remaining glass panes. A person in a ski mask stared back.

"Get out!!" Stacey screamed as she raised the club in self-defense. The figure hesitated. Then Stacey heard sirens and the intruder ran off. Just before the burglar disappeared, Stacey saw moonlight glancing off the blade of a large knife. She thought she might throw up. Megan Cahill had been stabbed to death.

A police car screeched to a stop in her driveway. Stacey ran out the front door. An older policeman with a slight paunch and a younger officer got out of the cruiser.

"He ran away through the backyard," she said, pointing around the side of the house.

"Calm down and tell us what happened," said the older officer.

"He's getting away," Stacey insisted.

"Who are we looking for? Can you give us a description?"

"He was wearing a ski mask and he's dressed in black. He took off toward the beach."

"Was he armed?"

"He had a knife."

The older man gestured to his younger partner. "See if you can catch up. I'll get a statement."

The young officer raced around the side of the house and the older man escorted Stacey inside. She turned on some lights.

"Why don't you sit down and catch your breath. My name is Ted Randolph. When you're ready, tell me what happened."

Stacey sat on the couch. Randolph pulled out a notebook and a pencil.

"I was asleep and something woke me. Then I heard the doorknob on the front door moving. I . . . I called 911 and got this golf club. Then he broke the glass in the back door and I raced in and smashed his hand."

"That was very brave," Randolph said.

Stacey reddened. "It was very stupid. He could have had a gun. But I wasn't thinking straight."

"What did this man look like?" Randolph asked.

Stacey started to answer. Then she realized something. "I'm not sure it was a man. I just said a man, but the intruder was dressed in black and wearing a ski mask and it was really dark. There's some moonlight but . . . I can't give you a description."

The younger officer walked in. "I didn't see anyone. He probably stayed on the side streets and it's too dark to see footprints if he ran down to the beach."

"Okay, let's check the back door," Randolph said.

Stacey turned on more lights and Randolph told his partner and Stacey to stay back so they wouldn't contaminate the crime scene. The back door opened into the kitchen and Stacey waited at the entrance to the kitchen area. Glass littered the floor near the door. Randolph skirted it and examined the door.

"Was the intruder bare-handed or wearing gloves?" he asked.

"Gloves."

"That means we won't get prints," Randolph said. "I'll write a report and have one of the lab techs come out in the morning. I can have someone take a look around tomorrow. It's too dark to find any footprints now. But I'll be honest. I don't have much hope that we'll get anyone for this. It was probably some kid. Do you have a place to stay tonight?"

Stacey had met some of Glen's friends but she didn't feel she knew them well enough to impose by asking to stay with them.

"No, I'll be okay. I don't think the person will come back. I'll probably just stay up until it's light."

"Tell you what," Randolph said. "We'll cruise by every once in a while until morning, but you're right, I doubt he'll come back."

The officers left fifteen minutes later and Stacey made a decision. She was certain that Glen would rush back if she told him what had happened and she didn't want to interfere with his work. But she couldn't stay alone in the house, either. The person who had tried to break in was no kid. Staying by herself in Palisades Heights was out of the question and she had just thought of a place she could go until Glen was back. Stacey booted up her laptop and figured out how to drive to Arlington, California.

CHAPTER FORTY-ONE

Stacey started her trip down the coast before the sun rose, stopping only for a quick lunch. A few times during the drive she thought she saw a dark car following her. The car was so far back she couldn't identify the make and there were times when she wasn't sure it was the same car. She decided that lack of sleep and her terrifying experience were making her paranoid.

Arlington was a beach town for the very rich, and its resorts and hotels were way out of Stacey's price range, so she settled for a motel in Graves Point, ten miles farther south. After checking in and unpacking, Stacey drove back to Arlington. She noticed the differences between the California resort and Palisades Heights immediately. There were millionaires with homes in Palisades Heights, but almost everyone with a house near the beach in Arlington was very wealthy, and while the businesses on Ocean Avenue catered to the middle class, the boutiques, jewelry stores, and upscale restaurants on the streets that led to the ocean in Arlington attracted a clientele that never had to count pennies.

The *Arlington Examiner* started publishing in 1947, and its offices were four blocks inland in a two-story brick building. Stacey told the receptionist that she was doing research for a novel and asked if back issues of the newspaper were available. The receptionist told her that all issues of the paper had been scanned into a computer and Stacey could access the files in the library on the second floor.

According to Jack Booth, Kathy Moran's parents had died when Kathy was in junior high school so Stacey figured that she would have been between twelve and fifteen years old when they passed away. An hour after she started scrolling through the back issues, a story caught Stacey's eye. Arlington residents Theodore and Marjorie Cromwell had been murdered during a home burglary. The Cromwells' twelve-year-old daughter had returned home from a sleepover at a friend's house and discovered their bodies. The daughter was named Katherine.

Stacey shuddered as she remembered how she had felt when she saw Megan Cahill's corpse. She tried to imagine how much more horrifying it must have been for a twelve-year-old to discover the bodies of both of her parents.

Stacey ran a search for stories about the Cromwells. Theodore's obituary said that his grandfather had started a business that had supplied uniforms to the armed forces during World War One and had then used the profits to diversify into other basic industries. Theodore was a lawyer who had served as counsel to several of the businesses. He had moved to California to oversee a West Coach branch of the original company that was manufacturing sportswear and had settled in Arlington. One line in the obituary caught Stacey's attention. Cromwell had been a well-known collector, but the obituary writer had not gone into detail.

Stacey was about to search for more information about

Cromwells' collection when the receptionist told her that it was five o'clock and the offices were closing. Stacey had been so focused that she only realized how exhausted she was when she stood up and swayed for a second. She decided to eat on the pier, then head back to her motel to catch up on her sleep.

The weather was balmy and the streets of Arlington were bustling. Stacey paused to window-shop and dropped into a bookstore to pick up a paperback novel. The receptionist at the newspaper office had recommended an Italian restaurant that sounded nice. The hostess seated Stacey outside where she had a view of fat seals frolicking under one of the piers that jutted out into the Pacific. Stacey ordered, then started reading her book. The intriguing plot coupled with the excellent meal and the view provided enough distractions to make her forget about the *Cahill* case during dinner. Stacey made the mistake of having a glass of wine. Lack of sleep and the soothing effect of the Chianti made her a little tipsy.

During the drive to her motel, thoughts of Kathy Moran and *Woman with a Gun* flooded back. If she hadn't been distracted, Stacey might have sensed that something was wrong when she opened the door to her room. She took a step inside and a figure in black rushed at her and buried a knife in her chest. Stacey was too shocked to scream but an adrenaline-fueled reflex shot out a foot that connected with the attacker's kneecap. Stacey staggered out of her room and lurched toward the motel office while her attacker struggled to stand. Moments later, Stacey collapsed in the crowded lobby and managed to cry, "Help me!" before she blacked out.

CHAPTER FORTY-TWO

The door to Stacey's hospital room opened and a barrel-chested man walked in. He had curly red hair, a pale freckled face, and green eyes and he was wearing a tan sports jacket over a black T-shirt and gray slacks. When he was next to Stacey's bed he held up a badge.

"Good afternoon, Miss Kim. I'm Detective John Coleman and I'm investigating your case. Do you feel up to talking about what happened at the motel?"

"I'm still a little woozy from the painkillers but we can talk."

"It sounds like you had a close call."

Stacey flashed on the attack and her eyes began to tear.

"Sorry," she said.

"You have no reason to apologize. I know cops who've been attacked. These are very brave, trained men and women, and they're all shaky after something like this."

"The knife just missed my heart," Stacey said. She sounded subdued. "The doctor said I'm lucky. He said I'll be as good as new when everything heals up. But I'm scared."

"You don't have to worry. There's going to be a policeman outside your door twenty-four/seven. And once you tell me who did this I'll lock them up and make sure you're never in danger again."

"Thank you."

Coleman pulled a chair over and sat next to Stacey's bed. The nurse had cranked it up and Stacey was sitting.

"I know you must be exhausted," the detective said, "so why don't we get right to it? And please tell me if you need a break. First, did you get a good look at the person who stabbed you?"

Before Stacey could answer Glen Kraft walked in. Coleman stood up quickly and placed himself between Glen and Stacey.

"I'm a detective and I'm conducting an interview with Miss Kim. You can't come in here."

"Wait," Stacey said. "Glen should stay. He knows the history of the *Cahill* case much better than I do. He should be the one to tell you about it."

"What is the *Cahill* case?" Coleman asked.

"Raymond Cahill was murdered ten years ago. That's why I was attacked."

"I've never heard of Raymond Cahill or the *Cahill* case," Coleman said.

"Neither had I until I saw the photograph."

Detective Coleman sat beside Stacey's hospital bed, listening intently and taking notes while Stacey and Glen told him about the murders in Palisades Heights.

"So you think Kathy Moran stabbed you?" Coleman asked when Stacey finished.

Stacey hesitated. She was certain that Kathy Moran had tried to kill her, but. . . .

"No, I couldn't swear that Miss Moran attacked me. There

were no lights on in the room and the person who stabbed me was dressed in black and wearing a ski mask, just like the person who tried to break into Glen's house in Palisades Heights. But who else could it be?"

Coleman rested his pencil on his notebook. "It could be anyone."

"What about the fact that Moran and Raymond Cahill both lived in Arlington?" Glen said.

"That hardly establishes proof beyond a reasonable doubt that Moran stabbed your friend. I had a forensic team go through your motel room and they haven't found any evidence I can use to arrest anyone for the attack. I can see why you would think Miss Moran is involved, but I can't arrest her based on a theory that's not supported by hard evidence."

Stacey was quiet for a moment. Then she got an idea.

"The doctors said that I'll be here recuperating for a few days. Could you bring me the file on the Cromwell murders?"

Detective Coleman hesitated for a moment. Then he smiled.

"Sure, why not? It's a cold case, and maybe you'll be able to dig up something. You certainly have a good imagination."

"Thanks. Even if I don't find anything, it will give me something to do."

"I'm sorry I've been so negative," the detective said.

"No, you're right. You can't arrest Kathy based on my feelings."

"I'll write up a report on the attack at the motel and give you a copy. Show it to Chief Melendez and tell him what you told me. No one looked at Moran before. Maybe he'll figure something out if he focuses on her."

The detective left and Glen took Stacey's hand. "I'm so glad you're going to be okay. When I heard you'd been stabbed . . ."

He choked up for a moment and Stacey squeezed his hand.

"And the attempted break-in must have been terrifying," Glen said when he'd recovered his composure. "You should have called me. I would have come back."

"I thought about it, but there wasn't anything you could have done, and I didn't want to interfere with your work."

Glen stared directly into Stacey's eyes. "I love you, Stacey. I really love you. You're the most important thing in my life and the thought that I could have lost you . . ."

Stacey teared up. "I love you, too. That's what I thought about when I came to after the operation. That I could have died and we would never . . ."

She stopped. Glen leaned over and kissed her.

"Ouch," Stacey yelped.

Glen reared back and reddened. "Sorry."

Stacey laughed. "Don't be. It was worth it."

CHAPTER FORTY-THREE

"The smoking gun" is a metaphor for a piece of incriminating evidence that seals a criminal's fate. In the *Cahill* case the evidence was quite literally a gun, although it wasn't technically a "smoking gun," because it didn't provide enough evidence to arrest Kathy Moran. In the old case file, Stacey found a list of things that had been stolen from Theodore Cromwell's collection. One item was a Schofield .44 Smith & Wesson revolver rumored to have been wielded by Wyatt Earp during the Gunfight at the OK Corral.

"This is just like the robbery-murder in Palisades Heights," Glen said as soon as Stacey told him about the Schofield.

"And it raises two interesting questions. Is the gun that was stolen from Theodore Cromwell and the gun that was used to murder Raymond Cahill the same weapon? If it is, how did Raymond Cahill come into possession of Theodore Cromwell's Schofield?"

"Remember my suggestion for your book?" Glen said.

"That Cahill bought the revolver from the person who stole it?"

Glen nodded. "Well, I just thought of another scenario. What if Cahill murdered the Cromwells and stole the gun? Is there anything in the reports about Cahill?"

"I haven't seen anything yet."

"We should ask Detective Coleman if Cahill's name ever came up in the investigation."

John Coleman opened the door to Stacey's hospital room and walked in with a man dressed in running shoes, jeans, and a kelly green short-sleeve shirt. Stacey put the newcomer's age at the late sixties because of his thinning gray hair and the wrinkles on his suntanned face, but the man was solidly built and it didn't look like he'd given in to old age easily.

"This is Lynn Merritt," Coleman said. "He retired from the Arlington Police Department five years ago and he's one of the detectives who investigated the Cromwell murders."

"Thank you for coming," Stacey said.

"There was no way I wouldn't, after John told me about the murders in Oregon and what you'd uncovered. The Cromwell case was one of my first as a detective and one of the few we never solved. How can I help you?"

"The woman I suspect in the Oregon murders is named Kathy Moran. Katherine is the name of the Cromwells' daughter. Do you know if they're the same woman?"

"I do. Katherine was a witness, so I had to keep tabs on her whereabouts in case there was ever a trial. She moved to Montana and was raised by an aunt named Selma Moran."

"Yes!" Stacey said as she broke into a grin. The men in the room couldn't help smiling.

"What's your next question?" Merritt asked.

"It would be an amazing coincidence if the gun that was used to murder Raymond Cahill and the gun that was stolen from Theodore Cromwell were two separate weapons, especially since Cahill and Cromwell lived in the same town and were both collectors. Did Raymond Cahill's name ever come up in your investigation?"

"Yes. Cromwell and Cahill were very serious collectors and occasional rivals for specific items. They were both members of the Arlington Country Club and a few of the other members heard them argue a couple of months before the Cromwells were murdered.

"When I interviewed Cahill he denied they'd argued. He told me that he outbid Cromwell for a rare coin. Cromwell offered to buy it, but Cahill said he didn't want to sell and Cromwell got upset because he needed the coin for his collection."

"Did you investigate Cahill at all?"

"I didn't put a lot of time in on him, but the people I talked to said he wasn't well liked. They felt that he'd made his money too fast and was full of himself. *Ruthless* was a word I heard a lot. If he wanted something he went full bore and wasn't concerned about who got hurt."

"Was he a suspect because of the theft of valuable items from Cromwell's collection?"

"Not really. We discussed the possibility but no one thought it was worth pursuing."

"What do you think now, knowing that there's a good chance that Cahill was in possession of the stolen Schofield?" Stacey asked.

CHAPTER FORTY-FOUR

"What happened to you?" George Melendez asked when Glen helped Stacey into the police chief's office and eased her onto a chair.

"You know that someone tried to break into my house while Stacey was there alone?"

Melendez nodded.

"Stacey was afraid to stay by herself, so she drove to Arlington, California, to look into Kathy Moran's background. That's where Moran grew up. While she was there, someone stabbed her."

"What?!"

"Kathy Moran's last name used to be Cromwell," Stacey said. "When she was twelve she was living with her parents, Theodore and Marjorie Cromwell, in Arlington, California. The Cromwells were murdered during a burglary and Kathy discovered the bodies.

"Raymond Cahill was living in Arlington, California, when the Cromwells were killed. Cahill and Theodore Cromwell were serious collectors and competitors at times for various valuable items. One item stolen during the robbery-murder was a Schofield .44 Smith and Wesson revolver believed to have been used by Wyatt Earp during the Gunfight at the OK Corral, the same type of rare antique that was used to murder Raymond Cahill."

"Is it the same gun?"

"I don't know. If it is, Kathy had one hell of a motive to kill Cahill with it."

"You think Kathy Moran killed Cahill to avenge her parents?" Melendez asked. He sounded incredulous.

"Shortly before the Cahills' wedding, Kathy took photographs for an article about the Cahills that appeared in the *Palisades Heights Gazette*. Raymond showed the reporter who wrote the article some of the highlights of his collection, including the Schofield. Kathy took a photograph of the revolver that was printed in the paper. If she thought that Cahill stole the Schofield from her father it would explain why she used that gun to kill Cahill. It also explains why none of the items stolen from Cahill's collection have surfaced."

"How does it do that?"

"Everyone assumed that greed was the motive behind Raymond Cahill's murder. If the motive was revenge, Kathy would have gotten rid of the items from the collection so they couldn't be tied to her."

"Okay, I follow you, but why would she murder Megan Cahill ten years later?"

"I don't know, but it would have been simple for Kathy to run down the beach from her house to Megan's place without being seen. Another thing, if she was working with Parnell Crouse it makes you wonder if she was really just taking pictures for a show when she saw Megan on the beach and snapped *Woman with a Gun* or if she was going to the Cahills' house to help Crouse kill Raymond Cahill."

"Do you have any proof that Kathy knew Crouse?" the police chief asked.

"No, but I've been thinking about that. Her law school at Berkeley isn't far from the Oakland Raiders stadium."

"This seems pretty flimsy to me."

"You're forgetting that someone tried to murder Stacey," Glen said.

Melendez looked at Stacey. "Could you identify the person who stabbed you?"

"No. I was staying at a motel. Someone was in my room. The lights were off and I was stabbed as soon as I opened the door. The person who attacked me was dressed in black and wearing a ski mask. And everything happened very fast."

"Was the person who tried to break in the same person who stabbed you?"

"I can't swear they were the same person."

"What do you want me to do, Stacey?" Melendez asked.

"I . . . I guess I want you to investigate Kathy Moran to see if she killed Raymond and Megan Cahill and Parnell Crouse and tried to kill me."

"I'll think about what you said, but there are some real problems with reopening the investigation. You can't swear Kathy tried to kill you, can you?"

"No."

"All of the evidence points to Parnell Crouse as the person who murdered Raymond Cahill. Unless we can establish a connection between Kathy and Parnell Crouse that's more convincing than this Berkeley thing, I don't see how you can tie Kathy to that murder."

"You can try to find out if Kathy has an alibi for the time

Crouse was murdered. Grady Cox should be able to tell you if Kathy showed up for her shift after Jack Booth finished interviewing her at the police station."

"You still haven't explained why Kathy would kill Megan Cahill—someone she barely knew—ten years after Ray's murder. If she was going to kill Megan, why not do it when she killed Ray?"

"I didn't convince him," Stacey said as she limped to Glen's car.

"He's definitely skeptical. But that doesn't mean he won't follow up by talking to Cox and reviewing the evidence to see if he missed something because Moran was never the focus of his investigation."

Stacey sighed. "He won't find anything. She covered her tracks too well."

"I think it's time for you to focus on your book and leave the police work to the police."

"I will," she agreed dejectedly.

Glen put his arms around Stacey and pulled her to him gently so as not to aggravate her wound.

"I love you and I can't bear to see you hurt. Stick to fictional crimes and let the police handle the real stuff so you can stay safe."

CHAPTER FORTY-FIVE

Jack Booth was working on a trial memorandum in a construction case when his secretary told him that Kathy Moran was calling. When they spoke at the gallery opening Kathy had been pretty clear that they weren't going to have a relationship so he wondered what she wanted.

"I need your help, Jack," Kathy said as soon as they were connected.

"What kind of help?"

"I need a very good lawyer."

"Why?"

"They think I killed Megan and Ray Cahill."

"Who thinks you killed the Cahills?"

"George Melendez and Gayle Sutcliff, the district attorney. I flew back from New York yesterday and they showed up at my house this morning. They wanted to know where I was when Megan was killed and if I worked on the evening Parnell Crouse was killed."

"They think you killed Crouse, too?"

"I don't know what they're thinking. But I'm certain that little bitch you're so fond of is behind this."

"Who?"

"Stacey Kim. I think she's convinced George and Gayle that I'm a mass murderer."

"Why do you think Stacey Kim has something to do with George's investigation?"

"She's been prying into my private life. She asked you about my childhood, and Grady Cox told me she asked him if I worked at the Seafarer the night Parnell Crouse was killed. I'm sure Kim is spreading rumors about me and I want it stopped."

"What did you say to Melendez and the DA when they asked you about the murders?"

"I'm not stupid. I did what I always advised my clients to do—I said absolutely nothing."

"Why are you calling me?"

"I want you to come down here. I want you to tell George and Gayle and that little bitch that I'll sue everyone who is part of this witch hunt if they don't get off my back."

"You know you can't sue the police and the DA if they're investigating you in good faith. Do you have any reason to believe either George or the DA have a personal reason to go after you?"

"Maybe that cunt is screwing Melendez."

"Come on, Kathy. Use your head."

Jack heard Kathy expel a breath. When she spoke again she sounded contrite.

"I'm sorry, but this is so unfair. I didn't kill Megan. I barely knew her or Raymond Cahill. If you don't count finding her on the beach, the dinner I had with Megan before the gallery opening was the first time I'd spent any time with her. What possible reason would I have to kill her?"

"Why don't I drive down and talk to George and the DA?"

"That would be great. My career wasn't going so well until the MoMA show. Now it's just starting to get off the ground again and I don't need this."

"I've got to wrap up some stuff but I can get down to Palisades Heights tomorrow afternoon."

"Thank you, Jack. What will I owe you?"

"Dinner."

"Come on. I don't expect you to work for free."

"I'll pick a very expensive restaurant. And don't worry. If you really need me I'll expect a retainer. But I won't know if you're in real trouble until I talk to Melendez."

CHAPTER FORTY-SIX

"Hi, George," Jack said when he was ushered into the police chief's office.

"Back in town so soon?" asked Melendez.

"It's business, I'm afraid."

"Oh?"

"You really upset Kathy Moran and she wants to know why."

"Why would she be upset?"

"Come on, George. She told me that you practically accused her of killing Megan and Ray Cahill and Parnell Crouse. I'd be upset if you accused me of being a serial killer."

"I never accused her of anything, Jack. I just asked her to clarify some issues that have come up recently. But the fact that she's hired a high-powered Portland lawyer is interesting."

"Can we stop playing games and will you tell me why the sudden interest in Kathy after ten years?"

"Look, Jack, I hope that I'm completely off base but I recently learned some very unsettling information."

"Such as?"

"Did you know that Raymond Cahill and Kathy's parents all lived in Arlington, California, when Kathy was twelve?"

"No."

"Well, they did. Kathy's father was a collector and he and Kathy's mom were murdered during a home burglary. One of the items stolen during the burglary was a .44 Schofield Smith and Wesson that may have been used by Wyatt Earp during the Gunfight at the OK Corral."

It took all of Jack's training as a trial lawyer to keep from reacting.

"It's also possible that Kathy Moran knew Parnell Crouse. She was in Berkeley at law school when he played for the Raiders nearby in Oakland."

"That's a stretch, George. Do you have solid evidence that they knew each other?"

"Not yet. But I'm taking a hard look at this case again since someone tried to murder Stacey Kim."

"What?"

"Stacey has been living with Glen Kraft. A week ago, Glen was in Eugene on business and Stacey was staying by herself. Someone tried to break into their house. Stacey scared off the intruder but she said that the intruder had a knife. Stacey was afraid to stay alone in Glen's house so she drove to Arlington to look into Kathy's childhood. She thought she saw a car following her from Oregon.

"Stacey conducted her research at the local newspaper office, had dinner, and returned to her motel. Someone was waiting in her room and stabbed her when she opened the door. She can't swear it was the person who tried to break into Glen's house but they were dressed the same."

"Is Stacey okay?"

"She was lucky. She's recovering nicely but she's scared to death and I don't blame her. As soon as she came back to town she filled me in on everything she'd discovered, including the fact that a Schofield was stolen from Theodore Cromwell's collection when he was murdered."

"Stacey interviewed me for her book and I got the impression that she's a good kid, but you don't have any basis for charging Kathy with Raymond Cahill's murder unless you can establish a connection between Kathy and Parnell Crouse that's more convincing than this Berkeley thing. No jury is going to convict Kathy of murder unless you can show she was in touch with him near the time Cahill was killed."

"You're probably right about that. But here's the thing: I tried to find out if Kathy has an alibi for the time Crouse was murdered. Grady Cox can't remember if Kathy showed up for her shift after you finished interviewing her at the police station."

"Which isn't surprising after ten years," Jack said.

"True, but a spectacular murder like that and Kathy being a witness . . . We hardly ever get a serious violent crime here, and that murder got national coverage. If Kathy went to work, it would be natural for her to tell Grady what happened and you'd think Grady would remember that night."

"It's still ten years ago."

"Even so." Melendez shrugged. "And Grady says he can't find any pay records for that night, so Kathy doesn't have a real good alibi for the time Crouse was killed. If she'd talk to me she might be able to prove she was working when Crouse was killed. That would be really helpful."

"Look, George, I feel very bad about what happened to Stacey. But novelists have vivid imaginations and I think you're putting too much stock in hers."

"Maybe, but you should think twice about representing Kathy. You were part of the prosecution team when Raymond Cahill and Parnell Crouse were killed, so you may have a conflict."

CHAPTER FORTY-SEVEN

Kathy chose a restaurant in a town several miles down the coast from Palisades Heights where they were less likely to be seen. She asked for a booth in the back. As soon as they ordered drinks, Jack told Kathy what the police chief had told him.

"Someone actually tried to murder Stacey Kim?" Kathy asked.

"After trying to break into her house. So you can see why George is taking this seriously."

"Sure, but everything rests on me knowing about the revolver, and I didn't. I was twelve when my parents were murdered. I was interested in boys, clothes, and music, not my father's antiques. I had no idea he owned Wyatt Earp's gun until George told me."

"It must have been horrible for you, having your parents die like that, then discovering the bodies."

Kathy looked down at the tabletop. "You have no idea. I went completely off the rails."

"What happened?"

"The only relative willing to take me in was Selma Moran, my aunt. She was a widow who lived in Sweet Prairie, Montana, a town that was as different from Arlington as Arlington is from the moon. I was still in shock when she moved me there and I hated everything about the place. I made my aunt's life hell.

"When I was fourteen I started running with a group of older kids. They were into drugs, burglary. My luck ran out finally and I was arrested in a house we'd broken into to get money for drugs. My aunt stood by me and the lawyer she hired arranged to get me into treatment so I could avoid a criminal record.

"The last straw was when I got pregnant in the summer before high school. My aunt was pretty progressive, and she arranged for an abortion, but she made it very clear that she was through with me unless I got my act together. When I started high school I made a real effort to walk the straight and narrow. My grades went way up, I stayed away from drugs and my old friends. Just before I left for college I changed my last name to Moran as a thank-you to my aunt and, symbolically I guess, to signal that I was starting a new life."

"I had no idea you had it so bad."

"Yeah, well, that's all in the past and I want the bad times to stay there. That's why I need your help. I'm sorry Stacey Kim was stabbed, but that doesn't give her the right to accuse me of murder. Can you nip this in the bud?"

"There's nothing I can do to stop George from investigating."

"Let him investigate all he wants. He's not going to be able to prove I killed anyone because I didn't."

The waitress brought their drinks. "I don't need this in my life right now," Kathy said when the waitress left.

"There's something else we have to discuss," Jack said. "George pointed out that I may have a conflict that would prevent me from representing you."

"What kind of conflict?"

"I was part of the prosecution team when Crouse and Raymond Cahill were murdered."

"That's outrageous. He's just trying to stop you from being my lawyer because he knows that no one on the DA's staff would have a chance against you in trial."

"I'll check with the bar, but I am concerned. I wanted you to know that you'll have to find another attorney if there really is a conflict."

Kathy reached out and covered Jack's hand. "Don't desert me, Jack. I need you."

"I'll do what I can," he said.

"Thank you."

Jack's attraction to Kathy was intense, and her touch and the intimacy of the situation were unsettling. Kathy didn't take her hand away. She looked into Jack's eyes. He felt a knot in his stomach and a stirring below that he fought to control.

"Let's forget about dinner," Kathy said, her voice barely above a whisper.

"Are you sure?" Jack asked.

Kathy let go of Jack's hand and opened her purse. Her eyes never left his as she pulled out a hundred-dollar bill and laid it on the table.

"Take me home, Jack."

Kathy rolled on top of Jack and draped a leg over his. Jack was slick with sweat and short of breath. Kathy ran a finger across his chest, feather light, just grazing his nipple.

"What was I thinking?" Kathy said. "We've wasted so much time."

Jack didn't answer. He was too spent to speak. He had waited fifteen years for this moment and it was everything he'd ever dreamed of and more. He touched Kathy's cheek. Then they kissed and Jack rolled over so that their bodies were touching. After what seemed like endless moments' kissing and stroking, Kathy's fingers strayed between his legs and Jack groaned. He returned the favor and they began to move together, both panting and straining until Jack couldn't stand any more. He rolled Kathy onto her back and pushed inside her. His eyes closed, his breath came faster, and moments later he left behind his last rational thought.

They rested, then they made love again, then Kathy drifted off to sleep. It took Jack a while to nod off, then he tossed and turned because he was having a really bad dream. He was wandering through an art gallery and the exhibit was a collection of horrible photographs of crime scenes and autopsies. Everywhere he looked, he saw eviscerated torsos, severed limbs, and hideous head wounds. The worst part of the head shots were the dead eyes that followed him when he walked by. One head was particularly disturbing. There was a gruesome entry wound in the temple and its mouth kept opening and closing, as if it were trying to tell him something. Dream Jack was compelled to lean toward the corpse's bloodstained and shredded lips in order to hear what it was saying.

Live Jack's eyes opened wide. His heart was beating rapidly. He was certain that his dream had something to do with the reason Megan Cahill had fled the gallery. He lay on his back, staring at the ceiling. His subconscious had tried to tell him something, but he couldn't figure out what it was trying to say. It had tugged at the corners of his mind while he slept, and now that he was awake, it was staying just out of sight, drifting away like morning mist whenever he thought he might grasp it.

Jack looked at the clock and saw that it was six thirty. Kathy was deep in sleep and Jack slipped out of bed and dressed quietly.

Then he drove back to his motel and showered. A little after seven thirty Jack knocked on Kathy's front door. She was barefoot, wearing shorts, a T-shirt, and no bra. She looked incredibly sexy sleepy-eyed with her hair tousled. Jack had stopped at a bakery and held out two cups of coffee and a paper bag that contained two croissants.

"I wondered where you'd gone," Kathy said as she stood aside to let Jack in. Jack walked out on the deck and set down the paper cups and the bag.

"I couldn't sleep. I was too worked up."

"Good," Kathy said with a smile.

"You were dead to the world."

"The sleep of the innocent," she joked. "Too bad that's not admissible evidence."

Jack laughed. "I don't think you have to worry. I've thought about everything George told me. He's nowhere near making a case that can be submitted to a grand jury."

"That's reassuring."

Jack took another bite of his croissant and a sip of his coffee while he stared out at the ocean. The sun was warm, the sea was calm, and Jack thought he could sit on this deck with Kathy by his side forever. Then he sighed.

"What's wrong?" Kathy asked.

"Life. I have to head back to Portland to take a deposition when all I really want is to sit here with you."

Kathy smiled. "What a nice thing to say."

"I can drive out again on the weekend," Jack said.

"That would be wonderful, but I'm going to East Africa for two weeks on a photo shoot for a fashion magazine."

Jack couldn't hide his disappointment. Kathy laughed again.

"Don't look so sad. I want to be with you as much as you want to be with me. I'll get in touch as soon as I'm back."

Jack broke into a grin.

"That's better," Kathy said.

Jack finished his coffee and stood up.

"I'll see you out," Kathy said.

As they walked to the door, Jack paused in front of a framed copy of *Woman with a Gun* that hung in the living room.

"What a fantastic achievement," he said.

"Thank you," Kathy said. Then she melted into Jack's arms. They held each other for a long moment before Kathy pushed him away gently.

"I'll see you soon," she said.

CHAPTER FORTY-EIGHT

Jack drove back to his motel to pack. He should have felt great but he felt uncomfortable. He remembered his horrible dream, and that made him think about Kathy's show at Ellen Devereaux's gallery, which, in turn, brought back a vision of Megan Cahill's rapid exit. What had spooked her? Jack concentrated, but he had no new insights by the time he parked outside his motel room.

Jack packed quickly. He had brought the catalogue of Kathy's exhibit with him and was just about to put it in his valise when a thought occurred to him. Jack remembered the two photographs that had been in Megan's line of sight right before she bolted. Jack turned to one of them and frowned. He'd brought his laptop with him so he could work and he booted it up.

Jack watched a lot of pro football but he had no clear memory of what Parnell Crouse looked like because Crouse had only been a backup running back. Jack had seen Crouse's face up close in the crime scene and autopsy photographs, but he had not studied his facial features because his attention had focused on the head wound that had killed him, a head wound like the one he'd seen in the photograph in his dream.

Jack used the Internet to find photographs of Parnell Crouse. The ex-Raider was clean-shaven in all of them, as he'd been in the crime scene and autopsy photographs. Jack studied the picture in the catalogue. He couldn't be 100 percent certain, but the man in one of the missing photographs—the morose and bearded man who was staring into the mirror behind the bar—looked a lot like Crouse.

Jack sat back. Megan Cahill was looking at Kathy Moran's photograph of her ex-husband just before she fled the gallery. She must have recognized Crouse in the photograph and reached the instantaneous conclusion that Kathy knew him and had never told her or anyone else that they had met.

Kathy had gone to Boalt Hall, the law school at the University of California in Berkeley, around the same time Crouse was with the Raiders, and Berkeley was not far from the Raiders' stadium. She must have met him while they were both in the Bay area. If Kathy was Crouse's accomplice in the murder of Raymond Cahill and she realized that Megan had recognized Crouse in one of her photographs, Kathy would have a strong motive to murder Megan Cahill.

Jack felt sick. In all the time he'd been involved in the Cahill case never once had he suspected that Kathy Moran was anything more than a witness. She'd fooled him and everyone else who had investigated the case. Jack closed the catalogue. *Woman with a Gun* was on the front cover. He stared at the beautiful, mysterious masterpiece and wondered how someone who could create great art could also kill in cold blood. He also wondered about their night together. When Jack left Kathy's house, he was as close to being in love with a woman as he'd been in ages. Now he wondered if anything that had happened between them had been real. Did Kathy care for him or was she manipulating him so he would defend her vigorously?

What was he going to do? He was Kathy's lawyer. He couldn't go to Melendez. Hell, he didn't even have enough evidence to accuse Kathy. All the photograph of Crouse proved was that she'd known him almost twenty years ago. Maybe Kathy had a reasonable explanation for concealing her connection to Crouse. Jack decided that he had to go back to Kathy's house and ask her about the photograph. Jack picked up the catalogue and stopped. He took another look at *Woman with a Gun* and that's when he saw it. Jack felt like the breath had been knocked out of him. He took a closer look and felt sick when he realized what he was seeing.

"We have to talk," Jack said as soon as Kathy opened her front door.

"My, you sound serious."

Jack was carrying the catalogue. He opened it to the picture of the bearded man.

"What are you showing me, Jack?"

"Do you recognize him?" he said, pointing at the picture.

"No, should I?"

"That man is Parnell Crouse."

"What?" Kathy said as she leaned forward.

"That's Crouse. Why didn't you tell the police that you knew him?"

"Because I didn't. I mean I had no idea who the man in that photo was. I took this picture when I was in law school. I used to wander around some of the down-and-out parts of Oakland and San Francisco, shooting scenes and people that interested me. I didn't date these guys. I didn't always ask their permission. So, if that is Crouse, I certainly didn't know who he was until you told me just now."

Jack wanted to believe Kathy. She sounded so sincere. But he was certain that she was lying. Jack closed the catalogue and pushed the cover photograph of *Woman with a Gun* across the table.

"I took a closer look at your masterpiece," Jack said. "You told me and the police officer who interviewed you right after Raymond was killed that you were walking toward the Cahills' house from the direction of the Seafarer when you saw Megan Cahill and took the shot, but this photograph was taken from behind Megan and slightly to the right. You took the picture when you walked down to the beach from the Cahills' house."

Kathy didn't move. Then she flashed a tired smile.

"So you figured it out. No one else ever has." Kathy laughed. "It's been in front of everyone's nose for ten years. I was so excited when the *Oregonian* wanted to publish my photograph on the front page. Once I let them, there was no way I could get rid of it. It was all over the papers in New York, L.A. Even I didn't see the problem until it was too late."

"No one took a hard look at the photo and no one would have any reason to take a hard look as long as no one suspected you of being anything other than a witness," Jack said.

"And I would still be safe if my wonderful photograph hadn't inspired that little bitch to write a novel about the *Cahill* case."

"What happened that night?" Jack asked.

"Megan was unconscious when I got there and Raymond was tied to the chair," Kathy answered. "Parnell had tortured him for the combination to the vault but he'd kept Ray alive, like I told him to, so I could finish him off. Crouse and I went into the vault and I loaded the gun. Then I told Cahill who I was. He begged me not to kill him. I asked if my parents had begged. He looked down and didn't answer. And that's when I knew he'd killed my parents just so he could have some shitty antique for his collection. I shot him, then I dropped the gun on the floor. I wanted everyone to think that robbery was the motive for Cahill's murder, so Parnell and I went into the vault so I could tell him what to take. When we went into the vault, Megan was out like a light. When we walked out, she was gone and so was the Schofield."

"Why did you take the photograph?"

Kathy's expression changed and she got the same dreamy look that had transformed her features when he'd asked her about the photograph ten years before in the interview room.

"I had to. It was so . . ." She shook her head. "I knew I'd never see anything like it again as long as I lived. That's why I didn't kill Megan. If I'd killed her I wouldn't have been able to show the photo."

"Weren't you afraid Megan would tell the police you'd shot her husband?"

"No, she was unconscious when I was in the same room with her, and I was in the vault when she came to. When I found her on the beach, she was in shock. But even if she were completely alert she wouldn't have known I had killed Raymond. If her memory came back she would remember Parnell, and I was going to kill him that night. So I took the photograph. Then I walked behind her and came up the beach from the direction of the Seafarer."

"How did you get Parnell Crouse to help you?"

"I took the photo of Parnell during law school in a bar in Oakland. His career was going in the toilet and his marriage was going south. After I took the shot I bought him a drink and we ended up in bed. He was a real stud in the sack so we had an off-again, on-again thing until I graduated and moved to Portland.

"After I did the photo shoot at Cahill's house and saw the

Schofield, I found him. He hated Megan. I told him we'd kill Cahill and frame Megan. He liked that idea a lot. I even told him he could keep everything we stole. Parnell was broke and he needed the money. He was easy to convince."

Jack digested what Kathy had said.

"What are you going to do, Jack? You can't tell George about my confession because you're my lawyer."

"I can't tell George what you've just told me in confidence but I can show him the photographs of Crouse and Megan. You didn't tell me about them. I figured out what they showed. George can draw his own conclusions."

"Don't do it, Jack. Why punish me for avenging my mother and father? We were meant for each other. We should never have put off being together."

Jack stood up. "I do care about you, Kathy, but this is just too big."

Jack picked up the catalogue and turned to leave. He was almost at the front door when he heard the hammer click. When he turned around, Kathy was aiming a handgun at him.

"You can't shoot me, Kathy. You know that. George is looking at you, but he doesn't have enough to go to a grand jury. If you kill me it will be like shining a spotlight on yourself. George will bring in the state police, the FBI, and someone else will look at *Woman with a Gun* and figure it out."

"I'll have to take that chance."

"No, you don't. Let me walk out of here. I do care about you. Now I know what Cahill did to you and I know the hell Gary Kilbride put you through. I'll make sure you get the best attorney. There will be a deal. Cahill killed your mother and father. Letting me go will work for you."

Kathy laughed but there was no humor in it. "If I'd just killed Raymond what you said would make sense, but you're conveniently forgetting about Parnell Crouse and Megan and Stacey Kim and Gary Kilbride."

Jack had forgotten about Kilbride, and the expression on his face showed it.

"Yes, Jack. I found out he'd been paroled, so I sent him the article from the *Gazette.* Then I lured him to my house with a promise to pay him off if he left me in peace. I got as much satisfaction out of killing that sadistic bastard as I did shooting Cahill."

"And what satisfaction will you get out of shooting me?" Jack asked. "My only sin is that I've been in love with you since the first time I saw you."

Jack saw something change in Kathy's expression and the hand holding the gun trembled for an instant.

"I'm going to leave," Jack said. "You can shoot me but you'll have to do it in the back and you'll have to get rid of my body and my car and hope that you've gotten rid of every trace of DNA I've left in this house.

"Our photographs are going to be on every front page and the TV news. You'll have to hope that no one at the restaurant remembers we ate together last night and left together. That includes the waitress who got the one-hundred-dollar bill as a tip for a meal we never ate.

"I meant what I said about going to bat for you. I can't imagine how it felt to lose your parents like that, and I can tell a prosecutor that Gary Kilbride deserved to die. But I can't do any of that if I'm dead."

The hand holding the gun trembled again. Jack turned slowly and walked toward the front door.

"Don't," Kathy said, but there was no conviction in her voice.

Jack reached for the doorknob.

"Don't, please," Kathy said.

Jack turned the knob. There was a shot but it plowed into the wall beside him. Jack walked through the door and toward his car. There were no more shots. His last view of Kathy Moran was through the open front door as he turned his car toward Ocean Avenue. She was standing where he had left her with the gun hanging at her side.

CHAPTER FORTY-NINE

George Melendez headed to Moran's place with two cars for backup as soon as Jack told him that Kathy had shot at him. When the police chief asked why, Jack told him that he couldn't answer that question because of the attorney-client privilege. Kathy was armed, so everyone was decked out in SWAT gear. Jack stayed in a police car while the officers cautiously approached the house with their guns drawn. When Melendez worked his way up the driveway he found the front door wide open.

"Kathy, this is George Melendez," he called while pressing against the side of the house. "Can you come out where I can see you? Jack said you had a gun. Can you throw out your gun and show me your hands? I don't want you shot by accident."

There was no reply.

"Come on, Kathy. You know me and you know I'll treat you fairly and I won't hurt you. I'd feel terrible if you were shot because we misunderstood the situation."

Melendez waited patiently. When there was still no reply, he told the men on either side of the door to cover him and he ducked inside. The living room was empty. The door to the bedroom was open. Melendez waited until his men were inside before calling out to Kathy again. When she didn't answer, he made his way to the side of the bedroom entrance. Then he crouched down and peered through a gap between the door and the jamb.

"Aw, no," he said a second later. Then he holstered his gun and walked into the bedroom.

Kathy was dressed and lying on the bed. She'd used a strip of rubber tubing as a tourniquet. The hypodermic she'd used to inject the heroin with which she'd overdosed was lying at her side.

An hour later, George Melendez and Jack Booth climbed the stairs to the offices of Baker and Kraft and asked to talk to Stacey and Glen.

"I've just come from Kathy Moran's house. Earlier this morning, Kathy threatened to kill Jack. Fortunately, she didn't follow through. She told Jack that she killed Megan and Ray Cahill and Parnell Crouse and she also confessed to masterminding the robbery-murder at Raymond's house to avenge the murder of her parents."

"Is she in custody?" Glen asked. "Is Stacey in danger?"

"Miss Moran is dead," the police chief said. "She committed suicide by taking an overdose of heroin."

Stacey's hand flew to her mouth.

"Did she admit to trying to kill Stacey?" Glen asked.

Jack nodded.

"So it's over," Stacey said.

"It is, and this case would never have been solved without your help," George said. "So I wanted to come here so I could thank you in person."

Stacey knew that she should have been ecstatic, but she felt empty. She also knew that she should hate Kathy Moran but she couldn't. Now that she was out of danger, she thought about why Moran had killed Raymond Cahill and she wondered what she would have done if her parents were brutally murdered and she learned the identity of the person who had destroyed her life.

"Why did Kathy threaten Mr. Booth?" Stacey asked.

"He figured out why Megan ran out of the gallery and what was wrong with *Woman with a Gun*. I'll let him tell you what happened."

"My God," Stacey said when Jack finished. "It was there from day one."

"But no one was smart enough to figure it out until Jack caught on," Melendez said.

"And I would never have given the photograph a second look if you hadn't found the evidence that pointed the investigation at Kathy," Jack added.

After Jack gave a statement at the police station, George Melendez told him that he was free to go. On the return trip to Portland he felt very bad. Jack flashed back to the morning. He was certain that Kathy was going to kill him, but there had been a turning point. It came when he said he loved her. He'd seen the uncertainty on her face and he'd seen the tremor in the hand that held the gun. Did he love Kathy? Was he capable of loving anyone? He thought he had loved Adrianna, his wife of long ago, but he'd cheated on her so often. Would he have done that if he loved her?

And was Kathy capable of love? She had spared his life and her hand had trembled. They were two broken people who had found each other, but Jack was uncertain of his feelings for Kathy or her feelings for him. And that uncertainty was his curse. How long would he live—twenty to forty years? Would he live those years alone without someone he loved and who loved him? He felt so sad and empty. When he left Kathy this morning he'd been happier than he could remember. There had been hope but that feeling had lasted less than an hour. Now it was gone and Jack had the sinking feeling that he would never recapture it.

CHAPTER FIFTY

Stacey stood behind the owner of the bookstore and waited for her to finish her introduction. It was the third week of her national book tour and she was running on fumes but she had not lost one ounce of enthusiasm. The woman was nearing the end of the introduction and Stacey took a quick look at the audience. *Woman with a Gun* had been an instant *New York Times* best seller and every seat was taken, but the person she was looking for was in the back row. She found Glen and smiled when he gave her a thumbs-up.

"And so it is with great pleasure that I present Stacey Kim."

Her host stepped away from the podium and Stacey took her place while the audience applauded.

"Thank you for coming out on this rainy night. I appreciate it. It's hard to believe that two years ago I had never seen Kathy Moran's mesmerizing photograph *Woman with a Gun*, and knew nothing about the tragedy that presented her with the opportunity to take it. It was luck that led me to take my lunch break at the Museum of Modern Art, where I saw an exhibition of Miss Moran's work celebrating the tenth anniversary of the award of her Pulitzer Prize.

"I had just received my MFA and I was in New York working on a novel, but I wasn't making any progress. But once I saw the photograph, I abandoned that book and vowed to write a book inspired by *Woman with a Gun.* But life is funny and research for the novel led me to discover the truth behind a ten-year-old murder mystery. So instead of standing here to talk about my novel, which remains unwritten, I am going to tell you how I helped uncover secrets that had been buried for more than a quarter of a century, how I almost lost my life, and how I ended up writing a true crime book that has become every writer's dream, a best seller."

ACKNOWLEDGMENTS

One of the most frequent questions I am asked is, "Where do your ideas come from?" With *Woman with a Gun*, the answer is very simple. Close this book and look at the photograph on the cover. I saw it for the first time when I was keynoting a writers' conference in St. Simons Island, Georgia. I was eating breakfast in Palmer's Village Café, a restaurant decorated with art from a gallery owned by the café owner. After breakfast I went into the bathroom to wash up. Over the toilet was one of the most thought-provoking photographs I have ever seen: a woman in a wedding dress, standing on the ocean shore, holding what I mistakenly believed to be a Wild West six-shooter. "What is going on here?" I asked myself. "Did she shoot her husband on her wedding night? Is she going to commit suicide? Is she waiting for someone who is coming ashore? Is she going to shoot that person?" I immediately ran out to the manager of the café and asked if I could buy the photograph. The next morning, I was told that Leslie Jeter, the brilliant photographer who had taken the picture, was willing to sell it to me. Voilà, I had the title of a new book, *Woman with a Gun*, and the book cover. Working out the story you have just read took a little longer.

I would like to thank Leslie Jeter for inspiring me. I want to thank my friend, gun expert and fellow writer Steve Perry, for informing me that the gun the woman in the photo is holding is not the ancient Western six-shooter in my novel, but most probably a modern-day Ruger.

I could not have finished this book without excellent editorial help from Claire Wachtel and Caroline Upcher. Thanks also to Hannah Wood, Heather Drucker, and all the other terrific people at HarperCollins.

Woman with a Gun would not have found a home at HarperCollins without the assistance of Jean Naggar and Jennifer Weltz, my intrepid agents and friends, and all the other wonderful people at Jean V. Naggar Literary Agency.

I also want to thank my longtime, fabulous assistant, Robin Haggard, for her research skills, and the home team: my daughter and writing partner, Ami Rome, and her husband, Andy, who administers my Facebook page; my son, Daniel; and my two rascally grandchildren, Charley (Loots) and Marissa Margolin.

Last but not least, I want to thank Doreen, my muse, who is gone but never forgotten.

ABOUT THE AUTHOR

Phillip Margolin has written eighteen novels, many of them *New York Times* best sellers, including his latest novels *Worthy Brown's Daughter, Sleight of Hand,* and the Washington trilogy. Each displays a unique, compelling insider's view of criminal behavior, which comes from his long background as a criminal defense attorney who has handled thirty murder cases. Winner of the Distinguished Northwest Writer Award, he lives in Portland, Oregon.